D0051997

Books Can Be Deceiving

"When murder disturbs the quiet community of Briar Creek on the ocean's edge, librarian Lindsey Norris springs into action to keep her best friend from being charged with the crime. A sparkling setting, lovely characters, books, knitting, and chowder! What more could any reader ask?"
—Lorna Barrett, *New York Times* bestselling author of the Booktown Mysteries

"With a remote coastal setting as memorable as Manderley and a kindhearted, loyal librarian as the novel's heroine, *Books Can Be Deceiving* is sure to charm cozy readers everywhere."
—Ellery Adams, author of the Books by the Bay Mysteries

"Fast-paced and fun, *Books Can Be Deceiving* is the first in Jenn McKinlay's appealing new mystery series featuring an endearing protagonist, delightful characters, a lovely New England setting, and a fascinating murder. Don't miss this charming new addition to the world of traditional mysteries."
—Kate Carlisle, *New York Times* bestselling author of the Bibliophile Mysteries

Praise for Jenn McKinlay's Cupcake Bakery Mysteries

Red Velvet Revenge

"With a rodeo, a road trip, and the delectable title *Red Velvet Revenge*, the Fairy Tale Cupcake bakers are back, lassoed into big trouble this time. You're in for a real treat with Jenn Mc-Kinlay's Cupcake Bakery Mystery. I gobbled it right up."
—Julie Hyzy, *New York Times* bestselling author of the White House Chef Mysteries

"Sure as shootin', *Red Velvet Revenge* pops with fun and great twists. Wrangle up some time to enjoy the atmosphere of a real rodeo as well as family drama. It's better than icing on the tastiest cupcake." —Avery Aames, author of *Clobbered by Camembert*

Death by the Dozen

"It's the best yet, with great characters, and a terrific, tightly written plot."   —*Lesa's Book Critiques*

"Like a great fairy tale, McKinlay transports readers into the world of cupcakes and all things sweet and frosted, minus the calories. Although . . . there are some pretty yummy recipes at the end."   —AnnArbor.com

Buttercream Bump Off

"A charmingly entertaining story paired with a luscious assortment of cupcake recipes that, when combined, make for a deliciously thrilling mystery."   —*Fresh Fiction*

"Another tasty entry, complete with cupcake recipes, into what is sure to grow into a perennial favorite series."
                              —*The Mystery Reader*

Sprinkle with Murder

"A tender cozy full of warm and likable characters and a refreshingly sympathetic murder victim."
                              —*Publishers Weekly* (starred review)

"McKinlay's debut mystery flows as smoothly as Melanie Cooper's buttercream frosting. Her characters are delicious, and the dash of romance is just the icing on the cake."
                              —Sheila Connolly, *New York Times* bestselling author of
                              Buried in a Bog

"Jenn McKinlay delivers all the ingredients for a winning read. Frost me another!"
                              —Cleo Coyle, *New York Times* bestselling author of
                              the Coffeehouse Mysteries

"A delicious new series featuring a spirited heroine, luscious cupcakes, and a clever murder."
                              —Krista Davis, author of the Domestic Diva Mysteries

Berkley Prime Crime titles by Jenn McKinlay

Cupcake Bakery Mysteries

SPRINKLE WITH MURDER
BUTTERCREAM BUMP OFF
DEATH BY THE DOZEN
RED VELVET REVENGE
GOING, GOING, GANACHE

Library Lover's Mysteries

BOOKS CAN BE DECEIVING
DUE OR DIE
BOOK, LINE, AND SINKER

Hat Shop Mysteries

CLOCHE AND DAGGER

CLOCHE
AND
DAGGER

Jenn McKinlay

BERKLEY PRIME CRIME, NEW YORK

THE BERKLEY PUBLISHING GROUP
Published by the Penguin Group
Penguin Group (USA) Inc.
375 Hudson Street, New York, New York 10014, USA

🐧

USA | Canada | UK | Ireland | Australia | New Zealand | India | South Africa | China

Penguin Books Ltd., Registered Offices: 80 Strand, London WC2R 0RL, England
For more information about the Penguin Group, visit penguin.com.

CLOCHE AND DAGGER

A Berkley Prime Crime Book / published by arrangement with the author

Berkley Prime Crime Books are published by The Berkley Publishing Group.
BERKLEY® PRIME CRIME and the PRIME CRIME logo are trademarks of
Penguin Group (USA) Inc.

For information, address: The Berkley Publishing Group,
a division of Penguin Group (USA) Inc.,
375 Hudson Street, New York, New York 10014.

ISBN: 978-0-425-25889-7

PUBLISHING HISTORY
Berkley Prime Crime mass-market edition / August 2013

PRINTED IN THE UNITED STATES OF AMERICA

10 9 8 7 6 5 4 3 2 1

Cover illustration by Robert Steele.
Cover design by Diana Kolsky.
Interior text design by Laura K. Corless.

ALWAYS LEARNING   **PEARSON**

For my brilliant editor, Kate Seaver.
You make my work sparkle and shine
and I can't thank you enough for all that you do.
You are wonderful!

Acknowledgments

Attempting to write about a foreign setting was a daring leap for me. Luckily, I had my agent, Jessica Faust; my editor, Kate Seaver; assistant editor, Katherine Pelz; and my family and friends to hold the net for me when I jumped. This is invaluable when you are taking a neck-breaking risk and so I thank each and every one of you.

I'd also like to express my eternal gratitude to my fellow authors Hannah Dennison, Rhys Bowen and Deborah Crombie for being willing to slog through the unedited galleys of *Cloche and Dagger*. As always, the generosity of the writing community leaves me humbled to be a part of it. Also, I'd like to thank my author friend Dorien Kelly, who introduced me to Andrea Blohm, a hat designer, who patiently answered my e-mails about the hat business and kept me from botching the details. And because it is all in the details, I'd like to acknowledge my cover artist Robert Steele for this truly brilliant cover. It's perfect.

Lastly, I'd like to tip my hat to the three men in my life who make every day a wonderful new adventure. Chris, Beckett and Wyatt, I love you!

Chapter 1

"Scarlett Elizabeth Parker, put down the MoonPie and listen to me," Vivian Tremont ordered.

I held my cell phone away from my ear and frowned at it. How could my cousin who was almost five thousand miles away and in another country know I was eating a MoonPie? I put it down on my coffee table and swallowed the bite of cookie, marshmallow and chocolate I'd just taken.

"I'm not eating a MoonPie," I said. Technically, it was not a lie since I had just put it down.

"Oh, please, I know you, pet," Vivian said in her crisp British way. "You always eat MoonPies when you're upset."

"How's business?" I asked. I had learned in my twenty-seven years of knowing her that a change of subject was the only way to throw Viv off track.

"Not good because I'm too busy worrying about you,"

she returned. Obviously, she was not to be thwarted today. "Now, here's what I think you should do."

Viv paused to take a deep breath and I thought about how much I disliked any sentence that had "you should" in it. Still, she was winding up for what sounded like it would be a lengthy monologue, so I decided to make use of the time by finishing my MoonPie.

"Now you know Mim left the hat shop to both of us," she said. "I know you had other career aspirations but since those have imploded, I think it's time for you to come to London and take up your half of the business."

I choked on a bit of cookie. I had to give it to her. I hadn't seen that one coming.

"I thought you said you weren't eating a MoonPie," she said.

"Well, actually, I'm choking on one," I said through my hacking cough.

"How can you eat that rot?" she asked.

"Aw, come on," I said. "I know you ate the box that I sent you for Christmas."

"I tried a nibble, to be polite," she said.

"Ha, you ate them and liked them. I know you did," I said.

"If I did, it was the child in me acting out, so it doesn't count because I can't be held accountable for what childish me does. Now moving on," she said. "What do you think of my idea?"

I paused before I answered. Mim was our grandmother, and when she had passed away five years before, she had left Mim's Whims, her millinery business, half to Vivian, who was already working for her, and half to me. Viv had been a natural fit. She had grown up down the street from the Notting Hill shop and had spent her teen and university years working with Mim.

As for me, I was born and bred in Florida, and although I had spent my school breaks with Mim and Viv, I didn't know squat about the hat business, which was why I had gone into the hospitality business after college, working at the posh Santiago Hotel chain headquartered in Tampa.

"Oh, come on, it's your legacy," Viv cajoled. "Besides, your life is in the loo, love. It's best you put some miles between you and that blighter who broke your heart—at least try it for a little while."

"Uff." I huffed out a breath as a sharp pain stabbed me somewhere in the vicinity of my chest, although it could have been angina from my steady diet of MoonPies, Pringles and French onion dip. I picked up the big box of MoonPies I'd scored at the Publix grocery store a few nights before. It was light, too light. I shook it. Empty. Damn.

"He isn't a—" I began, but Viv cut me off.

"No! Do not defend that pile of rubbish to me. The man led you to believe he was available and then you find out that he hasn't left his wife at all by walking in on a lavish anniversary party that he threw for her," she fumed. "I'm delighted that you lobbed chunks of five-thousand-dollar cake at him. It's a shame your escapade got recorded and went viral on the Internet, but it was no more than he deserved."

I felt my insides wither as they were clutched in the unforgiving fist of humiliation. I had watched the clip of the video, repeatedly, hoping my shame would become less horrific with each viewing. It never did.

On the grainy video, I looked like a deranged redheaded banshee, grabbing fistfuls of the gorgeous three-tier cake and flinging them at a man in an impeccable tuxedo, while he held up his arms and tried to protect his handsome face from a frosting pelting. The nicest comment posted about the video was that I had an arm like Nolan Ryan in his prime.

"I don't know, Viv," I said.

"How long has it been since you've showered?" she asked. "Or left your flat?"

"Three days," I said.

"That's it then, either you come here under your own power or I'm coming to get you," she said. Being two years older than me, Viv could be the teensiest bit bossy. "I'm booking you a ticket now for the first flight out of Tampa International tomorrow. Are you in?"

I thought about staying holed up in my apartment until I died. It had a certain appeal. Then I thought about fleeing the country to be with my cousin. It had slightly more appeal.

"All right," I agreed. "Book it."

Chapter 2

The platform of the underground was mobbed as the smokers hustled to get up onto the surface street to light up because the fumes in the tunnel weren't enough of a rush for their lungs. I was pushed aside as I dragged my rolling suitcase behind me and couldn't push back as I was weighed down with two carry-on bags as well. My Florida wardrobe was not going to cut it for April in London, so I had packed heavier than I usually did when I crossed the pond.

It had been three years since I'd come for a visit, which seemed an inexcusably long time now that I thought about it. Flying away from Tampa, I had to admit I hadn't been sad to see the city growing ever smaller in my window. Like the fading taste of something bitter, I hoped the memory of my humiliation would diminish just as quickly as the city.

The climb up the stairs was dicey but I made it, feeling like a mole popping its head out of its hole when I reached the street. I parked my bags and glanced around the Notting Hill Gate entrance to the underground, looking for Vivian.

She was always easy to spot because she used any opportunity in public to promote the shop by wearing one of her hats. Mim had been an extraordinary milliner and Viv had inherited her gift but also had her own flare of irreverence that had garnered her loads of press and quite a lot of clients among the titled elite.

I looked for an orange plume of feathers or a bright blue burst of glittery fronds in the shape of lilies, but no, there was nothing. Viv was typically late, I supposed. She had said she would meet me at the Gate and I had given her the time of my estimated arrival on the underground from Heathrow Airport, which had been less than an hour after I claimed my bags. There was no sign of her. I tried not to feel disappointed.

Vivian was an eccentric who not only marched to her own drummer but was usually the drum major of the crazy parade, so it really was expecting a bit too much to think she'd be waiting for me when I arrived. I hefted one of my carry-ons over my shoulder and began to pull my big bag with the other carry-on perched on top of it toward the street that would lead me to Portobello Road, where the narrow three-story building that was home to Mim's Whims was located.

I stepped off the curb when a tall man stopped in front of me and peered at a photograph and then at me and said, "Excuse me, are you Scarlett Parker?"

I looked at the man with all of my internal sensors on high alert. There had been quite a flurry of media attention after the cake debacle went viral. Even *Good Morning America* had wanted an interview. Honestly, did they really think I wanted to be a participant in my own humiliation? The morning after the video reached a million hits, I'd even found one lunatic with a camera on the balcony of my apartment trying to peer in my windows. Needless to say, I was just the teensiest bit paranoid about strangers who knew my name.

The man in question, however, was dressed in a sharply creased pair of khaki pants with a blue dress shirt and brown loafers. He was not hoisting a camera or a microphone and he seemed to be alone. He was also very handsome in an academic sort of way.

"Do I know you?" I asked.

"No," he said. He looked irritated by the question, but continued, "But I know your cousin Vivian and she sent me to collect you. I'm Harrison Wentworth."

"Nice to meet you," I said. I shifted my bags so that we could shake hands. His grip was firm but not crushing, and his hand was warm.

"Here, let me get those for you," he said. "I have a driver waiting."

He gestured to the car parked at the curb as he took my rolling case from me and the driver opened the trunk.

"Wait!" I grabbed my suitcase back from him. "I've never heard Viv say your name before. How do I know she sent you?"

He raised one eyebrow, and the flash of irritation I'd seen before looked to go into full-on annoyed now. The air was damp and cold and his cheeks had a ruddy tinge to them. His dark brown hair was brushed back from his face in careless waves and I noticed that his eyes were a bright emerald green.

"Nice to know Viv thinks so highly of me that she tells her partner all about my financial wizardry on her behalf," he said.

"Oy, I'm standin' in traffic 'ere," the driver called to us. "Are you comin' or what?"

Harrison Wentworth frowned at him. He dug into his pants pocket and handed me a photograph along with a note scribbled in Viv's distinctive handwriting, which stated the estimated time of my arrival at Notting Hill Gate. The photograph had been taken on my trip here three years ago. Viv and I had been sitting on the steps of our shop, wearing two of her outrageous hats. We had our arms around each other and were mugging for the camera with silly grins. I felt as if I'd aged a decade since that happy summer day.

"I'm surprised you recognized me from that," I said. I handed it back to him.

He tucked the photo back into his pocket and wheeled my bags over to the driver, who popped them into the trunk. Then he held the door open for me and we climbed into the backseat together.

"My uncle, my mother's older brother, is the one who took the photograph," he said. "He was to your grandmother what I am to Viv, well, and you, I suppose, since you're a proprietor as well."

"Mr. Turner! That's right," I said. I remembered the jovial, white-haired man who had come into Mim's shop almost every week to keep track of her books for her. Mim had had no business sense. "How is your uncle?"

"Retired," he said. "So, in other words, happy."

"Good for him," I said.

At that moment the driver punched the gas and we shot

out into the oncoming traffic, which was alarming not only because of the speed at which he was driving but also because I wasn't used to being on the left side of the road. I kept thinking we were going to have a head-on collision at any moment and I kept flinching accordingly, you know, as if that would help.

The driver took a sharp turn onto Portobello Road and I slid across the seat, pressing up against Harrison like a puppy looking for love. Mortified, I grabbed my armrest and hauled myself back to my side. When I turned to look at him, I found him studying me with an undecided expression, as if he wasn't sure what to make of me just yet.

"So, why did Viv send you?" I asked, trying to ease the awkwardness of the moment. "Did she have a client meeting and couldn't come herself?"

"No, not quite," he said. His face grew grim. "The fact is Viv couldn't come because she's missing."

Chapter 3

"Missing?" I repeated. "Define 'missing.'"

"Succinctly, it means I have no idea where she is," he said.

He did not look disturbed by this, a fact I found more than a little alarming. Granted, I'd been traveling for fourteen hours since I'd left Tampa yesterday evening and it was now a bit after midday, so my ability to process was impaired to say the least. Still, he seemed awfully cavalier about Viv's whereabouts being unknown.

I pressed my cold palm again my forehead in an effort to clear my head.

"Don't you think this is a cause for concern?" I asked.

"If it were anyone else, I might agree, but this is Viv," he said. "It's what she does."

He shrugged as if resigned to the eccentricities of my cousin. Now I know Viv can be, oh, how do I say it?

"Colorful" seems too nice but "odd" seems too negative, so she's somewhere in between "colorful" and "odd." I know this, but still it seemed wrong that she wasn't here when I arrived and I couldn't help getting a bad feeling about it.

"But she knew I was coming," I said. "Heck, this was her idea. She even bought my ticket."

"All I know is that when I was having my morning eggs and toast, a messenger came 'round with that picture and a note from Viv requesting that I meet you," he said. "When I called to ask about it, she didn't answer her mobile. I stopped by the shop on my way here, but it was locked up."

I stared at him. He seemed awfully calm about the whole thing, like serial-killer calm. I felt alarm bells ringing in my head and I pulled out my cell phone and called my Aunt Grace, Viv's mother. She lived up in the wilds of Yorkshire, but if anyone knew where Viv was it would be Aunt Grace.

It took a while for my phone to connect to hers and when it did, all I got was her voice mail. Drat. I left a message, hoping I didn't sound as worried as I felt; no need to incite a panic in the upper generation after all.

We passed the Earl of Lonsdale pub and my sudden need for a pint almost overrode all other reason. Harrison did not look the type to drink in the middle of the day, but it was the middle of the night my time, so I really didn't think I could be held accountable for my actions until after I was acclimated to the proper time zone.

The car pulled over to the curb with a lurch and bang. I gathered my purse and let Harrison hand me out of the backseat. The driver put my bags on the curb while Harrison paid him. I glanced up at the three-story white stone building with the jaunty blue-and-white striped awning and matching blue shutters on the windows of the two stories above.

Presently, the awning was tucked back against the building as Viv only put it out on market days or in the summer when every bit of shade was welcome. The large picture window boasted a new display. Wide-brimmed, white straw hats with cobalt-blue trim on the brim and matching hatbands on the crown were hanging in the window at all different heights and depths, making it look like a forest of floating hats. It lured me closer to the window and I longed to step through the glass and run through the hats, which I expect was just what Viv wanted passersby to feel.

I fished out my key. I'd had my own set of keys to the shop ever since I used to come over as a child. The door was the same bright blue as the shutters and on its wrought-iron-and-glass window the name "Mim's Whims" had been etched in thick white letters.

Dear Mim, five years gone and still not a day went by that I didn't think of her and miss her. I unlocked the door and pulled it open. The mild scent of lavender danced on the air like dandelion seeds, tickling my nose and making me smile. Viv believed the scent of lavender calmed her customers and so she always had lavender sachets tucked all about the shop.

The smell brought back memories of my last visit here and again I felt flattened by guilt that I hadn't made time to visit more often. I knew Mim would have been disappointed in me, and the realization stung.

"Do you want me to carry these upstairs for you?" Harrison asked.

Since he already had all three bags and was headed

through the door at the back of the shop that led upstairs it seemed a bit ridiculous that he was asking. Still, I called an affirmative after him, not that it mattered.

My eyes swept over the shop. Other than the hats that were on display, it looked exactly as I remembered it. Viv hadn't changed a thing. The same cobalt-blue and white decorated the inside of the shop. Built-in display shelves lined the store with hats perched on pedestals in every shape, size and color that could be imagined filling the floor-to-ceiling shelves.

There were several sitting areas with stiff upholstered armchairs posed around glass coffee tables that boasted the latest issues of *Look*, *Vogue* and *The HAT.*

Beyond the main shop was the back room, which was Viv's work area. It was a large space with windows that overlooked a tiny but lush garden in back. Viv was a birder, one of the many reasons she used feathers so much in her hat designs, and so the petite garden was filled with bird-houses, birdbaths and bird feeders. How had I forgotten being awoken every day to the cacophony of birdcalls? If it was anything like the last time, I'd have to get myself over to Boots, the pharmacy at Notting Hill Gate, and buy some earplugs.

A drafting table took up one corner with a desk and a computer beside it. From floor to ceiling were cupboards full to bursting with Viv's supplies, which were anything from bolts of wool and sinamay to bottles of fabric dye to bags full of feathers, ribbons and beads. A large worktable filled the center of the room and on it were several hats in various stages of production. It did not look like the work-room of someone who planned to be away. Harrison's words that Viv was missing sent a frisson of alarm through me. Surely she had just gone out unexpectedly to an appointment or something.

I returned to the shop to follow Harrison up the stairs to the flat above. My eye was caught by the large bulky object in the corner, Mim's old wardrobe, which had stood in that same spot for as long as I could remember.

It was a tall piece done in dark mahogany with two doors on top of three drawers. It still had the old glass drawer pulls. The feet of the piece were carved to look like claws around wooden balls while above the seam where the two cupboard doors met, a bird's head had been carved with its beak pointing straight out and its eyes watching me no matter where I stood. The top part of the wardrobe above the doors had been carved as if the bird's two wings were outstretched.

I'll be honest, when I was younger, the bird had freaked me out, but now it reminded me so much of Mim I was glad to see it. I ran my hand down the smooth front door, tracing the rich, red-brown grain with my fingers.

I heard a thump from upstairs and realized I should probably go tell Harrison which room was mine. With a last glance at the wardrobe, I turned to cross the room and go up the stairs. I stopped. Surely I must have imagined it. I turned back and looked at the bird.

"Don't wink at me," I said. I'm not sure if I said it aloud to reassure myself or to inform the bird that impertinence would not be tolerated; either way it wasn't the bird who answered.

"Excuse me, but I'm quite sure I didn't."

Chapter 4

I whirled around to find Harrison standing in the doorway with his arms crossed over his chest, looking at me as if he thought I was a couple of slices short of a loaf.

"I didn't mean you," I said.

"Because there are so many other people here for you to be talking to," he said.

"No, I . . ." I paused. There was no way that saying I was talking to the bird wasn't going to sound nuts. I knew this was one of those "better to shut my mouth and be thought a fool than to open my mouth and remove all doubt" moments. "Never mind."

"Fine," he said. He pushed off the doorjamb. "I put your bags in the pink room, the one that overlooks the back garden. Viv said that is your room when you're here."

I smiled. My room was still pink. Mim had let me pick out the paint color when I was twelve. I'd been at the peak of my girly-girl stage back then and the pink, if I remembered right, was a sort of retina-searing pink found only on Vegas showgirls and candy.

Harrison reached into his jacket pocket and pulled out a business card. "My number is on here if you need anything."

"Thank you," I said.

I realized that while I was uncertain about him, and he really wasn't the friendliest person I'd ever met, the alternative was that I was going to be completely alone. Surprisingly, that had even less appeal.

"Are you hungry?" I asked.

He looked surprised. "You want to go to lunch? I thought you'd be knackered from all of the traveling."

"Well, a girl has to eat," I said.

"I suppose we could do that," he said.

His enthusiasm for spending time with me really bowled me over, I have to say. Fortunately, my self-esteem was swirling in the bowl already so I wasn't put off by his less-than-enthusiastic response. Besides, I really felt like I needed to know more about Viv's absence and he was my best source.

"Excellent," I said. "Let me just go freshen up and we can go."

He opened his mouth as if about to announce an abrupt change of mind, but I dashed through the doorway that led upstairs, not giving him the opportunity to rethink the plan.

I pushed open the door at the top of the steps and stepped into Mim's sitting room. This had been my grandmother's favorite room in the house. Squashy furniture done in blue suede—yes, she was very partial to blue—bookcases that were full to bursting along one wall; an oval rag rug over the wooden floor and a large flat-screen television on the wall opposite the largest couch. This was the room where Mim spent most of her evenings.

Lace curtains covered the windows where houseplants sat on narrow shelves built onto the windowsill. It even smelled just like it used to, of lemon furniture polish and gingersnaps. I was hit with a longing for my grandmother so sharp and so deep that I gasped. I missed her no-nonsense ways and her ability to always move forward no matter what challenge life handed her. I know she would have scolded me severely for getting duped by a married man, but she also would have been able to lessen my shame with a few words of perspective and lessons learned. She was good like that.

I pushed my sadness down and strode through the room, through the kitchen and the dining room to the hallway. Here there were two doors, one that went into Mim's bedroom and the other that led to the uppermost floor where the two bedrooms Viv and I used were located. I knew Viv had moved into Mim's old bedroom a few years ago. It made sense since she lived and worked here. I wondered if she had done anything to her old room or if she kept it as a guest bedroom.

I opened the door and hurried upstairs. A small foyer split the two bedrooms, and I glanced into the one that used to be Viv's to see that it was neatly made up as if awaiting a guest. I turned and went into my old room. Wow!

How had I forgotten how pink my room was? In fifteen years, the paint hadn't faded at all. Not only that, but my Spice Girls poster—Viv and I had both been fans back in the day—was still on the closet door as if waiting for me to break into my dance moves and belt out "Wannabe."

When Viv and I worked out our routines, I was always Ginger Spice because of my red hair and even though she's a blonde, Viv was always Scary Spice, well, because she is.

I saw my bags sitting in the middle of my room and felt a shot of horror that Harrison had seen my room, still trapped in adolescence. Somehow this was worse than having him walk in on me in my underwear.

I quickly grabbed a change of clothes and my bag of makeup and went into the bathroom that separated the two bedrooms. A glance at the mirror told me that I looked as if I'd carried every one of the five thousand miles I'd just traveled on my face. Ugh! Small wonder Harrison had seemed less than enthusiastic about having lunch with me: I looked like a refugee and not a well-groomed one. This was going to take a major overhaul.

When I stepped through the door and back into the shop twenty-five minutes later, Harrison looked me over.

"I was beginning to wonder if you meant lunch today or Thursday," he said.

"Today," I said. And wasn't that just the cleverest quip back at him? I blame jet lag. I was definitely not at the top of my game.

"Shall we then?" he asked.

I unbolted the front door and led the way out. I turned and locked it after him.

"The Earl of Lonsdale is just down the road, and it is more of a locals' haunt," he said. "Are you up to it?"

"That's fine," I said. "Walking will feel good."

We walked side by side. Harrison kept his head up and his gaze at the horizon as if oblivious to my presence. I was getting the sneaking suspicion that he didn't like me much but I couldn't for the life of me figure out why.

"It's weird to be back here," I said. If he heard me, he didn't acknowledge it. Undaunted, I forged on. "I've changed, but the shop hasn't and my room certainly hasn't."

I glanced at him out of the corner of my eye. I had switched into my wedge heels to be taller but I still only came up to his ear. Still he ignored me. Now his dislike for me was becoming less of a suspicion and more of a fact. As far as I knew it was completely unwarranted, so I kept up my jabber, hoping to goad him into at least blinking at me.

"No, I guess as much as things change they also stay the same," I said. "Same old Portobello Road, same old antique shops and bookstores, yep, not many changes of note."

"Clearly, you aren't looking at things very closely then, are you?" He stopped walking and turned to face me, heedless of the other pedestrians who were forced to walk around us.

"What do you mean?" I asked.

He looked torn between irritation and amusement, but at least he was looking at me and really seeing me. It was a vast improvement on the man who refused to acknowledge me a few moments before. My vanity really didn't like for me to be ignored.

"I was inaccurate with you before. We have met," he said. "Seventeen years ago, in fact."

"We did?" I studied his face. In addition to the pretty eyes, he had a nice square jaw, full lips and arching eyebrows. I was quite sure we could not have met because he was handsome now so he must have been cute back then and I was not one to forget a cute boy, especially back then.

"Yes, Ginger, we've met," he said. "In fact, I asked you to go for ice cream with me but you stood me up so that you could chase after a dodgy football player."

My heart fell into my shoes with the speed of an express elevator. It was the nickname "Ginger" that brought it all back to me. There was only one boy who called me Ginger despite my attempts to get everyone to call me that. Hey, I was a kid and I thought it made me sound cool. I blinked at him as the recognition kicked in.

"Harry?" I asked.

Chapter 5

"It's Harrison now," he said. His tone was as dry as dust.

He turned to continue walking, but I grabbed his arm and turned him back to face me. I studied his features closely and then I shook my head.

"No, seventeen years ago, I was ten. I'm quite sure I could not have had a date with you as I was entirely too young," I said. This time I was the one who turned and started walking.

"It wasn't a 'date' date," he protested. He stopped me with a hand on my elbow. "But it was supposed to be the two of us going for ice cream, but you threw me over so you could stalk some older, and may I say inappropriate, boy."

"No, I think you must be *inaccurate* again," I said.

His lips twitched as if smacking away the smile that wanted to surface.

"Sorry but no," he said. "On this I am perfectly clear. One does remember the first girl who breaks one's heart, you know."

He said it so sincerely that I felt my breath catch. He had to be teasing me.

"No, I don't believe you," I said. I tossed my long auburn hair over my shoulder and resumed walking.

Now here's a little trick I've learned while watching my mom manage my dad my entire life. Quite simply, she has taught me that you will often get what you want much faster if you flirt. Yes, I know you could argue that it throws back the women's movement a century or two, but I prefer to think of it as a management skill, where the person on the receiving end of my attention enjoys being made to feel good, and I get what I want.

In this case because I knew very well that ten-year-old me had blown off Harry Wentworth in favor of chasing some stupid soccer player whose name I couldn't even remember, I was angling for forgiveness.

"How can you not believe me?" he asked. He fell into stride beside me. "I was a crushing twelve-year-old, who showed up at your grandmother's door ready to take you out for ice cream, only to discover that you'd gone off with your cousin to chase someone else."

I felt a spasm of guilt at how badly I'd treated him. Had I really been such a thoughtless girl? It appeared so. Given the recent events in my life, I had to conclude that the public humiliation I had just suffered was just what I deserved in the cosmic sense of karmic payback, and apparently, my transgression had accrued some serious interest.

"No, that's just not possible," I said.

He looked exasperated enough to throttle me, so I stopped walking and gave him a small smile.

"I would never have stood up a boy as handsome and charming as you," I said. "I'm quite sure of it."

His ruddy cheeks flushed a deeper color at the flattery and he no longer looked like he wanted to choke me. Instead, just as I'd hoped, he looked charmed and disarmed.

I rested my hand on his chest and leaned in close. "Whoever that horrid girl was who stood you up, well, you can be sure she regrets it now."

His mouth quirked up in the corner and this time he gave in and grinned. Then he leaned in close to me and said, "You're incorrigible as always."

"See?" I asked. "Nothing changes."

We settled into a snug, wooden booth with high walls, at the Earl of Lonsdale, and I immediately ordered a pint of Sam Smith's Nut Brown Ale and the cottage pie. There are certain things you just can't replicate in Florida, like real pub grub, and cottage pie was one of my favorites.

We were served quickly, and Harrison watched me as I ate with the gusto of a woman who enjoys her food. I really do. When I had demolished half of my plate and could slow down enough to actually taste my food, I glanced up to find him studying me.

"What?" I asked.

He just shook his head. I had a feeling that, although I'd been forgiven, mostly, for standing him up in our youth, he still hadn't made up his mind about me. I decided not to take it personally.

"So, when do you suppose Viv will be back?"

"No idea," he said.

"A day?" I persisted. "Two?"

"Scarlett." He said my name as if talking to someone who was slow, and I realized I preferred that he call me Ginger. I liked the way it sounded when he said it in his charming accent, but given our history, I really couldn't go requesting that, now could I?

"Yes, Harry," I said. Naturally, I used his old nickname to goad him, just a little bit.

"It's Harrison."

I had a feeling he'd be saying that a lot to me, but I nodded politely as if I got it.

"Viv is like, well, you," he said. He paused to take a sip of his Taddy Porter. "So, there's really no way to know when she'll return."

"What does that mean exactly?" I asked. "That she's like me?"

"Well, you and your grandmother and Viv all share one particular trait," he said. "My uncle and I have discussed it."

"You have, have you?" I wasn't sure how I felt about this. "And what trait would that be?"

"You all severely lack impulse control," he said.

I chewed thoughtfully on a bite of pie. Then I shook my head.

"I disagree," I said.

He raised his eyebrows.

"You do? Well, your cousin just up and left with no word other than for me to collect you. What do you call that?"

"That's just Viv's way. You said it yourself."

"Indeed, I did, but that doesn't mean it's normal. And your grandmother—"

"What about her?" I cut him off. He was treading on sacred ground there.

"My uncle said she was a wild one," he said. "Is it true that she threw champagne in Sir Roger Dunmore's face?"

"Hmm," I hummed noncommittally. That tale was definitely in the family lore; we seldom discussed it.

"Or that she fashioned a hat with a big fat grouse on it for Lady Tidwell?" he asked. "A grouse that, if one looked closely, which the unfortunate Lady Tidwell did not, was seen to be laying an egg?"

I put down my fork and studied my fingertips as if inspecting my manicure for chips. Yes, that was another tale we did not discuss.

"And then there's you, Scarlett," he said.

I put my hands on the edge of the table as if to brace myself from an incoming blow. I glanced up, forcing myself to meet his gaze. I owned my bad behavior and I would not flinch from whatever he had to say about it.

Still, the mortification from last week scalded my cheeks. He must have seen the silent suffering in my eyes, because he reached across the table and patted one of my hands.

"The bloody bastard got off easy if you ask me," he said.

I felt my entire body sag with relief and then I laughed.

"Thank you," I said. My voice came out a little choked up and I swallowed hard.

I hadn't spoken to anyone about the situation except Viv. I'd even fled the States without talking to any of my friends. It was nice to have someone, a virtual stranger, in my corner, especially when the social media outlets had portrayed me as a deranged-stalker type.

"Still, it proves my point, yes?" he asked. "No impulse control."

"All right," I said. "I'll concede your point, but only because you've been very nice. Now, back to business. What should I do if Viv doesn't return soon? I don't know anything about running the shop."

"Well, today is Monday so the shop is closed," he said. "But Viv has loads of special orders that need to be picked up, so you can't stay closed indefinitely. You'll have Fiona to help you."

"Fiona?" I asked.

"Pardon me." A young woman approached our table. "Sorry to bother you, but could I have a picture with you?"

"Me?" I asked. I glanced behind me to make sure there wasn't someone lurking in our booth that she was talking to. "I think you have me mistaken for somebody else."

"Oh, no, you're the American, yeah? The party crasher? The one on the Internet? My mates and I love what you did," she gushed. "You made a stand for women everywhere against lying, cheating ba—"

"Did I?" I interrupted her before she launched herself into a tirade. I looked at Harrison. "This is new. The last I heard the media was portraying me as a lunatic."

"They were!" she exclaimed. "Right up until those other two girls he was having a bit on the side with popped up."

Chapter 6

I felt the room give a lurch as my reality had its feet kicked out from under it.

"Other two girls?" I asked through gritted teeth.

"Oh, you didn't know?" she asked.

"No."

"They were all over the news yesterday," she said. "Apparently, your married beau got around and with the same story—that he and his wife were separated. One of the girls said she wished she could give you a hug for standing up for all of them. The other said she wished you'd hit him with something harder than cake."

I glanced across the table to see Harrison watching me with sympathetic eyes. It pushed me out of my stupor and I glanced back at the woman, who was still talking.

"They suspect there may be even more women in his

personal queue. So, you can see you're an inspiration," the woman said. "So how about a picture?"

She was a tall girl with a thick, black braid that hung forward over her shoulder. Her round face sported freckles, big brown eyes and an engaging grin. I liked her.

"I don't think—" Harrison began but I cut him off.

"Sure, I'd love to," I said. I decided right then and there I wasn't going to let the shame of the past own me.

Sadly, I wasn't as surprised as I should have been that there were others like me. If the word was now out that the rat bastard had lied to me, maybe I would even be able to show my face in the States again. Maybe.

Either way, it was time to pick my chin up and keep moving forward. What was the British saying? *KEEP CALM AND CARRY ON*. Yes, it was in reference to World War II and featured the crown of King George VI above the words. And yes, it was one of three propaganda posters, the only one that was never actually used during the war. Rather it was rediscovered fifty years later in Barter Books, a secondhand shop in Northern England. Still, it suited my mood at the present.

The girl handed her phone to Harrison, who shook his head, but snapped the picture as we stood with our arms draped over each other's shoulders like we were long-lost pals.

"Thanks," the girl said and hurried back to her table to show her friends.

Harrison stared at me, and I knew he was about to say it was just another example of my lack of control, but I forestalled him.

"Oh, don't be ridiculous," I said. "That story about me

is over a week old, no one cares anymore. Obviously, there are new fish to fry."

"Then why did the girl want to have her picture with you?"

"She probably had her heart ripped out by a married guy, too, and considers me a kindred spirit," I said.

"Or she's going to sell the photo to the tabloids and say you were a roaring good drunk," he said.

"So suspicious," I said. "I'm not that bad a judge of character."

"Do you even hear yourself when you speak?" he asked. Then he muttered, "'Not that bad a judge of character.' Ha! Probably thought the cheating toe rag was just misunderstood."

"I'm right here, you know."

He huffed out a breath but stopped muttering. I finished my pie while he did the same with his fisherman's pie just as the waitress came with the tab. I made to grab it, but he snagged it first.

"It's on me. Welcome to London," he said.

"Thanks, Harry."

I grinned when he rolled his eyes and grumbled, "Harrison."

It was a quiet walk back to Mim's Whims. Monday in the city was a bustling sort of day. Lots of pedestrians and cars, the frequent sounds of honking intermingled with occasional shouts.

Spring was longing to bust out in its full glory. I could see it in the box gardens that decorated a few of the buildings that we passed.

"You never told me who Fiona is," I said.

"That's right, your fan interrupted, didn't she?"

29

I ignored the sarcasm in his tone and gave him a pointed look.

"Fine," he said. "Fiona Felton is a student who is currently apprenticing in the shop. She's very quick. I'm sure she'll be able to answer any questions that you have."

"I didn't know Viv took on apprentices," I said. Again, I felt a twist of guilt that I hadn't been here in three years and was seemingly so out of touch. How could I have gotten so consumed with my life that I didn't even know the basics of Viv's?

"Fiona's the first."

As we approached the shop, I felt the weight of the meal and the pints, not to mention jet lag, relax me into a light stupor. It must have shown on my face, because Harrison took one look at me and relieved me of my keys.

He unlocked the door and pulled it open. Then he handed me my keys and said, "Lock up behind me and go get some sleep. I'll pop in on you tomorrow."

I nodded and patted his arm as I passed him. He closed the door after me. With a yawn, I turned the key in the lock and headed toward the stairs. Even my toxic pink bedroom was appealing in that it had a bed, and I was sure I could sleep for a month.

Out of the corner of my eye, I felt Mim's wardrobe bird watching me.

"Good night," I called, half expecting him to caw in response.

When I opened my eyes, it was to find another pair of eyes staring back at me just inches from my face.

"Ah!" I yelled and scrambled back across my bed while the person staring jumped back and yelled as well.

"Who the hell are you?" I shrieked.

"Fee, er, Fiona Felton," she gasped. She put her hand on her chest. "Oy, I think my heart stopped, yeah?"

"*Your* heart stopped?" I asked. "What are you doing in my room?"

"Harrison called me this morning and told me to check on you," she said. "When you didn't show up, I figured I'd better see if you were all right. You know, make sure you hadn't done anything drastic."

"Drastic?" I pushed the covers off and sat up. "Why would I do anything like that?"

She pursed her lips as if keeping herself from saying anything else.

"Oh, I get it, because my life is in the toilet," I said. I rolled to my feet and faced her. She shrugged, which I took as assent. "My life isn't that bad."

Again, she said nothing. Smart girl.

"Have you heard from Viv?" I asked.

"Just a message telling me to help you out while she's gone," she said.

"No indication of when she'd be back?" I asked.

Fee shook her head. I got a weird feeling in the pit of my stomach again. I just couldn't accept, even as eccentric as Viv was, that it was okay that she was missing. I reached over to the nightstand and checked my cell phone. There was nothing from Viv or my Aunt Grace. I would have to call my mother later and see if she could get some answers.

"Is that the time?" I asked.

Fee nodded. "That's why I came to check on you."

It was almost noon. I had slept for almost eighteen hours.

"I'm sorry," I said. "No wonder you thought the worst."

Fee gave me a weak smile, and I realized that she was nervous and no wonder. I could only imagine the bed head I must be sporting. Not to mention with Viv gone, she was being put in the position of getting the foreigner, me, who as co-owner was also technically her boss, up to speed. Poor thing.

At a guess, I'd put her age at twenty, maybe twenty-one. She had dark skin and dark eyes and her hair was a chin-length bob of corkscrew curls, some of which were a vivid shade of hot pink and one of which kept popping forward to hang over her right eye no matter how many times she shoved it back. She also had a nose ring and wore a spectacular amount of gold eye shadow.

"Tell you what," I said, trying to put her at ease, "I'll just grab a quick shower and meet you down in the shop."

"Want me to make a pot of tea?" she asked.

"That'd be nice," I said.

Fee bounced from the room with entirely too much enthusiasm, and I dug through my suitcase until I found my jersey tunic top in a nice olive green and a pair of black leggings. I'd been too tired to hang up my clothes yesterday and they had the suitcase wrinkles to show for it.

I decided I was too hungry to deal with it now and left the suitcase lid propped open in a lame attempt to air out my meager wardrobe. An overhaul would have to be done later. I took a quick shower and dressed, pulling on a pair of knee-high black boots to complete the outfit. I had no patience with my hair, so I twisted it into a topknot and put on just enough makeup to keep from scaring the customers away. Fifteen minutes from the time Fiona had awoken me, I headed downstairs.

I entered the shop to find Fee sitting with a customer in one of the blue sitting areas. I could tell from the tight expression on Fee's face that whatever was happening was not going well.

"No, no, I don't want that," the older woman was saying. "This is for my son's wedding. It has to make a statement but not be ostentatious. Where is Vivian, anyway? I thought I'd be speaking with her. Really, is it so much to ask for some knowledgeable service?"

Chapter 7

"May I help?" I asked.

Fee looked at me as if I'd just thrown her a life preserver.

"Mrs. Abbingdon, this is Scarlett Parker," Fee said. "She is Vivian's cousin and an equal proprietor in Mim's Whims."

"A pleasure to meet you, Mrs. Abbingdon," I said.

Mrs. Abbingdon gave me a dubious look and only took my hand with the tips of her fingers.

"Would you care for some tea and biscuits, Mrs. Abbingdon?" I asked.

"I'm feeling a teeny bit peckish," she said.

"Fee, could you—?" I began, but Fee interrupted me.

"Right away," Fee said. Her thick-heeled shoes almost left skid marks on the floor, so fast was her departure.

My offer of tea was twofold. First, I was starving and second, whenever I dealt with clients at the hotel, I always fed them. People were more at ease over food, plus, they felt you went the extra mile if you fed them, which made them infinitely more manageable.

"You're Vivian's cousin?" Mrs. Abbingdon asked.

"Yes, our mothers were Mim's daughters," I said. "I grew up in the States, but I spent all of my vacations here with Mim."

"So, you're half British?" Mrs. Abbingdon asked.

"The good half," I joked with a wink.

Mrs. Abbingdon chortled and I knew we were going to get along just fine. While we waited for refreshments I told her stories about how Viv and I used to play in the shop while Mim greeted customers and designed her hats. I ruefully admitted that I had no talent at millinery but that Viv was a genius.

Mrs. Abbingdon patted my hand and assured me that I was probably more talented than I knew. I knew it wasn't true, but I let her comfort me anyway.

Fee brought a tray loaded with tea and a plate of shortbread as well as cheese, crackers and a pile of grapes.

"Nice job," I whispered to her.

"I was about to say the same to you, yeah?"

Fee left the tray with me and disappeared into the back room again. Once Mrs. Abbingdon had noshed her way through two cups of tea, half a plate of cookies and a good portion of the cheese, I managed to direct her back to the topic of the hat.

She was going to be wearing a lilac suit with purple trim and we determined that her hat ought to match. I was certain that Viv could match the swatch Mrs. Abbingdon brought from her dressmaker and we determined that her best look would be a hat shape reminiscent of the one the Queen wore to the Duke and Duchess of Cambridge's wedding.

By the time Mrs. Abbingdon left, the tea had grown cold and I was feeling the teensiest anxiety that I was taking on work of which Viv wouldn't approve. I'd also felt my phone vibrating during our chat and it had about killed me not to check it. What if it was Viv? I suspected it would drive Mrs. Abbingdon away, however, so I waited.

As soon as the door closed after Mrs. Abbingdon, I checked my phone. It was my Aunt Grace who had called, and she left a message that essentially said it was no big deal that Viv had up and left before I arrived. Like Harrison, she seemed to think that was just how Viv was and I shouldn't worry. Still, I couldn't shake the bad feeling I had about it.

I hauled the tray back into the workroom, which housed a small kitchenette in the corner. I set the tray on the counter to be dealt with later and approached the workbench where Fee was embroidering a cluster of five-petal, pale blue forget-me-not blossoms onto a narrow dark green hatband.

"That's lovely," I said.

Fee glanced up from her work and grinned.

"I have to ask," she said. "How did you manage to keep your patience with Mrs. Looksee?"

"Mrs. Looksee? You mean Mrs. Abbingdon?" I asked. "The patience part was easy. She's like a chicken on a nest, she just needs to fuss a bit and then she's fine. She's really very sweet, but I did agree that Viv would make her a hat for her son's wedding, lilac with a purple trim. Is this doable?"

Fee's eyes went wide and she goggled at me as if I suddenly suggested we give away all of our hats for free.

"Oh, no, I overcommitted, didn't I?" I asked. "Viv is going to kill me."

"No, no," Fee said. She kept staring at me as if in shock. "It's just, well, in all the years Mrs. Looksee has been coming into the shop, she's never actually bought anything. That's why we call her Mrs. Looksee."

"Never?"

"According to Viv, never, not once," Fee said. "What sort of magic did you work on her?"

"No magic," I said. "Just, you know."

"No, I don't," Fee said. "But now I see what Viv meant."

"What do you mean?"

"When Viv told me you were coming, I asked if you were a milliner, too, and she said no, but that you had other gifts," Fee said. She picked up the hatband and resumed stitching. "Now I see what she meant."

I didn't, but I didn't say as much. I heard the bells on the door chime and the sound transported me back twenty years, and I remembered being a little girl, playing in the shop when a customer came in.

Mim had the same temperament as Viv. They were artists first and businesswomen second. I'd known Mim to get obsessed with a particular hat style or a color—there had been an infamous chartreuse stage—or if she'd found a vintage hat that she wanted to make over, it positively took over her brain.

We'd had cold tea and burnt dinner frequently when she was swept up by an obsession of the moment, but neither Viv nor I had minded. There was something spectacular and otherworldly about Mim when she'd been consumed by her creative fire. I'd always admired her devotion to her art. I had tried to follow in her footsteps like Viv, but I didn't have any talent for millinery.

Unlike Mim and Viv, I was a people person. I enjoyed talking to people. Everyone had a backstory and they were almost always interesting, which is what drew me to the hospitality industry.

Thoughts of my ex flitted into my head and I felt my spirits tank. While I'd been helping Mrs. Abbingdon, I'd completely forgotten the rat bastard. I was tempted to see who these other two women were, the ones the girl at the pub had told me about, but I didn't really want to know. It wouldn't do me any good, and really, my self-esteem was already at an all-time low as it was.

Instead, I straightened my back and headed out into the shop to see who had arrived. I was suddenly very grateful that Viv had sent for me. It was a relief to have something to think about besides my personal life.

"I'll go see who that is," I said to Fee and strode toward the door.

I had just stepped into the doorway when I collided with a solid male shirtfront.

"Oh, are you all right?" Harrison asked. He grabbed me by the elbows and steadied me on my feet.

"Sorry," I said. I glanced up at his concerned green gaze and smiled. "That was clumsy of me."

"Not at all," he said. "It was my fault. I should have called out a hello so you knew I was coming."

"Eh." I shrugged. I really had no idea what I meant or why I had a sudden feeling of awkward between us.

"You look like you got some rest." He let go of my arms.

"Practically slept the day away," I said.

"Well, if that's what it takes for you to sell to Mrs. Look-see then I say you should lie in every day," Fee said.

Harrison's brows rose up on his forehead and he studied me with renewed interest. "You sold a hat to Mrs. Look-see?"

"Mrs. Abbingdon," I corrected them both with a look. "She was very sweet. I think she just needed someone to listen to her."

Harrison and Fee exchanged a look I couldn't interpret, but I didn't get the feeling they were mocking me, so I let it go.

"So, have you heard from Viv?" I asked him.

"No, but I didn't really expect to," he said. "I take it you haven't either."

"No," I said.

"Not to worry," Fee said. I saw her looking at me in understanding. "Viv's an artist. She lives life her own way."

"Indeed," I agreed.

I remembered on my vacations spent with Mim and Viv that I always felt like the stabilizing force. I was the one who liked a schedule and liked to be on time. Viv and Mim were never on time and loathed to commit to any sort of itinerary. That was probably where I had first learned to work with challenging personalities.

It had obviously served me well. Right up until I had found myself hurling cake at the lying, cheating no-good rat bastard I'd been dating. I had to admit I hadn't managed that one well at all.

"Well, if all is right and tight here, then I will get back

to the office," Harrison said. "Is there anything you need, Scarlett?"

"Not that I can think of," I said. "I haven't checked the state of Viv's kitchen but I know there's a Tesco right down the road, so I can stock up on whatever I need there."

"All right," he said.

There was an awkward pause where he seemed to want to say something but then thought better of it.

"Go on with you," Fee said. "She's got me. I can help her with anything that might come up."

"Right enough," Harrison said. "'Bye then."

"'Bye," Fee and I said together.

"What's got his trousers in a bunch?" Fee asked. "He's not usually so knotted up."

"I don't know," I said. But a bad thought flitted through my head. "You don't think he actually knows where she is but isn't saying, do you?"

To my surprise Fee paused to consider it. I had thought since she knew both Harrison and in many respects Viv better than I did, at least when it came to day-to-day living, that she would reject my idea. But she didn't, which made me wonder.

"What is their relationship?" I asked.

"Relationship? You mean are they seeing each other?" Fee asked. "Romantically?"

"Yeah, I guess that's what I'm asking," I said.

"Well, he does come around quite a bit," Fee said. "Of course, a lot of that is because Viv has no head for business. You know, he always has to pull her out of some financial tangle or another. But come to think of it, they do attend some events together, you know, social functions, like the annual milliners' ball, and Viv gets invited to a lot of fashion events. I expect you'll be going to those, too, now that you're here."

I felt my chest get tight. I had stopped listening when she said that Harrison and Viv attended a lot of social functions together.

I reviewed the facts. Viv was missing. Harrison had met me at the Gate in her place. Why would he do that? Oh, sure, he had said she'd sent him, but the note was just a listing of the time and place of my arrival in her handwriting. It wasn't a personal note asking him to pick me up in her place.

I felt the blood rush into my ears with a whoosh. What did I really know about Harrison Wentworth? If he and Viv were dating and she went missing, wouldn't he be suspect number one if there were any foul play? Wasn't it always the person involved with the person who went missing who was the chief suspect?

Was Harrison Wentworth not just Viv's business manager and boyfriend but the reason she'd gone missing as well?

Chapter 8

I did not share my fears with Fee, partly because I didn't want to freak her out and partly because I didn't want to be perceived as a lunatic just yet.

I spent the rest of the afternoon familiarizing myself with the shop's inventory. Viv had obviously been going through a restoring-vintage-hat phase. The workroom had a cupboard full of old hats of all shapes and sizes, and out front one of her floor-to-ceiling display racks boasted everything from narrow-brimmed trilbies to trendy fascinators.

It seemed mandatory that I try a few on, so I spent a good half hour in front of one of the many freestanding mirrors placed about the shop, trying on hats and turning this way and that. My red hair clashed horribly with the magenta hats, but I found a divine olive green number that I was pretty sure was going to find its way into my collection.

When I lived in Florida, I had been a sun hat and visor sort of girl. In fact, I rarely went outside without them because I have the genetic predisposition to being part crustacean. In other words, if I spent a half hour in the tropical sun, I was soon red enough to sport claws and a snappy tail.

I glanced through the floating hat display to the street outside. It was a cozy gray day. Maybe it would even rain. I found myself looking forward to it as a nice change from the land of eternal sunshine.

Fee left the shop early on Tuesdays and Thursdays. She was still a student, slogging through classes in the hope that she would run a shop of her own one day.

"I'll see you tomorrow, yeah?" she called on her way out the door.

"I'll be here," I said.

The posted hours for the shop meant we were open for one more hour. I figured I could handle anything that came up. Now here's the thing about me, in case you missed it: when I am wrong, I am so very wrong.

Ten minutes before I would have turned the dead bolt, drawn the shades over the windows and door and called it a day, the door was yanked open with unnecessary force, setting its bells jangling and sounding more like an alarm than a pleasant ringing announcement of a customer arriving.

The woman who strode in was wearing a leopard-print dress that hugged her bodacious curves. She had on matching leopard-print shoes. A Coach bag dangled from her arm and her jewelry was not what one would wear for an everyday errand but rather the stuff of walks down a red carpet somewhere. Unless of course, she considered Mim's Whims that auspicious an outing but I suspected not. Rather, I think she was what the Brits call a toff, showing off her wealth, well, because she could. We had a lot of those in the hotel industry in Florida as well.

Her black hair was scraped back from her flawless face, a face that left even me staring at her in wonder. It wasn't a face that had been manufactured by nips and tucks and injections of toxins. No, it was a perfectly oval face with arching brows over luminous aqua-colored eyes, a narrow nose and perfect full pink lips.

"May I help you?" I asked.

The woman looked me up and down. "You're not Vivian."

"She's on vacation," I prevaricated. That sounds so much better than saying 'I lied,' doesn't it?

The woman turned and handed her purse to the man behind her. He was handsome but not overly so. In fact, he was of medium height, medium build, with pale skin, brown hair and hazel eyes and made an impression about as exciting as a glob of mayonnaise as he stood in the shadow of the beauty beside him.

"Vacation?" the woman asked.

I gathered from her tone that this was unacceptable. I wondered if Viv had a special order for the woman and I hoped like heck that there was a paper trail for it.

"When will she be back?" the woman asked. Her voice was curt and it was easy to see that she was irritated.

"Any day now," I said. Not a total lie because for all I knew it could be any day.

"You obviously don't know who I am," the woman said.

I wasn't sure if she was slamming me for being a foreigner or for being ignorant shop help, but I didn't want Viv to lose an account because of me.

"Of course, I know who you are," I bluffed.

One of her thin eyebrows rose higher than the other and I knew I had messed up somehow.

"Of course she knows you, Lady Ellis, or should I say The Right Honorable Countess of Waltham, adored wife of Earl Ellis of Waltham and beloved by all," the man beside her said. He put his hand over his chest and gave a mock bow.

He rose and stared at me in amusement. He licked his overly large lips as if I were a tasty morsel about to be devoured. Ew. I assumed from his mocking tone that he was Earl Ellis and he knew quite well that I had no idea who they were.

Nuts! The first customers I have to help all by myself and they are members of the peerage. I knew from my training at Mim's side that the proper address for Lord and Lady Ellis would be to address them first as "Lady Ellis" and "Lord Ellis" and then as "my lady" and "my lord." I scanned my brain trying to think of a way to save myself.

A quick glance at the woman, who was a beauty but also immaculately groomed, led me to believe that she logged a lot of time in front of her mirror. Anyone who spent that much time gazing at her reflection was definitely vain. It was easy for me to deduce that the best way to manage this woman was to appeal to her narcissism.

I inclined my head and said, "Lady Ellis, it is a pleasure to have you in our shop. My cousin mentioned you particularly when we discussed the business during her absence."

"Did she?" Lady Ellis's eyebrow lowered and she looked intrigued.

Vivian is a wild card, but like Mim, her hats have always been sought after by those who can afford them, because she is a gifted milliner. To have a favored designer like Viv talk about her would do more for Lady Ellis's vanity than any hollow praise I could offer her.

"She did," I said. "She was quite effusive in her praise of how beautifully shaped your head is."

I glanced at her through my lashes to see if she was looking mollified by my words. I saw her raise a hand to her head and pat the hair that was scraped back into a tight bun at the nape of her neck. Then she smiled.

"Vivian said that? How interesting." Her eyes met mine and she said, "My garden party is in four days. I'd like to pick up my hat now."

"Certainly," I said. There was no need to ask if it was a special order. Lady Ellis was not the type to buy off-the-rack. Whatever she had requested, I was quite sure it was one of a kind.

We kept a computer out front that was networked to the computer in the workroom. I opened the file on the desktop where Viv kept all of her accounts. It was a straightforward system that had a special-order file. Within the file the clients were listed alphabetically, then the hat they ordered and the price and whether they had paid or not.

I scanned the list, looking for Lady Ellis. I checked under the "L's" and the "E's" and the "V's." There was nothing. I could feel Lady Ellis watching me, and my heart began to pound. There was no help for it, without Fee or Viv to consult, Lady Ellis was just going to have to come back.

"I am so sorry, my lady," I said. "But there is no listing for any hat on order for you."

She stared at me as if my words were incomprehensible to her. Then her eyes narrowed and she said, "I'm afraid that is completely unacceptable."

Chapter 9

Lord Ellis leaned on the counter and smiled. It wasn't a knee-slapping-that's-a-funny-joke smile. It was a closed-lipped, wicked smile as if he was taking a twisted delight in her disappointment or my dilemma or both. Either way, it gave me the creeps.

I turned my attention to Lady Ellis. "I'm sure my assistant will be able to locate your hat for you. If you'd like, I can deliver it to your home personally."

"No, I don't like," she said. "I want my hat, for which I paid an outrageous sum, and I want it now."

"Do you know what it looked like?" I asked. I could feel myself getting flustered. I had assumed having her hat delivered to her home would calm her, but no.

"No, I don't," she said. "Vivian promised me a one-of-a-kind creation, something that would be the envy of all of my guests. As for me, I sincerely hope it was created to bring attention to my eyes."

I met her gaze. Her eyes were spectacular, and I could imagine that Vivian would have been quite inspired to match their unusual hue. They were a light teal or a dark aqua depending upon how the light shone into them. I glanced around the shop to see if perhaps Viv had put the hat she had created for Lady Ellis on display.

"It won't be out here. I told you it was to be kept a secret," she said. She sighed. I knew it was to let me know that she was finding the entire situation tedious.

I felt a prick of irritation with her but an even deeper stab with Vivian. How could she take off and not leave decent records? It was completely irresponsible. I didn't care how brilliant Viv was with her designs: if she annoyed a client with the stature of Lady Ellis, the business was going to go belly-up before her clever fingers could save it.

"Let me just go check in back," I said. "Can I offer you refreshments while you wait?"

"No, thank you," Lady Ellis said. "We are in a hurry, after all."

"Yes, my lady," I said. Suddenly, I felt as if I were in an episode of *Downton Abbey*, playing the part of a clumsy American.

I hurried into the workroom, thinking that if Vivian didn't get back soon, we were going to have some issues, namely, me throttling her.

Although Fee had given me a quick tour of the studio portion of the shop, I hadn't really paid much attention because this was not my area of expertise. Oh, I knew a lot of hat terminology, such as crown, brim and blocking. I'd have to have been in a coma all these years not to have picked up on most of it.

Still, although I admired pretty ribbons and cool hat shapes and what could be created by putting these things together, my brain was more geared toward appreciating the finished result. The few hats I had attempted in my youth always ended up looking like chowder pots and not very attractive ones at that.

I opened all of the cupboards and drawers and I checked all of the shelves. I saw loads of supplies and lots of half-done projects but there was nothing that I thought Viv would have concocted to accentuate Lady Ellis's eyes.

Going out front empty-handed was going to be like facing a firing squad without a blindfold. I straightened my shoulders. There was nothing to be done for it. I could almost hear the low tones of a dirge playing in my head as I dragged my feet toward the front.

Lady and Lord Ellis were browsing the shop when I returned. Lord Ellis was trying on a trilby hat in front of one of the mirrors while Lady Ellis tipped it to sit jauntily over one of his eyes. They were laughing together and for a moment I thought the bad news might not be received as poorly as I feared. Again, I was so wrong.

"I apologize, Lady Ellis," I said. "But I didn't locate any special projects in Vivian's studio."

The smile vanished from Lady Ellis's face as if I'd slapped her. I got the feeling she did not often hear the word "no." The man with her gave a low whistle like a teapot that was about to reach optimum boil.

Frantically, I glanced around the storefront. There had

to be something here that would appease her. Again, I knew I should focus on her vanity.

"It could be that your hat is such a special creation that Viv didn't want to leave it where anyone could see it," I said. "I'm sure that must be it. In fact, I wouldn't be surprised if Vivian was hoping to have you model it for the shop."

"Model?" Lady Ellis asked.

She looked interested, so I ran with it.

"Oh, yes," I said. "We do put out a catalog and our Web site features Viv's exclusive designs."

Lady Ellis studied me as if trying to figure me out. "Do you really think Vivian would want me to model one of her hats?"

"I think she'd be honored," I said.

Lady Ellis gave me a smile that reminded me of the one Lord Ellis had worn a few minutes ago. It was a smile devoid of warmth but rather seemed to take its delight in something sinister. No wonder they were a couple.

I tried to figure out why my words amused her but before I could latch on to an answer, Lord Ellis called to us from Aunt Mim's raven-topped wardrobe.

"Excuse me, but what's in here?" he asked.

"Nothing," I said. At least, Mim never used to keep anything in there. I supposed things could have changed.

Suddenly, it all made sense. I wanted to smack my hand to my forehead but I refrained. Of course, Vivian had probably kept Lady Ellis's hat in there. That was the only explanation.

"But let's check just in case," I said.

I crossed over to the wardrobe and turned the old-fashioned iron handle on the cupboard door. It opened with an ominous creak.

The scent of lavender wafted out into the room. Viv had obviously filled the wardrobe with the calming sachets. I sincerely hoped they worked if we found the wardrobe empty.

There was no need to worry, however, as I swung the other door open, there it was. Perched on a pedestal was a gorgeous, teal-colored cloche trimmed with a wide satin ribbon in a matching teal and finished with a brilliant cluster of Swarovski crystals set into the satin ribbon in an art deco diamond pattern. Viv had outdone herself.

"That—" Lady Ellis paused and glanced at her husband as if seeking his approval. He nodded, which of course he should have because it was a fabulous hat. I shifted from foot to foot, wondering if I was going to get reamed if she didn't like it. Of course, she was crazy if she didn't like it, and I had a good mind to tell her that.

"—is it," Lady Ellis continued. Then she smiled at me. "Well done."

I felt myself relax just the slightest bit. The Ellises exchanged delighted smiles, and I was so relieved it was all I could do not to jump up and kiss the raven on the beak in gratitude.

"Let me just box it up for you," I said.

"Yes, and while you do that, we can talk about my photo shoot," Lady Ellis said. Her eyes gleamed, but I couldn't tell if it was with delight or malice.

Chapter 10

When I closed and locked the door behind them, I felt a moment's panic that I now had to come up with a photographer by Friday, which was Lady Ellis's preferred day to meet for the photo shoot. Like a wet dog, I shook it loose, refusing to let it dampen my evening. I turned and leaned my back up against the closed door, surveying the shop.

Okay, yeah, the panic had me by the throat and it was not letting go. In fact, it seemed to be squeezing my air passage tighter and tighter.

"Viv, when you get back, we are going to have a long chat," I said. "It is completely unacceptable to leave me here alone with insufficient records."

It felt as if the word "alone" echoed back at me from every corner of the room like ghostly specters swooping down on me. I realized I had never been in the shop, or the house for that matter, by myself. Last night I'd had jet lag and a couple of pints to knock me out, but now I just had worry.

Worry about Viv and where she was and why no one was as concerned as me, worry that Harrison knew more than he was telling and quite possibly had something to do with Viv's disappearance. Worry that I now had to find and hire a photographer to take pictures of Lady Ellis modeling her hat. And lastly, worry that there was nothing decent to eat in the kitchen upstairs.

My stomach rumbled and it seemed to me that the last worry was now the most pressing. If I didn't eat, then I would be too weak to solve any of the other issues.

Of course, another problem for me was that there weren't any MoonPies in the UK. Yes, they did have Jaffa Cakes, a sponge cake with a burst of orange in the center and coated in dark chocolate, and I planned to stock up on those. But I really would have enjoyed a marshmallowy, gooey bite of decadence right now, or you know, a whole box of them.

I didn't want to go upstairs to find the cupboards lacking, so I decided to go out and forage for my food elsewhere, and if someone else cooked it, all the better, as I am a chef of absolutely no skill. I can't even boil water for tea. All right, I probably could, but I was resistant to learning.

Somewhere in my formative years, I noted a serious imbalance of the domestic arts in my family. When I was little, my mother stayed home with me. She said it was to nurture and raise me right but mostly I remember jumps off the roof with bedsheet parachutes being thwarted, so I always look at it as more of a quelling of my personality rather than a shaping of my good sense.

Anyway, with Mum home all day, it made sense that she

cooked. My father worked as a chemist, so he came home from his laboratory every night to a home-cooked meal. When I got older and my mother started her career as a professor of literature at a nearby university, she worked a full day like Dad but then came home and still cooked.

My father didn't know how to cook and had no interest in learning. On nights when my mother didn't cook and had to work late, Dad and I had cereal for dinner. I think it was then that I realized that the division of labor was less than equal in my house, and I determined that the best way not to get stuck carrying the load was to make sure I didn't know how.

My former boyfriend, the rat bastard, had found this to be a charming trait of mine. I'm sure it was because he never actually left his wife, like he said he did, and she probably did all of the cooking. Did I mention he's a rat bastard?

Viv kept an umbrella stand by the back door and one glance out the window told me that the overcast day was going to prove to be a soggy evening. As I shut off the lights in the shop on my way to retrieve an umbrella, I stopped by the wardrobe and peered up at my friend the raven.

"Nice work today," I said. "I'm going to the Tesco, do you want anything?"

He watched me but not even the tiniest caw passed his beak.

"Fine then, but I don't want to hear that you're hungry when I come back with yummy food and you have nothing to eat."

Still, he maintained his wooden silence.

"I'm talking to a carved bird," I said. "Viv, you'd better come back soon before I am full-on crackers."

There was no reply, which was not a big surprise, which I took to mean that I wasn't completely around the bend just yet.

I grabbed Viv's umbrella. Naturally it was not a plain black affair, no, hers was orange with pink polka dots. I was going to feel like there was a strobe light on me as I made my way down Portobello Road. On the upside, it would be very difficult to misplace.

I locked the shop door and headed out. It was only a light drizzle, so I didn't pop open my carnival tent to cover my head, but instead lifted my face up to feel the dampness bathe my skin. I felt as if I was still washing off the five thousand miles of travel, the day spent in the shop and my worries about so many things I couldn't control.

As I walked down the familiar road, I noted the changes that had happened over the years. Mim's Whims had been in the same spot for over forty years. Newly widowed, Mim had come to Notting Hill mostly because after the upheaval it had suffered during the riots of the late 1950s and the scandal of the early '60's, she found it cheap to buy in, but also she was charmed by the area, which seemed to have resisted all attempts at gentrification over the years. Mim was a rebel and the area definitely spoke to her wild side.

Mim had scrapbooks stuffed with photos of the hats she'd made for various members of the royal family as well as those that were particular favorites of hers. I used to spend hours as a child poring over the old albums, asking her questions about the people and the events they attended. I found it fascinating.

I paused beside an old shop. Its awning was tattered and it desperately needed some paint. It looked tired, like an aging beauty queen who refused to stop wearing her tiara and sash. I tried to remember what business had once been here, but I couldn't pull it out of my memory banks.

I saw a man inside the shop. He was moving around the empty space unpacking crates. Curiosity got the better of me and I pressed my face to the glass.

He bent over and used a crowbar to pry off the top of a flat wooden box. He moved the lid aside and removed a layer of packing material. Beneath it, I could make out a large, framed photograph. Was he opening a gallery?

He glanced up just then and saw me. Not knowing what else to do, I waved. He waved back.

Since I didn't move away, and I'm not sure why I didn't, he straightened up and crossed to the door. I heard the dead bolt click as he unlocked it. He pushed the door open and poked his head out.

"I'm sorry. I'm not open for business yet," he said.

The streetlamp on the corner shone on his face. He was black with close-cropped dark hair. He was of medium height but had a solid build. He wore all black except for the wink of diamond studs, large ones, in his earlobes.

"No, I'm the one who is sorry," I said. "I didn't mean to disturb you, but I was curious to see what sort of shop you're opening."

"Well, if I ever get it going, it will be a photography studio," he said.

"What a perfect location for it," I said. "My cousin and I own the hat shop up the street."

He looked me up and down as if considering me. I gave him my best wide-eyed ingénue expression.

"I'm Andre Eisel," he said.

"Scarlett Parker," I said.

We shook hands and I noted that his was warm whereas mine had grown cold from the chilly evening air.

"Would you like to see the inside?"

"I'd love to," I said. I stepped forward before he could change his mind.

There are no such things as coincidences. I firmly believe this, and the fact that he was opening a studio just when I needed a photographer, well, I was not going to let the opportunity go by. Even if he wasn't interested in taking Lady Ellis's photograph, surely he would know someone who was.

The main room was stark with no furniture, just wooden flooring and white walls with large, framed photographs leaning up against the walls. They were mostly cityscapes from all around London. That was bad luck, but I was determined.

As he led me around the small space, telling me about his plans to sell his original works, teach classes and take professional jobs, I thought all might not be lost. A stack of portraits was against the back wall and I asked if I could look at them.

I don't know a whole lot about photography, but the portraits had a quality to them, a certain angle or maybe it was the lighting that made me feel as if I was being let into the person's innermost being.

"Wow, these are really good, Andre," I said. "You have real talent."

"Thanks," he said. "With some of them I was just mucking around, but a few are keepers."

"Are you looking for work in portraiture?" I asked.

He narrowed his eyes at me. "Not particularly, why?"

"I'm in dire need of a photographer this Friday; would you consider it?"

"What's the job?" he asked.

"A portrait of Lady Ellis, wearing her new hat from my shop."

"Earl Ellis's wife? Lady Victoria Ellis?" he asked.

"Do you know them?" I asked.

"Of them," he said.

He put his hand on the back of his neck and tipped his head in that direction while crossing his other arm over his middle. I'm no expert on body language, but it looked to me as if he was torn. I was curious about why, but I was more desperate for him to agree to take the job, so I let it go.

A rapping on the glass door brought our attention around. While I'd been inside, the drizzle had surged into a downpour and only now I noticed the steady beat of the rain against the glass windows.

Standing outside in a trench coat with his collar up stood a fair-haired man, holding a plastic bag full of takeout food.

He looked soaked to the skin and suddenly I was grateful to have brought Viv's hideous umbrella.

"Oh, that's my partner, Nick Carroll," Andre said, and he hurried forward to open the door.

"Is he a photographer, too?" I asked.

"No, he's a dentist," Andre said. "And my life partner."

"Oh."

"What? Don't I give off enough poof?"

"Well, honestly, no, you don't," I said.

Andre grinned. "That's all right. Nick more than makes up for it."

I had no idea what he was talking about until he opened the door and Nick came in.

"It's bucketing out there and me without my brolly," Nick said. He kissed Andre's cheek. "Why did you let me go out without it, love? I'll catch my death and then you'll miss me."

Andre grinned. "I would at that."

"Who's the ginger?" Nick asked. He handed the food to Andre and put his hands on his hips as he looked me over.

"Manners, please," Andre said. "This is Scarlett Parker, a neighbor from down the street."

"Scarlett?" Nick asked. "I like that." He gave a little growl out of the corner out of his mouth. "It suits you."

"Thanks," I said. I couldn't help smiling.

Nick shrugged off his coat and hung it on a rack by the door. He looked to be a bit older than Andre, with thinning blond hair and a pleasantly plump shape.

"Of course, you'll join us for dinner," Andre said.

"Oh, no, I don't want to intrude," I said. "I've taken so much of your time as it is. If you'll just think about the job, I can pop back tomorrow to discuss it further if you'd like."

"What a lot of tosh," Nick interrupted me. "You can't go out in that. You'll drown before you get to the corner. Besides, I can never make up my mind when I order Thai food so I order too much and there is plenty. I hope you like it spicy."

Then he winked at me and disappeared into the back room.

"See?" Andre asked. "He more than makes up for me."

"Are you sure it's no trouble?" I asked.

"Positive," he said.

"All right then," I said.

I hung my coat on the rack by the door and put my umbrella beside it. Then I helped Andre clear off the lone table in the back of the room, while Nick brought plates and flatware and, bless him, a bottle of wine and three glasses.

It was one of the best meals I'd had in a long time. Andre and Nick were both delightful storytellers and they shared with me how they'd met—the traditional way, drunk in a pub. They'd been together for five years and seemed to be looking forward to a long and happy life together.

It wasn't until we'd cracked the third bottle of wine that Nick made the connection I'd been dreading.

"So, Scarlett, I know this sounds crazy, but I'm sure I've seen you before."

"It's not crazy," I said.

"But you just arrived yesterday," Andre said. "And you're from the States. How could Nick have seen you before? Are you an actress?"

"Not in the traditional sense," I said.

They exchanged a confused look.

"Do you really want to hear my tale of woe?" I asked.

"Yes!" they said together.

Chapter 11

"I'm an Internet star," I said with a hair toss.

Andre looked confused. Nick frowned.

Obviously, that wasn't enough of a clue. I was going to have to tell them the whole sordid story. It was just as well. They would put it together eventually, just like the girl in the pub yesterday, and at this point in our friendship, I'd rather they heard it from me.

"Do you have your Internet hooked up?" I asked.

Nick leaned over the table to reach into his briefcase, and he pulled out a tablet computer. He fired it up and handed it to me.

"Is this adult viewing only?" he asked.

"No!" I protested. "Sheesh, I'm not a porn star."

"Pity," Nick said with a grin.

Not surprisingly, I was able to type "party crasher" as I'd been nicknamed by the press into Google and the video gone viral came right up. I turned the tablet toward them and they leaned over it while I drained my glass and lifted the bottle of wine to fill it again. After a few seconds, Nick stared up at me with wide eyes.

"I've seen this before. That's how I know you. It's you, oh my god, it *is* you!"

"Shh!" Andre hushed him. "Oh! You got him right in the face!"

"Wow, that was no little cupcake tower you decimated," Nick said. "Wait! Is that the wife?"

"Yeah, apparently, there was a twenty-five-thousand-dollar diamond necklace decorating the top of the cake," I said.

"But you just hefted off the top tier and chucked it at him!" Andre's eyes were huge.

"Yeah, I was pretty lucky I didn't take out one of his eyes with that necklace."

Andre looked at me, and I could see he was pressing his lips together in an effort not to bust up. Nick had his head down and his shoulders were shaking as he did his best to squash his own laughter.

"Go ahead," I said. "Yuk it up before you hurt yourselves."

The dam broke. They basically had fits while I sipped my wine and waited.

"Better now?" I asked when they began to wind down. This, of course, set them off to laughing again.

When Nick began to wipe his eyes, I thought we might be in the clear.

"Well, you really frosted him, didn't you?" Andre asked.

And they were off again.

"She could have gotten an ASBO for cake and battery." Nick chortled.

I sighed. Luckily, I'd spent enough time in the UK to know that an ASBO is an anti-social behavior order, a fairly common citation, otherwise I might have been offended.

"That would have been the icing on top," I quipped. They both stopped laughing. "What? That was good. 'Icing,' 'top,' oh, come on."

"Oh, love," Nick said with a sad shake of his head.

"I should have gone with 'cherry on top.'"

"No, that's ice cream," Andre said.

"It doesn't matter," Nick said. He reached across the table and patted my hand with his. "We like you anyway."

"I still think 'icing' was clever," I said.

"Let it go now," Andre said. "So, tell us how you found yourself in such a layered situation."

Nick spewed his sip of wine across the table and they were doubled up with laughter again.

"Really?" I asked. "'Layered' trumps 'icing'? Ugh, no fair!"

I huffed, but it was impossible to stay mad at them. When they'd recovered themselves, I gave them the entire story from how I'd met the rat bastard and dated him for two years, thinking he was separated, to how I walked in on the anniversary party he was hosting for his wife.

"Oh, I'm so sorry," Andre said.

Nick nodded, looking too choked up to speak. All mirth was wiped from their faces and they looked at me with pity. I think I preferred the laughter.

"Don't feel bad for me," I said. "Feel bad for his wife. It

turns out he had a few more girls on the side. I can't imagine how she'll ever forgive him."

"If he's throwing twenty-five-thousand-dollar necklaces at her, I imagine she'll dig deep enough to find forgiveness in her heart," Andre said.

"Or her wallet," I said.

"And now you're here with us," Nick said. He lifted his wineglass and toasted me. "To Scarlett and her new beginning."

"To Scarlett," Andre said.

"To me," I said.

We touched our glasses together and for the first time since I'd arrived I felt as if I was coming home.

"So, Andre, what do you think about taking Lady Ellis's portrait?" I asked. "I'll pay you and I'll make sure she understands that we both get to use the photograph for our businesses."

"Lady Ellis?" Nick asked." You mean the Countess of Waltham married to Earl Ellis of Waltham?"

"Yes, that's right," I said. "Do you know her?"

"Who do you think gave her that gorgeous smile?" Nick asked. "She's a very powerful lady."

"So it would be good for the business to take her portrait?" Andre asked.

"It would be excellent," Nick said.

"So, Friday morning, Andre, are you willing?" I asked.

"And able," he said.

"To new business opportunities," I said and raised my glass.

"And to new friends," Nick said.

We killed off the third bottle and the two of them insisted upon walking me home. They lived above Andre's studio just like I lived above the shop. It made me feel more secure to have friends right down the street.

Oh, I knew some of the shop owners from spending my vacations here, but I imagined they remembered me as the very loud child I once was, not as the grown-up I'd become. And if they saw the video of me that had apparently circled the globe, well, then there was no chance of proving my maturity whatsoever.

It was probably the wine, but I found, as I hooked my arms through Andre's and Nick's and the three of us sang a horrid rendition of Katy Perry's song "Peacock" as we skipped down the street, well, I really didn't care what anyone thought of me at the moment.

Mim's Whims came into view just as I busted out into a knee-raising, arm-flapping part of the song. It took me a moment to realize that Andre, who really couldn't dance, and Nick, who was surprisingly good, had stopped moving.

"Come on, guys," I said and continued to sing, " 'I want to see your—' "

Nick was shaking his head back and forth and his eyes were huge. Andre pointed to something behind me.

"What?" I asked, freezing in place as if this would somehow make me less visible. I tried to be quiet but I think my voice was made louder by the dampness on the air. "Is it a cop?"

"Lucky for you, no," a voice said from behind me.

I whirled around to find Harrison, leaning against the front door with his arms crossed over his chest wearing a frown so deep it looked permanently etched into his face.

Chapter 12

Introductions were awkward. But Harrison seemed less suspicious upon learning that Nick was a dentist, which was interesting, given that most people do not have the warm fuzzies for dentists. I think he lent Andre and me an air of respectability in our shenanigans that we were lacking on our own.

"I'll stop by tomorrow to discuss," I whispered to Andre as I hugged him good night. He nodded.

" 'I want to see your peacock,' " Nick sang into my ear when he hugged me, and I giggled.

I waved as they strolled back to their apartment and yelled, "Good night!"

"Shh," Harrison hushed me. "You are aware of how loud you're being, yes?"

"Am I?" I asked at top volume. I was perhaps feeling the teensiest bit ornery.

"Scarlett, don't you know the whole of London is on CCTV?" he asked, sounding thoroughly annoyed.

"Sure," I said. I remembered that they had installed closed-captioned cameras all over London. Mim had been very much against it as a privacy issue.

"So, your behavior is undoubtedly being recorded somewhere," he said.

"So what?" I asked.

"So, I think you've had more than enough attention from your bad behavior being filmed lately, don't you?"

Ouch! I felt as if he'd slapped me, but I had to concede the point.

"Fine, Harry," I said in a much lower volume this time.

It took me a moment to fish my key out, but by the time I found it, Harrison had the door unlocked. "It's Harrison," he said with a sigh. "I have a key, too. Viv likes me to keep a spare for her in case she locks herself out."

"Uh huh," I said. I wasn't sure how I felt about that. To me it was just more evidence that he and Viv were more than friends and business partners.

"After you," he said and gestured with his arm for me to enter.

I didn't bother to turn the lights on until I got to the back room. I put Viv's umbrella away and hung up my jacket. I turned to find Harrison watching me.

"What?" I asked.

"I might have known," he said.

"Known what?" I asked. But I didn't wait for his answer. I was cold and required a piping-hot beverage. "I'm going to make tea. Would you like a cup?"

"Do you know how to make tea?"

"No," I said. "I was hoping you'd offer."

I shivered. Although Florida was a damp state, it was significantly hotter than London, and I couldn't seem to get the chill out of my bones.

Harrison rolled his eyes and moved to the little kitchenette where he put the kettle on. I figured this was a good chance to get him talking about Viv, so I could determine what exactly their relationship was and see if he knew more than he was saying.

"So, what did you mean, you 'might have known'?" I asked.

"Nothing," he said. He took the tea tin out of the cupboard over the sink and began to spoon loose tea into the steel infuser.

"Oh, no," I said. "You can't say something like that and not explain it."

He looked up from the cobalt-blue teapot into which he'd just put the infuser. He was giving me a slightly annoyed face, and I had a feeling the wine was making me more demanding than charming, but still, I wanted to know what he meant, and I wasn't above badgering to find out.

"Oh, come on," I said. "I'll just keep bugging you until you tell me."

"Honestly, I meant nothing by it," he said.

I shook my head, indicating that this was unacceptable.

"Fine, it's just that I was worried that you'd be curled up in a little ball of sad and lonely because Viv isn't here, so I came over here in the pouring rain to check on you and what do I find? You skipping down the street, singing at top voice with your two new best friends," he said.

"And that's a bad thing?" I asked.

"No," he said. "It's not bad. It's not normal, but it's not bad."

"I get the feeling you don't like me very much," I said. "In fact, you seem to suffer from a case of permascowl when I'm around."

His lips twitched, but he didn't smile or laugh.

"It's not that I don't like you," he said.

The kettle began to whistle and he turned away as if relieved by the interruption.

He filled the teapot with hot water and then covered it while the tea steeped. As if done with our conversation, he foraged through the cupboards until he found a canister of McVitie's Hob Nobs, a rolled oat biscuit with a layer of milk chocolate on it. He put some out on a plate for us to share, and I reached for one, surprised to find that I was hungry.

"Then what is it?" I asked.

"What is what?"

"If it's not that you don't like me, then what is it that makes you look so grumpy when I'm around?" I asked. I had a feeling he was being deliberately obtuse, but what the poor man did not realize was that I had staying power.

"I'm not grumpy," he growled.

"So you're just doing an impression of a grizzly bear for grins?" I asked.

"We don't have bears in England," he said. "And that's my point. I don't think you belong here either."

"So, *I'm* the bear?" I asked. I was getting confused.

"Uff!" He let out an exasperated huff and then poured the tea. "That's not what I meant."

"Well, what did you mean?" I asked. I waved my hands

at him. "Because this little tap-dance thing you're doing is giving me a headache."

He pushed my cup of tea at me, and I met his gaze and held it. It hit me then just what a handsome man he was. He had changed his clothes from earlier and was now wearing jeans and a forest green crew neck sweater. It made his eyes appear darker and more mysterious.

"Sorry," he said. "I guess what I'm trying to say is that I don't think you belong here and you should probably go back to the States as soon as possible."

Chapter 13

"Oh, you do, do you?" I asked.

Now normally, when there is an opinion expressed that is different from mine, I assess the situation, study the person and try to see their point of view. Then I determine the best way to devise a compromise that will meet both of our needs and let us go forth from there.

Maybe it was the wine, maybe it was the way his dark hair was falling over his forehead in an annoyingly attractive way, or maybe it just bugged me that he seemed to have taken a dislike to me, which frankly, is not how most people respond to me.

I am a people person. I am all about getting people to yes, meeting their needs, helping them to have not just a hotel stay but an experience. Granted this wasn't a hotel and he wasn't a guest of mine, but still, what had I done to make him dislike me so?

Oh, yeah, I stood him up when we were kids. Well, sheesh, that was seventeen years ago. Move on, already.

"Are you still mad at me for standing you up?" I asked.

"What?" he asked and then quickly said, "No!"

I ignored my tea and stared at him, willing him to be straight with me.

"Besides," he added. "You said you didn't."

He met my gaze with a steady one of his own. I raised my eyebrow in question and he mimicked me. Game on.

Suddenly, it all came rushing back. That summer as children when he'd been staying with his uncle and I'd been here with Mim. There had been a whole pack of us shop owners' kids, running amuck up and down Portobello Road daily until we were sent to nearby Kensington Gardens to play.

I remembered Harrison now as he had been then, a tall, skinny boy with big feet and messy hair. He'd been smart and funny but had seemed to be in a constant battle with his elbows and knees as if he just couldn't seem to get them all going in the right direction at the same time.

Oh, he'd had the potential to be good-looking even then, but I'd had my eye on what's-his-name. What was his name? How sad. I really couldn't remember the boy I'd had a crush on.

As I locked stares with Harrison, it was hard for me to believe anyone could have outshone him, even as awkward as he had been then. With our fellow wild things, we'd engaged in all sorts of games from ghost in the graveyard and freeze tag to staring contests, silent contests, and the impossible no-laughing contest, all were staples from that lazy summer.

I usually won the staring contest, Viv was best at the

silent contest, definitely not my gift, and we both failed at the no-laughing contest, primarily because Harrison always made us laugh with his quick wit and silly expressions.

The memory made me nostalgic for days gone by. It made me miss Mim. I felt a tear well up, and I knew I couldn't blink it away. I saw Harrison watch the tear track down my cheek and he looked as if he wanted to say something, but he didn't.

He didn't blink either, because whoever looked away first lost. For some reason I couldn't fathom, beating me seemed very important to him.

The sound of the clock ticking and the steady beat of the rain against the window kept time to our showdown of wills.

My eyeballs started to dry out. He grinned as if certain of his victory, as if he could tell I was at the breaking point. Not going to happen, bub.

I forced myself to think of something else. I pretended his pupil was an access point to another world and I focused on that as if I could tunnel my way inside of him and see his soul. He leaned in closer and narrowed his eyes, and it was then that I noticed the greens of his irises were full of heat and not the angry kind.

I felt my own eyes widen in surprise and for the first time I thought Harrison Wentworth might be more than I could handle.

A crash at the window made us both jump and turn toward it, ending our childhood game of a stare down in a definitive draw. I hopped off my stool and hurried toward the window. It appeared that one of the shutters had come loose and the stiff wind blowing outside had it slamming against the side of the house.

Mim had installed new windows to reduce the draft just a couple of years before she died. I unlocked it and it slid open easily. I then tried to figure out how to pop the screen.

"It'll be easier if I do it from outside," Harrison said.

"But you'll get soaked," I argued.

He was out the door before I could press my argument.

It was "bucketing" out again, as Nick had said. I watched helplessly through the window, letting the rain in, while Harrison wrestled the shutter back against the side of the house. It took him a few moments to latch it back, and I knew he was going to be soaked to the skin by the time he came back in.

I met him at the door with a batch of fresh tea towels from the drawer in the kitchenette. I blotted off his shoulders while he toweled his thick head of hair. I draped the towels on his shoulders and he left one on his head.

"Come sit and have your tea," I said. "It will warm you up."

He clutched the towel under his chin and gave me a coquettish look. In a high falsetto, he said, "Just a spot of tea, dear, and only half a biscuit. They go right to my arse, you know."

It was a spot-on impression of Mim, and I busted out in a belly laugh. How had I forgotten his ability to mimic people? He was never cruel, but he always managed to capture the person's mannerisms and say something that I could hear the person saying, but when Harrison did it, it was hilarious.

He lifted up his teacup and took a noisy slurp, still with his head in a tilt like Mim held hers.

"My grandmother did not slurp her tea," I said.

He raised an eyebrow at me and said, "Oh, no, I was imitating you."

"Oh, you!" I snatched up the tea cozy and threw it at his head.

He laughed and caught it before it connected. We were quiet for a moment, enjoying each other's company. Now I felt ridiculous for thinking he could have any knowledge as to Viv's whereabouts. Maybe the events of the past week had caused me to become more suspicious. If so, I hoped it wore off. I didn't like thinking the worst about people.

Now that Harrison and I seemed to be friends again, I couldn't resist asking, "Do you really want me to leave?"

Chapter 14

"Yes," he said with no hesitation whatsoever.

"Ah," I gasped. My feelings were hurt. I admit it. I'd thought we were joking around and getting our old friendship back, but no. He still wanted me gone. Fine!

I lifted my cup of tea and took a big sip. It was still hot but not scorching, so I drained it and plunked it back down onto the table.

"Oh, look at the time," I said. I pointedly glanced at my wrist. And no, I don't wear a watch.

He got it in one. "You want me to leave."

"Why would I want that—just because you want me to leave the country?" I asked.

The sarcasm dripped so thickly off my tongue I was surprised it didn't leave spots on the counter.

"I hurt your feelings," he said. He came around the counter to stand beside me.

"You told me that I should go home as soon as possible," I said. I refused to look at him and addressed the top of the counter instead. "How is that supposed to make me feel?"

"I just don't think you're a good fit for the business."

"I sold a hat to Mrs. Looksee," I reminded him.

"Listen, I didn't think you'd take it so personally," he began, but I cut him off.

"Really?" I asked. Now I turned to face him. I was losing my temper. I never lost my temper. Had my unfortunate experience with the rat bastard altered my personality? Well, wouldn't that just be a lovely parting gift from that relationship? "Well, I did take it personally, and you know what I think? I think you have an ulterior motive for wanting me gone."

"What possible motive could I have?" he asked.

"I think you know what happened to Viv, and you don't want me to figure it out," I said.

"Hey!" Now he looked outraged, and I found that quite satisfying. "What exactly are you accusing me of?"

"I think you know where Viv is," I said.

"That's ridiculous," he argued. "Why wouldn't I tell you?"

I pressed my lips together. There was nothing I could say that wouldn't sound bad.

His eyes widened as he figured it out all on his own.

"You are mental!" he said. "Do you really believe I had something to do with Viv's disappearance?"

"Aha!" I said. I poked him in the chest with my index finger to drive my point home. "Right there. You called it a disappearance. Why would you call it that if you didn't know something?"

"I don't know anything!" he protested. "I swear."

"I don't believe you," I said.

"What do you believe then, Ginger?" he asked.

He was several inches taller than me and I probably should have been intimidated with him looming over me, but I wasn't. I met his stare. I figured he was using my old nickname to soften me up, but when I studied his face, he just looked angry. Maybe when he thought of me, he thought of me as "Ginger" and the nickname came out by accident. Either way, there wasn't much point in holding back now.

"I think you and Viv are romantically involved," I said.

Now he laughed, and it wasn't a mirthless laugh, he was actually amused. "Dating? Me and Viv?"

"Yes," I said, but I knew I sounded less sure. "And the person involved with the person who is missing is usually the culprit."

"Culprit of what?" he asked. "What exactly are you accusing me of?"

"I don't know," I admitted. "But I don't trust you."

"Well, at least we have that in common," he said.

"You don't trust me?" I asked. Now I was offended.

We were mere inches apart and I was feeling feisty enough to do some bodily damage on him. It was a shocking thought as, other than the cake incident, I was not generally a brawler.

"You really think Viv and I were romantically involved?" he asked and I nodded. "Let me ask you this, did she ever mention me as her boyfriend?"

"No," I said.

"And you and Viv talk frequently?" he asked.

"Well, it used to be weekly, but the time change makes it difficult," I said. "So, it's been less lately."

Yeah, big fib. It had been a lot less for the past two years while I'd been dating he-who-should-have-choked-on-cake. Yes, I can admit it. I dropped everyone and everything for him. Only now that I was five thousand miles and a global humiliation away from him did I see how much I had sacrificed for him. It made me queasy.

"Still, if she and I were involved, don't you think she would have mentioned me?" he asked.

"I don't know," I said. "Are you married?"

"No." He held up his left hand so I could see it had no wedding band. "But here's an interesting theory you might enjoying chewing on, Ginger."

"What's that, Harry?" I asked. His brows lowered at the use of his old nickname. Point to me.

"Since I'm not romantically involved with Viv, and as far as I know, she isn't seeing anyone, that would leave whomever she's in business with as the most likely suspect, don't you think?"

It took a few moments for his words to register and when they did, I gave him a hearty shove, catching him off guard and sending him back a few paces.

"Me?" I cried. "You think *I* had something to do with Viv's disappearance?"

Chapter 15

"As the person who inherits the business if anything happens to Viv, wouldn't it make sense that the one most likely to do her harm is you?" he asked.

"No, it wouldn't," I said. "I was in Florida with my personal life imploding, so no, it doesn't make sense."

"How do we know you were in Florida?" he asked. "How do we know that whole video thing you did wasn't just a part of your ploy to cover your tracks when you got rid of your cousin?"

"Stop it!" I cried. "Just stop it. It's not true."

"Fine. My work here is finished," he said and he wiped his hands together. He strode to the front door without looking back. "Lock up behind me!"

I heard the door slam behind him and I was left alone in the kitchen with a rapidly cooling pot of tea that seemed like a perfect metaphor for the tentative friendship I had begun with Harry, er, Harrison.

I cleaned up the kitchen, feeling equal parts confused, angry and sad. Was Harrison right? Was I the most likely suspect in my cousin's disappearance? Is that why he didn't like me? Did he suspect deep down that I had whacked my cousin to get my clutches on the family business?

I swung from hurt to some serious rage. I'd had enough hurt to last me awhile, so I settled in on a nice slow-burning rage. I reheated my cup of tea in the small microwave and called my mom.

It was a five-hour time change from London to New Haven, where my parents were currently living as my dad, who had retired from lab work, was now teaching chemistry at Yale University. My mom had retired from teaching literature and now worked as a freelance editor. It was early evening so I hoped she'd be home.

The phone rang three times before she picked up. I hadn't checked in since the morning after I arrived and they hadn't answered then so I'd only left a voice mail.

"Hello?" she answered. Her accent wasn't as thick as it once was, but it still had her lovely English lilt that always soothed me.

"Hi, Mum," I said. My voice wobbled and I cursed myself. What was it about calling my mother that reduced me to a three-year-old with a case of the sniffles?

"Oh, love," she said. "What's wrong?"

The dam burst and I let loose. I had tried to spare my parents the news of the nasty breakup, the video gone viral and getting sacked from my job. Instead, I had told them I was just hopping over to London to see Viv for a long-overdue vacation. God love them, my parents hadn't questioned me.

Once I finished whining and crying and wound down and ended the story with Viv being missing and no one taking it seriously, not even Aunt Grace, my mother's sister, my mother waited for a beat as if absorbing all that I had told her.

"Now, Scarlett," she said. "I know you were trying to spare Dad and me, but the truth is we already knew about the video."

"You did?" I blew my nose.

"One of your father's colleagues showed it to him," she said.

Oh, poor Dad!

"Why didn't you say anything?" I asked.

"We knew you'd tell us when you were ready," she said. "Although I did have to hide your father's license and credit card; the day after we saw the video, he was planning to fly to Tampa and give that rat bastard a good thrashing."

"So, you're not disappointed in me?" I asked.

"In you? Never. In the choice you made? A little bit," she said. Like Mim, my mother seldom candy-coated it. "Dearest, I know that deep down, you probably knew that this man was hiding something, otherwise he would have wanted to meet your family and you never brought him home to meet us, did you?"

"No, he was always busy," I said.

We were both silent for a moment as I realized how truly stupid I had been, because that's always fun, isn't it?

"Do you realize that this is the first time since you turned sixteen that you haven't had a boyfriend?" she asked.

"No, that can't be," I said. "I've been single before."

"Two weeks between boyfriends doesn't count," she said.

"I've gone longer than that," I protested.

"No, pet, you haven't," she said.

She sounded so sure that I didn't press it and instead changed the subject.

"But, Mum, what should I do about Vivian?" I asked. "Don't you find it peculiar that she wasn't here when I arrived, considering that she sent me the ticket and all?"

"If it were anyone but Viv, I would," she said. "But you know how she is."

"Yes, but—"

"Remember the time she came to Florida to visit and then vanished for three days because she found out that a woman on Key West had a collection of rare wooden hat forms and she wanted to see them?"

My mother had been in a panic that Viv had been kidnapped or crashed her car by driving on the wrong side of the road. Then as now, Viv had left no note or anything, but simply returned a few days later and with several hat forms she'd managed to charm out of the woman for a decent price.

"Yes, I remember," I said.

"And then there was the time she was in Italy with your Aunt Grace and discovered that there was a Borosilicate glass bead auction in Murano and she just went, leaving Grace to fend for herself in Venice."

I heaved a sigh. All of this was true and just the tip of the iceberg when it came to Viv and her artistic whims.

"I really think Viv will turn up when she catches whatever she is chasing."

"I suppose you're right."

"Of course, I'm right," she said. "Now enjoy your time in London, and you might consider taking a time-out from men and relationships, don't you think?"

"I suppose," I said. I knew I sounded cranky and I couldn't help it.

We chatted for a few more minutes, and I paced about the shop, checking that the windows and doors were locked, while we talked. When we hung up, I felt better about Viv, but not much else. I was still mad at Harrison, and I still thought he knew more than he was telling.

Before I left the kitchen, I decided to go through Viv's desk. Maybe she kept a calendar on her computer that would tell me where she was or if I was really lucky maybe she had an automatic sign-in on her e-mail and I could snoop through it. No, I had no qualms about doing this. If she didn't want me to snoop, she should have left me more information before she up and abandoned the ship.

Sadly, Viv's desk was a lot like her personality, seemingly neat with a whole lot of clutter going on underneath. Just because all of the stacks are tidy does not mean there is any order to them. Receipts and bills were stacked together along with fashion catalogs and a few greeting cards.

Her computer was not much better. I could not break into her e-mail no matter how hard I tried, and her file system was not a system so much as everything was saved on her desktop and therefore covered the main screen with documents and photos with nothing filed in any sort of order. I had no doubt that she could find anything on here, but it gave me the feeling of looking for a pearl in a pile of oysters with nothing to show for my effort but a whole lot of shucking.

I quit. I switched off the lights and said good night to the carved bird. Per usual, he did not respond. He was going to have to be named if we were going to keep having these late-night chats, even as one-sided as they were.

"What do you think of Ferd?" I asked him. Nothing. "Come on, you can be Ferd the bird. It can be short for Ferdinand, if you prefer?" Still, nothing. "Fine, think on it and get back to me."

I dragged myself upstairs. I debated searching Viv's room, but it was already well past midnight and I figured if her room was anything like her computer or her desk it would give me a scorching headache. It could wait until tomorrow, then.

With face washed and teeth brushed, I climbed in between my cold sheets. I pretended to run in place to warm the sheets up and when they were not so icy, I lay still and listened to the rain beat on the glass window as if looking for a tiny crack or crevice to sneak its way into the warm house.

I was more hurt and angry at Harrison's insinuation that I had something to do with Viv's disappearance than I liked. It shouldn't have bothered me that he thought so lowly of me. Then again, didn't I think the same thing about him? I wondered if it bothered him.

There had to be a way to track where Viv had gone: receipts, billing statements, something. Fine, maybe she was out of cell phone range and with spotty access to her e-mail. Still, I wanted to see evidence that she had bought plane tickets or made a hotel reservation somewhere.

Then again, as her business manager, did Harrison do that for her? If he did, why didn't he tell me? Because he had something to hide. It was the only explanation.

Well, tomorrow he could just explain it to the police. I didn't care what my mother or Aunt Grace said. I had a funny feeling about Viv being missing that I couldn't shake, and I was going to report her missing tomorrow. We'd just see how Mr. Harrison Wentworth felt about that. Ha!

The last thought that flitted through my head before I conked out was that for the first time in days, I felt as if I was getting a little of myself back. I was making decisions and taking action. It felt good.

I was still irritated with Harrison when I woke up in the morning. I frowned when I thought of him. I couldn't believe that he had, oh so nicely, pointed out that I might be the cause of my cousin's disappearance. Jerk! I was still hopping mad at him, and if I did see him, I thought it likely that I might not be able to squash the urge to kick him, in the shin, of course.

The shop opened at ten, so I waited until Fee arrived for work and then I decided to take an early morning stroll in the neighborhood. I picked up a hot cup of coffee from the Starbucks on Portobello and then made my way over to Ladbroke Road, where the local police station sat on the corner.

When I had decided upon this course of action this morning, it occurred to me that popping in to talk to someone about the situation with Viv might be the best, as in the least hysterical, way to handle the situation.

I glanced up at the large stone building that housed the Notting Hill police station. It was intimidating, and for the first time I wondered if I should go ahead with my plan. It wasn't as if Aunt Grace or my mother or Harrison seemed overly concerned about Viv, but still I felt like I should tell someone just in case something was wrong.

I leaned against the stone rail that jutted out from the building while I pondered my motives. Was I doing this just to get even with Harrison for accusing me of having a vested interest in Viv's absence? If I was honest, that was a part of it. The innocent side of me shouted that if I was guilty I would never go to the police, so this would prove it.

But the part of me that had a funny feeling about Viv being missing didn't care. I hadn't been able to shake the feeling since I arrived that there was something wrong with Viv's not being here.

That decided it. I pushed off the rail and strode toward the station. A constable passed me on his way out and tipped his rounded hat at me. I smiled in return and lifted my coffee cup to take a long, bracing swallow.

When I glanced up and saw who was coming out of the station, I choked on my inhale. Harrison Wentworth, looking annoyingly impeccable in a charcoal-gray suit, was walking with another man dressed in brown slacks, a dress shirt with a tie and a buff-colored jacket. They were walking out of the station together and appeared to be having an intense conversation. It was almost as if he sensed me standing there, and before I could dash away or hide, Harrison glanced up and met my stare.

Chapter 16

He stopped in his tracks and the man beside him stopped, too, and followed the line of his gaze. He was older than Harrison, with a thatch of light brown hair that was going gray and a thick mustache that was doing the same.

"You!" I cried. I pointed my finger in Harrison's direction to remove any doubt as to who I was shouting at.

"How did you know I was coming here today? And what are you trying to do—accuse me?"

"Calm down, Ginger," he said. His hands were raised in the international palms-out sign for "I have no weapon," "stop right there" or "I surrender." It was hard to say which one it was or if it was a combo of all three. Frankly, I didn't care.

"What did he tell you?" I asked the other man as they stopped in front of me.

The man reached up and stroked his mustache as if it

was something he did to give himself a minute to ponder the situation before him.

"Detective Inspector Franks, this is Ms. Scarlett Parker," Harrison said. "She is the cousin of the woman I was telling you about, Vivian Tremont."

"What did you say?" I snapped at Harrison.

This was unbelievable. How could he? I glowered at him. I was absolutely convinced that he had something to do with Viv's disappearance now. He was no doubt trying to take the suspicion off himself and dump it on me.

"Inspector Franks," I said, addressing him in what I hoped was my most earnest tone. "I don't know what Harrison has told you, but my cousin was supposed to meet me two days ago, but when I arrived *he* was there, and I think he knows more than he's saying."

Inspector Franks considered me from under some spectacularly bushy eyebrows. I wondered if he'd let them run wild to balance out his mustache. Despite the facial hair, his deep-set, brown eyes were sharp with intelligence. I got the feeling he didn't miss much.

"You're American?" he asked.

"Half," I said. "My mother is British."

"Where'd you live in the States?"

"Florida," I said.

"The South?" he asked. "The homeland of country music."

"Technically, I think that's Nashville, Tennessee," I said. "A bit further north."

He didn't appear to hear me. "I've got the pipes of Alan Jackson."

"Excuse me?" I asked.

Harrison was watching our exchange with interest, which turned into amusement when Inspector Franks broke into a barrel-deep baritone and starting singing about the Chattahoochee. No, I'm not kidding.

I had to give it to him. He certainly sounded as if he could be the six foot four Georgian. Still, I felt the need to get this situation back on track.

"You really are wonderful, Inspector Franks," I said. He looked pleased at the compliment and Harrison gave me a look with one eyebrow raised that said he knew what I was trying to do. "But back to my cousin Vivian . . ."

"Yes, of course," he said. "I suppose I should save the singing for the pub."

He gave a good-natured chuckle, and I had to admit that I liked him. He seemed so reassuringly unflappable.

"Upon Mr. Wentworth's report, I did some checking," he said.

He preened his mustache again and glanced at Harrison as if still assessing him. I liked that. Inspector Franks was no pushover.

"It seems your cousin is somewhere in Africa buying supplies for her hat shop," Inspector Franks said. "I had a nice chat with your aunt this morning, who got an e-mail from Vivian last night, and I called one of our liaisons over there and he is going to check on her."

"Why isn't she e-mailing me?" I asked.

"Sounds like she doesn't have great Web access," Inspector Franks said. "Maybe one e-mail was all she could get out."

That seemed an awfully convenient answer. I frowned.

"Look, as soon as I get a line on her from our people I'll

call you," he said. "Her mother isn't worried. There's no reason you should be."

He sounded so pragmatic. What could I say? That I had a feeling? That the man next to him was not to be trusted?

"Thank you," I said. I sensed it would be bad form to push it.

Inspector Franks wished us both a good day and went back into the imposing police station, singing as he went.

"So, Harry, how did you manage that?" I asked.

He raised his eyebrows. "I don't know what you mean and it's Harrison."

"Yes, you do," I growled. "Harry."

I turned on my heel and stomped back down Ladbroke Road, which would take me to Kensington Park Road, which ran parallel with Portobello Road. I was so mad I was surprised the sidewalk beneath my feet wasn't crumbling under the force of each step I took.

"Ging—uh—Scarlett," he called after me.

I ignored him, mostly because I was afraid that if he got within my reach, I would chuck my coffee at him and that would be a sad waste of a good cup of java.

He was undeterred, however, as he caught up to me and matched his longer stride to my shorter one. I ducked around a mother pushing a stroller and he met me on the other side.

"Scarlett, just listen to me," he said. "It's not what you think."

"Huh," I scoffed. I picked up my pace.

"You think I went to the police first to try and shift suspicion away from myself and onto you, don't you?"

I drew up short. Okay, I hadn't expected him to admit it.

I turned to face him and almost collided with a business-woman in spiky heels and a pretty plum-colored suit.

"Sorry," I said as I scooted to the side.

Harrison followed me and we found ourselves pressed up against a short wrought-iron fence.

"That's exactly what I think," I said. "Now I know that I haven't been the best cousin or business partner, but I'm going to find out where Viv is and what's going on with her and you can't stop me."

"Do you really think I would try?" he asked. "I came to the police station because I think you're right."

It was the genuine tone of worry in his voice that caught my attention and held it. I studied his face. His green eyes looked concerned, but there was something else there. He knew something that he wasn't telling me.

It was then that I noticed he looked pale, as if he hadn't been sleeping well, and his thick, dark hair had tracks in it as if he'd run his fingers through it repeatedly.

What did he know? And more importantly, how could I get him to tell me?

Insulting him was obviously not the best plan. I wasn't sure why Harrison caused my stellar people skills to evaporate, but if I wanted to know what exactly was going on then I had to make my next move carefully.

Chapter 17

I'm a toucher, so I went for the tactile maneuver. I've found that people respond well to a pat on the hand or a half hug. It breaks down barriers and builds a rapport, especially if people are not being straight with you.

I put my hand on his forearm in a comforting gesture. I gave it a light squeeze and then met his gaze, making sure I looked sympathetic.

"You really are anxious about Viv, aren't you?" I asked.

He blew out a breath as if relieved. "I'm trying not to be, but yeah, there's something off here. She always contacts me when she travels."

He glanced at my hand resting on his arm, and I quickly removed it. That is the other secret to being a toucher: don't linger into awkward. That had been borderline. We exchanged a quick glance, and I began walking back to the shop. Harrison fell in beside me.

"She did e-mail Aunt Grace," I said. The irony that I was now comforting him was not lost on me.

"Yes, and that's definitely a good sign," he said. "Listen, I'm sorry that I was dismissive when you were trying to tell me that it was odd that Viv wasn't here to greet you. She is a wild card, but that was out of character even for her. She adores you, and she was so excited that you were coming."

"Does that mean you don't really think I had anything to do with her being missing?" I asked.

He had the grace to look a bit embarrassed. "I never thought that. I just wanted you to see how easy it was to twist the facts and accuse someone."

"Oh." I frowned.

"This is where you say you never thought I had anything to do with it either," he said. His tone was as dry as toast.

I broke into a surprised laugh.

"I missed my cue, didn't I?" I asked.

"By a kilometer or two," he said.

I thought about our first few meetings. Did I really think Harrison had anything to do with Viv being missing? I dug deep all the way to my core. No, but there was a lingering doubt. I just couldn't shake the feeling that he knew more than he was saying. Of course, up until a week ago, I would have said I was pretty good at reading people, but the rat bastard had taken care of that. Still, I didn't trust Harrison completely.

"I don't think you're the reason she's missing," I said.

"Clever." He gave me a small smile, letting me know he was very much aware that I hadn't absolutely absolved him.

"Do you think Inspector Franks will be able to find her?" I asked.

"I don't know," he said. "I guess it depends on how far his reach extends. I have some business associates that I am going to meet with today. I think they might be able to help us, and you can contact your aunt and see if you can get more specifics."

I gave him a sideways glance.

"What?" he asked.

"Are we working together on this now?" I asked.

He gave me a slow smile and again I was struck by how handsome he was.

"Truce?" he asked, holding out one hand.

"Truce," I said. I took his hand in mine. It was large and warm and his fingers folded around mine gently but firmly. It was a good handshake. If you can measure a person by their handshake, then Harrison Wentworth was a good man. Still, I was going to keep an eye on him.

We continued on to the hat shop. When we turned onto Kensington Park Road, he stopped me with a hand on my arm.

"Do you remember this corner?" he asked. He had a twinkle in his eye as if the memory he had of it was a good one.

"Given that I walked past it just a half hour ago, it would be hard for me to forget," I said. I knew full well that wasn't what he meant, and he gave me an exasperated look that told me he knew I was teasing.

"We got busted here," he said. "You, me, Viv, Dean, Clarissa, Chester and some others. I can't remember their names."

The names he did mention brought back faces from the

past like specters. We had been such an unruly gang of preteens.

"Wow, I haven't thought of that group in years," I said. I glanced around the corner where we stood and then I remembered.

"Chester! He was the one."

Harrison broke into a grin and I knew he was sharing the same memory.

"We were spitting out watermelon seeds and he nailed that passing car," I said. "And it turned out to be Prime Minister John Major's car."

We exchanged a wide-eyed glance.

"The Specialist Protection officers were not amused," he said. Again, classic British understatement.

"I can't believe they let us go," I said. "I remember thinking they were going to arrest us and that Mim would never forgive me and I'd never be allowed back into the country again."

"As I remember it, you worked your magic on the officers and the Prime Minister," he said.

"I don't know about that."

"Oh, sure, you started with big, limpid eyes," he said. He batted his eyelashes at me and I felt my mouth tip up in one corner. "Then you were so polite as you asked questions about how dangerous their jobs were and then told them how grateful we were to have such brave men looking after our distinguished prime minister. I think Chester vomited on his shoes."

"That's gratitude. I was saving his bacon," I said.

"Remember we all ran to Kensington Gardens and hid for the rest of the day?" he asked.

"We were afraid to go home." I laughed at the memory. I began to walk again, feeling as if ten-year-old me had joined us. I had to squelch the urge to skip just to see if it felt the same.

"But we got hungry," he said.

"Well, watermelon will only take you so far," I said.

The foot traffic on the sidewalk was thicker than it had been earlier. Several times I had to swerve around mothers with toddlers and elderly people. After a block, Harrison took my elbow and turned me onto a narrower and less busy street.

The strong breeze that had been at our backs vanished and I felt myself relax. London in April felt like winter in Florida with cool days and brisk breezes.

I used to be pretty quick at converting Celsius to Fahrenheit in my head, but like any skill it goes dormant without use, and I had to really think about it now. The BBC weather report this morning had said it expected the day to be partly cloudy and fifteen degrees. I knew that was somewhere around sixty degrees but I had a feeling it was still in the fifties. I was glad I had worn my thick wool sweater and jeans.

Of course, this made my thoughts veer to Vivian. I wondered where she was and if she had packed the right clothes. Was she scared, lonely, drunk? It was maddening not knowing.

At the door to the hat shop, Harrison stopped.

"I'll call you if I hear anything," he said.

"Likewise."

"She's fine," he said. I wondered if it was to comfort me or him.

"Sure," I agreed. My voice lacked conviction and his gaze met mine.

He looked as if he wanted to say something but then thought better of it. In a surprise move, he put a hand on the back of my neck and pulled me close as he planted a kiss on my forehead.

It was an oddly comforting gesture and I found it made my throat get tight. I swallowed hard.

"We'll find her," he said.

I nodded, unable to speak. And I was surprised to find that I believed him.

Friday morning, I met Andre at his studio. It had been two days since I'd seen Harrison and I hadn't heard from him or Inspector Franks in the interim. I tried to tell myself that no news was good news, but I wasn't buying what I was selling.

I had called Aunt Grace every day and she still seemed to think everything was fine, but I was beginning to think she had a deep case of denial going. It was now five days since I'd arrived without a word from Viv. There was no way this was normal.

Andre said he knew where the Ellis Estate was and had agreed to drive since he had to haul equipment, and I had no car and no idea of where we were going.

We met in front of his shop at ten o'clock. He had several bags of equipment that he was stuffing into the trunk of his tiny car. Compared to the ridiculously giant gas-guzzlers I was used to in the States this felt a bit like trying to wedge myself into a go-cart, the wrong side of a go-cart for that matter.

He merged into the traffic on Portobello Road and took

several turns through Ladbroke Grove, heading south toward Kensington.

"Are you sure of the address?" I asked.

"Harrington Gardens?" he asked. "Of course. Don't forget I spend my days photographing London and all of its surrounding neighborhoods. Nick accuses the old girl of being my mistress."

"Does he really mind?" I asked.

"Well, I offered to take pictures of him in the buff if it would make him feel better, but he said the mere offer made it unnecessary," he said.

I could see Nick saying that and I smiled. A car honked and I whipped my head around to see if they were honking at us.

"You can't take every bleat of the horn personally," Andre said.

"Sorry, I'm just not used to it."

"No worries, we're almost there," he said. "I swear surface traffic in London moves at about five kilometers per hour. Mercifully, we're not at peak driving hour otherwise it would take us forever."

We turned left onto Kensington High and I could see Kensington Gardens on the left. I promised myself that I would take a long walk there at the first possible chance. The large park disappeared as Andre wound further south into Kensington.

After a few more short turns, he pulled up along a row of beautiful homes in the heart of Harrington Gardens. I felt my jaw thunk into my lap. The narrow mansions were built of terra-cotta brick with ornate stone facings and stone mullioned windows.

"Wow," I breathed, and Andre laughed.

"I know what you mean," he said. "I did a little research and found out that Lord and Lady Ellis's Dutch colonial home was built in 1883 by the architects Ernest George and Peto for the second son of the Earl of Leicester."

"No wonder Lady Ellis seems to think she's all that," I said. "I would, too, if I lived here."

"No, you wouldn't," Andre said. "Being a toff is not your style."

I took that as a compliment.

We stepped out of the car, and while Andre unloaded his equipment bags, I stared up at the four-story, pointy-roofed mansion with awe. A stone angel peered down at me from the third floor. Its chubby face was so much more pleasant than the sharp-beaked raven on top of Mim's wardrobe that I made a mental note to see if the raven could be carved to look more like a fat cherub. Viv would never go for it, of course, but it made me smile to think of it.

The front door was recessed within a stone archway. A thick wooden door was set back, and I led the way up the three short steps into the alcove with Andre on my heels hoisting his bags onto his shoulder as we went.

I rang the bell, which I could hear echoing in the house. Andre rocked back and forth on his heels while we waited. I had to curb the urge to hum or whistle. I'm not very good at waiting, Harrison would probably say this was another sign of my lack of impulse control.

The door opened and a stout woman in sensible black shoes and a severe black dress that covered her from neck to knee greeted us.

"Good morning," she said. She peered at us through

rimless glasses that perched on the end of her long, thin nose. "You are the photographer and the hat-shop girl."

It was dismissive the way she said it, and it wasn't just her broad accent that made it sound so. Calling me a "hat-shop girl" made me feel as if she was calling me a "coat-check girl," and I wondered if she thought we should have used the servants' entrance.

"I'm Ms. Parker and this is my associate Mr. Eisel," I said. "I believe Lady Ellis is expecting us."

The woman reared her head back as if surprised that I wasn't as easily intimidated as she'd thought. I felt like telling her that in the hotel I once worked in I was in charge of an entire fleet of chambermaids and I certainly was not going to take any attitude from a housekeeper, but I refrained.

"Follow me," the woman said, and turned on her heel to lead the way.

I gestured to Andre to go first, so I could shut the door behind him. For such a stout lady, the housekeeper moved at a solid clip, and I had to hurry up the short steps and across the marble floor of the reception hall to catch up to her. I barely had a chance to take in the white walls, which were rectangles of wainscoting that reached from floor to ceiling with a brilliant crystal chandelier overhead.

The housekeeper, gargoyle, what have you, led the way into a narrow lift. Andre and I squeezed in after her and she pushed the button for the second floor. I expected it to lurch and creak but it was a smooth ride, and we arrived in seconds on the second floor.

"Wait here, please, whilst I announce you," she said.

We waited in another receiving area while she went through a large door on the left.

"Cheery old gal, isn't she?" Andre asked.

"A regular beam of sunshine," I agreed.

Again, Andre rocked on his heels. This time, I did hum. It was equal parts nerves and boredom. I was stressed that the shoot go well and Lady Ellis be satisfied, but I was also anxious about being gone from the shop all morning and leaving Fee in charge.

Of course, if Viv were here, I would not be feeling so edgy. In fact, if Viv had been here from the beginning, we never would have had the kerfuffle of me not being able to find Lady Ellis's hat and getting roped into this photo shoot.

Honestly, I was becoming torn between rage at and worry for Viv. My Aunt Grace had forwarded the e-mail that Viv had sent her, but of course, it didn't say where she was or when she'd be back, just that her phone was out of range and she had little to no access to the Internet. I swear I could just wring her neck.

Just when I was about to ask Andre what he thought might be taking them so long, a shriek sounded from the door the housekeeper had just gone through. I exchanged a startled glance with Andre.

"Mouse?" I asked.

"Ew, I hate vermin," he said. He clutched his equipment to his chest and stood on his tippy toes as if this would elevate him out of the fuzzy critter's climbing range.

The door to the room was yanked open and the housekeeper staggered out. Her face was deathly white and she slumped against the wall.

"Lady Ellis is . . . dead!" she cried and then she fainted with a crash that shook the floor.

"Oh my god!" Andre shrieked in a pitch so high I didn't think I could reach it if I tried.

"Call an ambulance and the police," I said. "She may have given herself a concussion. And don't move her. I'll go check on Lady Ellis."

Andre dumped his equipment on the floor and began scrambling in his pants pocket for his phone.

I hurried through the door into an enormous bedroom done in regal shades of purple and gold. My brain refused to acknowledge what the housekeeper had said. Surely Lady Ellis was just asleep. She was young. How could she be dead? I glanced at the bed first, but it was neatly made up with a large mass of throw pillows.

I turned and noticed a sitting area in front of two French doors that opened up onto a balcony. The small couch and matching wing chairs were empty and the doors to the terrace were shut. I crossed the room looking around the floor for any evidence of Lady Ellis. I was about to leave when I noticed another door that opened into a dressing room.

I could see that the lights were on inside and as I stepped into the room, I noted that it was larger than my bedroom in Mim's house. My gaze swept down from the racks of clothing to the forest-green carpet and there, lying on the floor just beyond the velvet chaise lounge, I saw the pale, cold form of Lady Ellis, sprawled in the center of the room, wearing nothing but the hat Viv had created for her.

Chapter 18

"Lady Ellis!" I cried. She didn't respond.

I stood frozen in the doorway. It felt as though my heart had locked up on a beat and I moved forward on legs that were operating on muscle memory instead of strength. Working at the hotel, we were required to know the basics of first response. I sifted through my gray matter, trying to remember what the hell I was supposed to do.

And then it came to me in a brain flash that looked remarkably like the PowerPoint we'd had to sit through. Assess victim's responsiveness. Well, she hadn't answered me, so that was none. Check for an obstructed air passage. Okay, I moved to stand beside her now, but as I looked down, I felt bile splash up against the back of my throat. There would be no need to check for an obstruction.

She was lying on her left side in a pool of blood that had been absorbed into the deep-green carpet. Her right hand was clutching a bloody knife as if she had just pulled it from her side before she collapsed. Her eyes stared vacantly up at me and I forced myself to kneel and check the pulse point in her neck just to be absolutely sure.

Her skin was cold and hard. Lady Ellis was dead.

"Help is on the way!" Andre cried as he raced into the room behind me.

"Don't come in here!"

I turned to hold him off by putting my hand up, but I was too late. He'd come in already. He took one look at Lady Ellis and spun around racing back into the hallway, where I heard him retch.

Amazingly, the housekeeper was roused by the sound of Andre vomiting into what looked to be an extraordinarily expensive vase. Tears coursed down her cheeks and she was shaking.

"Are you all right, Mrs.—?" I asked.

"Stone," she replied. She glanced back at the bedroom door. "Lady Ellis—"

"Is dead. The police are on their way," I said.

"Oh." Mrs. Stone let out a moan and I looked at Andre. He had finally pulled his head out of the vase.

"Are you all right?" I asked.

He just looked at me as if there really was no answer to that question. I couldn't argue that.

There was a pounding knock on the door below. I hoped it was the ambulance people and hurried toward the stairs across from the lift. I ran down the two flights until I was in the reception hall. I crossed to the door and opened it.

Two people, a middle-aged man and a young woman, both wearing dark green uniforms with fancy patches on their left sides and the initials NHS on the right stood in the doorway.

"Upstairs," I said. "Two flights. An older woman fainted and, well, there's something else."

"Are you all right?" The woman asked me as the man hurried past me up the stairs.

I shook my head. "But it's not me who needs care. Please upstairs hurry."

I knew the shock of the past few minutes was kicking in as my speech was becoming disjointed. The woman frowned and rushed past me to follow her colleague.

I wasn't sure whether to follow them or to wait for the police to show up. A knock on the door made the debate irrelevant.

A uniformed officer, a constable, was at the door. He was young with a round face and concerned eyes. He was wearing the traditional rounded hat with his badge on the front of it. Mim always liked those hats. His uniform consisted of dark pants, a short-sleeved, white dress shirt with a dark gray vest over it which carried a radio on his shoulder and a Metropolitan Police patch on his left front.

"Upstairs, second floor, hurry," I said and pointed.

At this point, that was about all I could get out. To his credit, he asked no further questions but took the stairs at a run, yanking the radio out of his shoulder as he went.

He was gone only moments when another constable appeared. He, too, went upstairs, obviously in communication with his colleague. I waited in the hall uncertain of what to do.

Much like a middle-aged lady, the house was well cushioned with years of living. I heard no noise coming from above and was grateful.

The second constable reappeared, looking pale and shaken. He had a long face and he had pushed his hat back as if trying to get some oxygen to his head.

"I'll need to ask you some questions, ma'am," he said.

I nodded. There wasn't much I could tell him, but I was willing to try. We began with my name and why I was here, and then I gave him a brief description of the events that led up to us finding Lady Ellis.

His partner's voice sounded in his radio and he excused himself to go back upstairs.

Andre came down the stairs and stayed with me in the reception hall. He looked pretty weak and shaky, so we huddled together, feeling like intruders in the drama that was unfolding.

I had left the door open after the second constable had arrived, knowing that more would be coming and that I didn't really want to be the designated greeter.

Sure enough, in minutes two plainclothes detective inspectors arrived. I was shocked to see that one of them was Inspector Franks.

"Ms. Parker," he said.

"Inspector Franks," I said. I was taken aback. What were the odds that he would be here? And then I had a horrible thought, and I felt all of the blood drain from my face as if someone had pulled a plug.

"Is it Vivian?" I asked. My voice was shaky. "Did you hear something about my cousin?"

"Oh, no!" He held out his hands in a "stop" gesture as if he could wave me away from the bad direction my thoughts were going. "The Kensington Borough includes Kensington, Chelsea and Notting Hill. I just happened to be at the

Kensington Station when the call came in. When I heard your name over the radio, I took the call."

I thought I saw him give me a speculative glance, but then he continued, "I'm sorry. I haven't heard anything about your cousin."

"Oh." The air whooshed out of my lungs and I felt Andre's arm brace me around the waist.

"Sit, Scarlett, before you fall over," he said.

He led me to a padded bench in the corner and I sat, feeling dizzy and a bit like vomiting myself. I briefly wondered what Andre had done with the vase but then I didn't want to know.

"This is my colleague, Inspector Simms," Franks said.

I glanced up and gave him a faint smile. He was considerably younger than Franks and was built solid. He had a thick head of brown hair, ruddy cheeks and pale brown eyes under eyebrows that met in the middle, forming a unibrow. He looked very forbidding, which I supposed was a good thing for a detective inspector.

"Can you tell us what happened?" Franks asked.

I let Andre take the lead, and he explained that we had come to take photographs of Lady Ellis and had found her "in her unfortunate condition." I had never thought of being stabbed to death in such polite terms, and I gave him a look.

"She was knifed," I said. "Through the heart."

As I said the words, Andre blanched and made a gurgling noise in his throat like he might be sick again, so I pulled him down to sit beside me and had him place his head between his knees.

"Simms, go up and have a look, I'll join you shortly," Inspector Franks instructed.

The younger of the two detectives disappeared up the stairs while Franks turned to me.

"Ms. Parker, may I ask you a few questions?"

"Certainly." I nodded. I figured the sooner they were done with us the sooner we could get out of there. Honestly, the whole experience was giving me a case of the wiggins.

"When did you last speak to Lady Ellis?" he asked.

"Tuesday night," I said. "She came by the shop and picked up her hat. There was a bit of an issue because I couldn't find it at first, but then I did, and she agreed to have her photo taken."

He nodded and ran his index finger and his thumb over his mustache as he considered his next question. "Mr. Eisel, you're the photographer?"

"Yes, I own a studio in Notting Hill, near Scarlett's shop. She asked me to take the pictures, and I agreed because Lady Ellis said we could use the photos for publicity purposes."

Franks raised an eyebrow as if that didn't seem quite right. I couldn't fault his logic. This wasn't the sort of house where one expected the resident to go along with being photographed unless it was for the society page.

"I only met Lady Ellis the one time," I said. I was picking my words extremely carefully, and he leaned closer, listening attentively. "But she struck me as being someone who valued appearances very highly."

He leaned back and studied me. He gave me a nod and I knew he understood exactly what I was saying, that Lady Ellis had been quite vain.

"Can you two wait here?" he asked. "I may have more questions."

"Of course," I said.

Inspector Franks turned and headed up the stairs.

Andre and I sat quietly for a moment and then I said, " 'Unfortunate condition,' really? Chicken pox is an 'unfortunate condition.' "

"I didn't want to overstate it," he said. He sounded a bit defensive.

"Fat chance of that," I said. "What would you call a shooting, I wonder, a bellyache?"

"No," he protested. "I would probably say they had lead poisoning."

My mouth popped open, and then I snorted. Andre looked back at me with an expression of comical horror on his face, causing me to snort again, which made him laugh. This made me chuckle so I clapped a hand over my mouth which made him laugh and clap a hand over his mouth, too. We turned away from each other, knowing that eye contact would probably set us off again.

"All right, Scarlett?" he said after a moment.

"We're going to blame that on hysterics," I said.

"Agreed, it was terribly bad form," he said.

I cautiously turned back to face him. We glanced at each other and we both nodded. We were okay now.

"I wonder how the housekeeper is faring," I said.

"I can't believe she didn't hurt herself," Andre said. "Mrs. Stone certainly hit the floor like twenty stone."

I twisted my mouth to keep from smiling and gave him a quelling look for the hideous play on words.

"Should we go up?" he asked. "I need to get my equipment and get back to the shop. Plus, sitting here is giving me the crawlies."

"I don't suppose there can be much more for them to ask us," I said.

Together we made our way up the stairs. The constables and the detectives were huddled together while the paramedics seemed to be finished with Mrs. Stone. They passed us at the top of the stairs as they were on the way down.

Inspector Franks looked grim.

Andre and I waited uncertainly. I met Mrs. Stone's gaze and crossed over to where she sat, looking distraught.

"Can I get you anything?"

"Thank you, miss, but no," she said.

She looked as if she would be undone by the kindness, and I reached down and patted her shoulder. She waited a moment and then patted my hand in return.

"Ms. Parker," Detective Franks called me over. "When you went into the dressing room, did you touch anything?" he asked.

"No," I said. "Well, I've been trained in first aid, so I did check her pulse point in her neck, but that was it. I didn't move her or touch anything."

"And when you went in she was unclothed?"

"Yes," I said. "Except for the hat."

"And that is your hat?" he asked. His sharp brown eyes were trained on me like two laser points on my face.

"Not mine, no," I said. I didn't mean to be obtuse, I was just hitting overload and not processing as well I should have been.

"Let me rephrase that. Is that hat from your shop?"

"It is the hat my cousin designed for her that she picked up on Tuesday, yes," I said.

"And you still haven't heard from your cousin?" he asked.

"No, not a word," I said.

"Do you know what sort of relationship your cousin and Lady Ellis had?" he asked.

Oh, I didn't like where that was going.

"As far as I know, it was purely business," I said. "Honestly, Viv never mentioned Lady Ellis to me, and Lady Ellis never said anything when I met with her about knowing Vivian in anything other than a millinery sense."

"It's interesting though, isn't it?" he asked.

"What?"

"She was in her dressing room, a robe would have been appropriate attire or even a towel, but there is no evidence of either. The only thing Lady Ellis was wearing was the hat from your shop."

Chapter 19

By the time Andre and I were done with the police, I was more than ready for a pint or three. Sadly, I'd left Fiona in the shop alone all morning and my conscience was refusing to let me take any more time away even to self-medicate.

Inspector Franks had made it quite plain that he would be stopping by the shop to discuss Viv's whereabouts. I tried not to worry. After all, it wasn't as if the two situations were connected. Perhaps it was the universe taking charge of getting Viv to come home. I would call my Aunt Grace and tell her what happened and she could tell Viv, assuming she heard from Viv, and then Viv would hurry home and all would be well.

"Is your cousin really missing?" Andre asked. We were once again in his compact car, crawling our way through the midday traffic back to Notting Hill.

"Her mother says she's been in touch and her business

manager—you remember Harrison from the other night—
said she does this all of the time," I said. "They think it is
perfectly normal for Viv, which it is, but Harrison did admit
that she doesn't usually stay out of touch with him."

"But you don't think it's normal?" he asked.

"No, I remember when she took off to go buy satin ribbons from a textile house in France once, and then there
was the time she took off to Belgium because she became
obsessed with a lace maker over there, but this, this feels
different to me."

Andre turned to look at me. His dark eyes were worried.
"If there's anything I can do . . ."

His voice trailed off and I patted his shoulder.

"You are so kind, Andre. I'm so sorry I got you into this
mess," I said. "What an awful morning."

"Most especially for Lady Ellis," he said.

"Indeed," I said.

He turned onto our street and I was relieved to see Mim's
Whims looking just fine. Not that I'd had any doubts, but
my anxiety was in overdrive.

"How is your stomach?" I asked. "Have you leveled out?"

"I got sick into a coil glass piece by Adam Aaronson,"
he said. He sounded shocked and appalled. "I may never eat
again."

He stopped on the curb and I climbed out. "I'll call you
later."

"Do," he said. "If I don't hear from you, Nick and I will
be over later to check on you."

"Bring wine," I said, and he smiled.

I closed the door and hurried into the shop. It was empty,
which, while not great for business, was good for me,

because I was thinking I might need to go have a little cry to get myself together.

I was halfway across the floor when Fee came rocketing out of the back room with Harrison on her heels. I hadn't seen him since our chat the other day, and I found that I was irritated with him for not being in touch with me.

"You might want to go upstairs," Fee said. Her eyes were wide with alarm.

"What did you think you were doing?" Harrison spoke at the same time as Fee. His eyes were narrowed in anger.

"Huh?" I asked. I couldn't process both of them at the same time.

"Too late," Fee said with a sigh and she slipped back behind Harrison.

"Fee said you were at Lady Ellis's," he snapped.

He stepped forward until he was looming over me. Here's a new discovery: I don't like it when people loom.

"Yes, but—" I began, only to be interrupted.

"And that you were having that photographer from down the street take pictures of her for the shop's Web site?"

"That's right, but—"

"Are you mad?" he asked.

"No, but I'm getting there," I said through gritted teeth.

"What could you be thinking?" he cried. "Don't you know the history between Viv and Lady Ellis?"

I froze. There was a history between them? I glanced at the wardrobe. I swear the raven was smirking at me. *Oh, sweet Ferd the bird, please tell me it was a grade-school scuffle, a rivalry over the best pigtails. Please!*

"What history?" I asked. I noticed my voice sounded

faint, and I hurried over to one of the sitting areas before I toppled over.

"Simply put, Victoria Ellis hates Viv because her husband, Rupert Ellis, has been in love with Viv since they went to university together."

"What?" I cried. This was not happening.

"Which part didn't you grasp?" he asked. "Lady Ellis hating Viv? Or Lord Ellis still being in love with Viv? Or the insane fact that you're going to put Victoria Ellis on the Web site?"

His tone was sharp and I might have taken offense if I wasn't already completely freaking out.

"All of the above," I said faintly.

"I didn't know either," Fee said. I think it was to make me feel better, but Harrison's green-eyed glower was having none of that. He gave her a scathing look and she pressed her lips together lest she say anything else of comfort.

Lady Ellis hated Viv. Lady Ellis had been wearing Viv's hat and nothing else. Inspector Franks had already remarked upon it. Oh, no!

Before the floor came rushing up to meet me and I fell face-first off the seat, I put my head in between my knees much as I had instructed Andre to do earlier.

This was bad. This was very, very bad. I'd had no idea.

"But why would Viv have designed a hat for Lady Ellis if they hated each other?" I asked from my crouched position.

"Lady Ellis hated Viv," Harrison said. "Viv couldn't really care less about Lady Ellis. You know how she is."

I nodded, keeping my head down. Viv was the original

I'm-rubber-and-you're-glue girl: nothing ever stuck on Viv because she genuinely didn't care how people felt about her.

I could only imagine what Inspector Franks was going to make of this. Maybe he wouldn't find out. Maybe if Harrison kept his big mouth shut, no one would find out.

"Are you all right?" Fee asked. I must have looked pretty bad, because she pushed past Harrison to get a better look at me. "It's not that bad. You can put Lady Ellis off about the photo being on our Web site, yeah?"

"Oh, no, it is that bad—worse actually," I said. I looked up and found them both watching me. "When Andre and I arrived at Lady Ellis's estate to take her picture, we found her dead."

Chapter 20

They stared at me. Fee's mouth formed a perfect *O* and Harrison looked as if I'd slapped him.

"When you say 'dead,' you're not talking dead tired, are you?" he asked.

"No," I said. "I'm talking stabbed-in-the-heart, fatally-wounded dead."

"A crime of passion," Fee said. "It had to be."

"Did you talk to the police?" Harrison asked. He looked stiff, as if his body couldn't move because his mind was churning through the facts as I shared them.

"Yes," I moaned. I pressed my forehead into my palms as I remembered. "And, of course, the inspector who showed up on the scene was Inspector Franks."

"Of course it was," Harrison said. His tone was bitingly sarcastic and it scraped on my very last nerve.

"Do you mind?" I asked.

"Mind what?" he demanded.

"Not being so damn condescending!"

"I would if you would stop mucking up every situation you find yourself in," he retorted.

"How is this my fault? How could I have possibly known that Lady Ellis would be murdered?"

"You couldn't have," he said. His voice was scathing. "But if you knew anything at all about your cousin, you would have known about her relationship with the Ellises."

"Oh, that's ridiculous," I said. "And I do know my cousin."

"Really? I thought you said you two talked. I thought you said you were close!" Harrison accused. He was looming over me again and I really hated it.

"We do. We are!" I hopped to my feet, rising up on my tiptoes to be closer to his height.

"Everyone just calm down," Fee said. She took a step forward, looking like she wanted to step between us but was uncertain of how to do it.

I stepped back from Harrison and blew out a breath, trying to calm myself.

"Viv and I are close. But I can't remember some guy from her university days, and she never mentioned any issues with Lady Ellis."

"You said before it wasn't her style to care what others thought of her," Fee reminded Harrison. "It's quite logical that she might not have said anything to Scarlett."

I gave her a small smile of gratitude and she nodded at me. I felt like I had at least one ally, and I suspected I was going to need her.

Harrison looked like he wanted to chew through a chair cushion. I couldn't blame him. This whole thing was a mess. I could only imagine what would happen when word got out about what Lady Ellis was and wasn't wearing.

I debated not telling them. I mean, maybe, the police would keep it quiet and no one would find out about the hat. Then again, I tried to picture Harrison if he heard it on the news and not from me. I heaved a sigh. Full disclosure seemed the only way to go.

"There's one other small detail," I said. "Really, it's nothing, I'm sure."

"Oh, dear god." Harrison sank down into a chair. He rubbed a hand over his eyes. "Let us have it then."

"When we found Lady Ellis, or more accurately when her housekeeper, Mrs. Stone, found her, well, she was naked except for one article of clothing."

Both Fee and Harrison looked at me expectantly.

"The hat Viv made for her," I said.

"No!" Fee said while Harrison swore under his breath.

"Were there any press there?" he asked.

"No," I said. "I got the feeling the police were trying to keep it quiet until her husband arrived."

Harrison ran both hands through his hair. I supposed that was better than wrapping them around my neck as I suspected he would have liked to.

"I need to make some calls," he said. "Excuse me."

"Would you like some tea?" Fee asked as we watched him stride into the far corner of the shop.

What I really wanted was a good cry, but I'd be damned if I'd do it in front of Harrison.

"That would be really nice, Fee, thanks."

She patted me on the arm and headed into the back room. I glanced up and saw the bird on the wardrobe, staring at me as if amused by the disaster I found myself in.

"Oh, put a sock in it," I said. I rose from my seat and followed Fee into the back. I may not be able to make a pot of tea, but I could certainly get a tin of biscuits out of the cupboard, not that I thought I'd be eating any.

Fee and I were standing over the pot while the tea steeped when Harrison came back into the room. His ruddy cheeks were redder than usual, which made his eyes an even brighter shade of green.

I noticed now that he was dressed as if he'd been at the office, in gray flannel pants and a crisp, white dress shirt. There was no sign of his jacket or tie. I noticed he had a broad-shouldered but lithe build without an ounce of fat on him. Not the norm for a guy who spent his days crunching numbers and certainly not for a guy who cleared up the pile of fisherman's pie I'd seen him devour a few evenings before.

Then again, he struck me as being a bit of an A-type personality. He probably worked out every day and drank water by the gallon. Unlike me, who only ran if someone was chasing me and who only drank caffeinated or alcoholic beverages.

"I checked and the story hasn't gotten out yet," he said. "At least the media hasn't picked up on anything. Scarlett, do you think your photographer is trustworthy?"

"Andre?" I asked. "Absolutely. The poor man barfed. Believe me, he's not going to tell anyone about it."

"He didn't take any pictures of her, did he?" he asked. "You know, to sell to the tabloids?"

"No, he never even unpacked his equipment," I said. I was irritated on Andre's behalf. "I really don't think he's like that."

"You can't be too careful," Harrison said. "Look, I have to get back to my office. If you hear from Viv, call me or have her call me immediately."

"I will," I promised.

"Do you have the number to my mobile?" he asked.

"No," I said.

"Put it in now," he said. It wasn't a request. I took out my cell and added him to my contacts.

"If the police come by, call me, and I'll come right over," he said. "And whatever you do, don't say anything else to them about Viv. Just stick to 'I don't know,' all right?"

"Yes, sir," I said. If he noticed my sarcasm, he didn't say anything. He turned and left without so much as a good-bye.

"Man, he's bossy," I said to Fee. "How does Viv put up with him?"

"Well, he's not hard on the eyes, now is he?" Fee asked.

"I hadn't noticed," I lied.

She looked at me and laughed as if she knew full well that I knew exactly how good-looking Harrison Wentworth was. She took the cozy off the teapot and poured us each a cup.

"Who do you suppose murdered Lady Ellis?" she asked.

"No idea," I said. "Isn't it usually the person closest to them? Like the husband?"

"Oh, that'll cause a stir in the gossip pot," Fee said. "Lord Ellis accused of murdering his wife."

"Well, we don't know," I said. "I mean, as far as I know,

it could have been the housekeeper. She was the only person there aside from us."

"Why would a domestic stab her boss?" Fee asked. "Kind of a lousy plan to skewer the heart that feeds you."

"I don't know," I said. "Maybe she was driven to it from being at Lady Ellis's beck and call for years and finally she just snapped."

"Do you really think she did it?" Fee asked.

I thought back to how Mrs. Stone had staggered out of the bedroom door and promptly fainted. No, I didn't really see her as a suspect. I sipped my tea and absently nibbled on a biscuit.

"No," I said. "Unless she has another job performing in a theater on Shaftesbury Avenue, I don't think there is any way her reaction to what she saw was anything other than genuine. It was a gruesome sight."

A shudder rippled down my back as I recalled seeing Lady Ellis's pale naked body against the deep green of her floor. I had a feeling the image of her sightless eyes and her hand clutched around the knife that had killed her were going to haunt me for some time to come.

Chapter 21

It was late afternoon when Inspector Franks and his partner, Inspector Simms, arrived at the shop. I had been expecting them, but still it made me nervous. I could only hope that they had no idea that Viv and Lady Ellis had a history.

As soon as they came through the door, I gave Fee a small nod to indicate that she should call Harrison. Much as I hated to rely upon him, I didn't want to get Viv into any more trouble than I already had.

"Good afternoon, Ms. Parker," Inspector Franks said. He stroked his mustache, and I remembered his love of country-western music. Too bad Viv didn't have any American cowboy hats around the shop. I'd have tried to charm, okay, bribe, him with one.

"Inspectors," I said. "Can I get you anything?"

"Water would be great," Inspector Simms said.

It was the first time I'd really gotten a look at him. I'd

been too upset earlier. His thick unibrow made him seem like quite the Neanderthal, but when he gave me a small smile he looked almost boyish. At best, he only had a few years on me.

I gestured for them to take a seat while I went to get a pitcher of ice water and some glasses. Fee was on the phone with Harrison while I made up the tray. I threw on a pile of grapes and some cheese and crackers, which I'd picked up yesterday to snack on, just to sweeten the pot, as it were.

I sat across from the inspectors, who looked comically out of place in the hat shop. Inspector Simms kept looking around as if hoping no one would see him here. Franks helped himself to the cheese and crackers and I realized with the morning they'd had, they probably hadn't had a chance to eat anything. Simms verified this by reaching gratefully for a handful of grapes.

"Ms. Parker, has there been any word from your cousin?" Inspector Franks asked.

"No, why?" I asked.

"It's troubling me that our murder victim was wearing only the hat your cousin made for her," he said. "Most especially because your cousin is missing."

This hadn't sat well with me either, but I didn't like the way it sounded, so I felt the need to take a defensive stand, although neatly cushioned in a polite tone of voice.

"You've spoken to my aunt," I said. "So it's not so much that she's missing as we're just not sure of where she is."

"Yes, but your aunt has only heard from her by e-mail," Franks said. "That bothers me."

It bothered me, too, but I didn't say as much.

The bells on the door handle jangled and I glanced up to

see Harrison stride into the room. He looked confident and he smiled at Inspector Franks with a careless charm that I admired, particularly because I was freaking out on the inside.

He shook hands with both inspectors and then gave me a warm smile.

"How are you, Scarlett?" he asked. He was playing it cool, as if he hadn't been yelling at me just a few hours ago. I gave him a small nod to signify that I understood.

"Well, there's been an unfortunate occurrence with one of our clients," I said. I wanted to pat myself on the back for my own way with understatement.

"Really?" Harrison asked as if this was news.

"Yes," Inspector Franks answered for me. "Which is why we're here."

"So, it's not about Vivian then?" Harrison asked. "When I saw you I'd hoped . . ."

"No, Mr. Wentworth," Franks said. They exchanged a look as if there was more to their conversation than the rest of us were aware of. "Unfortunately, we've had no luck in locating Ms. Tremont. However, one of her clients was found murdered this morning."

"No!" Harrison sounded positively shocked and for a moment even I forgot that he already knew.

"I'm afraid so," Inspector Franks said. He gave Harrison a considering look. "Lady Ellis was found stabbed, wearing only a hat from this shop, and Ms. Parker here was one of the first to find her."

Harrison sat down beside me and took my hand in his. "Oh my god, are you all right?"

He looked so genuinely solicitous that I almost fell for

it. Then I remembered how bossy he'd been, and I took my hand out of his and said, "I'm fine."

He raised his eyebrows at me and I looked away, pretending that I didn't get his silent message to go along with him. What did he think I was going to do? Tell the police he already knew all of this? Then again, why didn't he want them to know?

I gave him a sideways glance, but he'd already turned back to Inspector Franks.

"Do they have any suspects yet?" he asked.

"We're still following several leads," Franks said.

Harrison nodded as if that was about what he expected.

"Ms. Parker," Inspector Franks said. "Would you mind telling us again exactly what you saw and heard this morning while you were in the Ellises' home? No detail is too small."

"Not at all," I said.

I proceeded to tell them exactly what I had told them before. I had no new details for them, which I'm sure was a disappointment, but the truth was, I had a feeling Lady Ellis had been dead for a while before we found her, otherwise how could her carpet have been so saturated with blood? I shivered at the memory of the carpet.

"All right?" Harrison asked, and I nodded.

Simms helped himself to another handful of grapes and as he munched he looked at me. After a good swallow, he asked, "Did you see anything that struck you as out of the ordinary when you entered the Ellises' home?"

I blew out a breath and thought about it. Andre and I had been talking when we pulled up. I remembered climbing out of the car and studying the house while I waited for Andre to get his equipment.

"Honestly, I was so taken by the house that I didn't really notice if anyone was out and about around us," I said. "The only person I saw was the housekeeper, Mrs. Stone, when she let us in."

"How was she when she greeted you?" Franks asked.

"Rude," I said.

I saw Franks suppress a smile.

"Not anxious then?" Simms asked.

"No," I said. "She was very calm and very condescending, but after she found Lady Ellis, well, she fainted."

The inspectors both nodded. I had a feeling Mrs. Stone was in the clear.

"What about Lord Ellis?" I asked. "Has he been told about his wife's death?"

"Yes," Franks said. He heaved a sigh. "The media's gotten hold of the story as well, so brace yourself. If they find out you were there, they'll be knocking your door down next."

As if in response to his words, the bells on the front door jangled. I glanced up to see an elderly woman and a younger version of herself come through the door. Not media but customers.

I rose to greet them, but Fee was already coming from the back. She glanced over at me and gave me a small nod, letting me know she would handle it. I took my seat again.

"How should I handle the press?" I asked. I felt my stomach twisting itself into knots. Not again. I really couldn't bear to be in the bull's-eye of the media again.

My face must have reflected my angst because Harrison rested his hand on my back, right in the middle of my shoulder blades as if trying to prop me up and comfort me at the same time.

"You can close the shop if you need to," he said. "You don't have to deal with all of this."

I was so grateful, I almost wept. But then, I thought of our customers and how disappointed Mim would be if I drove our business into the ground because I closed up because of a few pesky reporters.

"No, it's all right," I said. "I can handle it."

Inspector Franks was watching both Harrison and me with a speculative gaze. I did not want to tell him about my woes with the media, so I quickly shoved aside my dread.

"Is there anything else I can help you with?" I asked.

"We're going to need to search the shop and your cousin's private residence," Inspector Franks said.

"Why?" I asked. Probably I should have just said "okay," but I wanted to know what they could possibly be looking for in here.

"We have to find your cousin," he said. "With the victim clothed only in a hat that your cousin made for her, and your cousin being missing, well, it just leaves too many questions."

"Surely you don't think there's a connection?" Harrison asked.

"At this point, I'm not ruling anything out," Inspector Franks said. "Especially since Lord Ellis has confessed to being in love with your cousin Vivian and that his wife hated her."

Chapter 22

"How did that come up?" Harrison asked. I could see his jaw clenching furiously and I could tell he was keeping his temper in check by sheer force of will.

"The hat," Simms said. He had finally stopped eating and I noticed the tray I'd brought out had been cleaned of all but two crackers. "When Lord Ellis heard that his wife was wearing only the hat from this shop, he became quite distraught."

Franks and Simms exchanged an uncomfortable look and I took that to mean that Lord Ellis had made quite a spectacle of himself. I tried to picture the smarmy Lord Ellis, who had been here just a few days before, looking distraught. I couldn't picture it.

"I expect any man would be upset to hear that his wife was stabbed to death, never mind what she was wearing," Harrison said. He put a hand on my shoulder and I took it to mean that I shouldn't contribute to this portion of the conversation.

"Agreed," Franks said.

"If you'd like to begin your search in the shop," I said. "I can show you the upstairs where Viv and I live, when you're ready."

"Thank you for your cooperation, Ms. Parker," Franks said.

"We can start with her office area in back."

We all rose and I led the inspectors toward the workroom. Fee was still helping the mother and daughter, who were happily settled in another sitting area, trying on hats. They were looking at bright colors and fun shapes so I suspected that this was a happy event for which they were buying their hats.

Fee glanced at us as we passed and I gave her what I hoped was a reassuring smile. Mercifully, the back room was nice and tidy, with only a bit of clutter on the worktable from where Fee had been stitching some fine netting onto the brim of a black fascinator.

"Thank you, Ms. Parker," Inspector Franks said. It was clear he wanted me out of the way while they searched. "We'll let you know when we're ready to look into the other rooms."

"All right," I said.

"You look a bit peaky," Harrison said. "Let's step outside and get some fresh air."

It wasn't a request. He took my arm and led me out the back door into the tiny garden Viv kept at the back of the house. A fountain trickled in one corner while a trailing rose bush, its red leaves just bursting as they had not yet turned green, climbed up the back of the house and along one wall of the small, bricked-in courtyard.

"Come here," he said.

"Where?" I asked. There was no room out here. Where were we supposed to go?

He opened his arms. "Here."

I raised my eyebrows at him. Shocked.

"I want you close so we can't be overheard," he said. "It'll look like I'm comforting you."

A slow, burning flush filled my cheeks, but I stepped into his arms, and he rested his hands lightly on my hips.

"Now listen," he said.

He was all business, and I tried to clear my head and pay attention, but I was having a heck of a time concentrating. No man had touched me, well, since hotel security had hauled me out of the reception hall and tossed me into the street, but that really didn't count. And before that, well, I had thought the rat bastard had so little time for me because he was such a workaholic, yeah, not so much.

My nose was just inches from Harrison's shirtfront. He smelled good, really good. It was a bay-rum, man smell. I liked it. I was trying to decide if it was his soap or his laundry detergent when I heard him huff out an exasperated breath.

"Ginger, are you listening to me?" he asked.

"Of course," I lied.

"Then what did I just say?" he asked.

Busted! I tipped my head up to find him staring down at me. I figured he was going to be mad, but instead he studied my face and a small smile tipped up the corner of his mouth.

"You have no idea, do you?" he asked.

"None," I admitted and he laughed.

"What were you thinking about?" he asked.

I noticed that we were still in our huddle, neither of us backing up, and I was abruptly aware of him, Harrison Wentworth in all his masculine glory, just inches from me. I felt my face grow hot and I took a quick step away from him.

He tipped his head to the side and studied me for a moment, and then a charming smile parted his lips. He looked wickedly intrigued.

Mercifully, the back door opened and Inspector Franks popped his head out. "We're ready to check the rest of the house, Ms. Parker."

"Absolutely," I said.

Saved! I turned to go, but Harrison caught my hand and dragged me back up against him. It looked as if he were giving me a quick hug, but his lips were pressed right into my ear when he breathed the words, "Here's the short version: say nothing."

I stepped back from him and our eyes met. I knew he was saying that I shouldn't volunteer any information to the inspectors, undoubtedly because Viv was now in a precarious spot given how Lord Ellis and Lady Ellis each felt about her.

I gave him a tiny nod and hurried to the door, and the inspector moved aside to let me pass. I did not look back at Harrison but I felt him watching me as I disappeared into the house.

They were very thorough in their examination of our living area. Still, I wasn't sure what they were looking for, and I got the feeling they weren't either. Viv hadn't been here since Sunday. Obviously, Lady Ellis had been killed well after that. Surely they didn't think she'd gone into hiding, then come out and killed her and then gone back into hiding again. It didn't make any sense.

Whatever their feelings toward her, Viv was completely apathetic toward the Ellises. She didn't have enough feeling for either of them to have done something like that.

"How is business?" Inspector Franks asked me. "Prosperous?"

"Yes, very much so," I said. "Viv is a popular designer and her custom hats are quite expensive."

"So, no financial woes then?"

"None," I said. I knew what he was thinking. That if the business were in trouble, Viv would whack Lady Ellis so she could have a crack at the earl, thus solving any financial difficulties she might have. It was a theory, a good theory; it just didn't hold up.

Harrison and Fee were downstairs when we came back into the shop from above. Per Harrison's instructions, I had said nothing of any consequence during their search and had mostly spent the time trying to stay out of their way.

I closed the door to the upstairs behind me and turned to walk the inspectors to the front door. Harrison joined us as we crossed the room.

"You'll let us know if you hear anything about Vivian?" he asked.

"Of course," Inspector Franks said. They shook hands. "And if you hear from her, you'll let us know."

It wasn't a request, and he was looking at me when he said it.

"Absolutely," I agreed.

As we approached the front door, it was abruptly yanked

open and a reporter and a camera crew shoved their way inside.

"There she is!" The reporter yelled. "The party crasher!"

The moment became surreal; everything slowed down and sound became muted as I watched the reporter lunging at me.

Chapter 23

I braced myself for impact, squinching up tight with my eyes shut and my arms drawn in, because he certainly didn't appear to be slowing down, and being wedged between Harrison and Inspector Franks didn't give me anywhere to go.

The impact never came. I opened one eye and noted that both inspectors were examining the ceiling as if looking for termites and Harrison was walking back into the shop, clapping his hands together as if he'd just taken out the trash.

I glanced over his shoulder and saw the reporter sitting on the curb with a look of shock on his face, as if uncertain of how he'd gotten there. The cameraman behind him was looking equally stunned.

I glanced back at Franks and Simms. Both were still looking up.

"There is some really excellent brushwork on the paint

job on your ceiling," Simms said. Then he looked back down and grinned at me.

I grinned back, realizing that they had been studiously examining the ceiling so as not to see Harrison manhandling the reporter.

"I'll see you out, Inspectors," Harrison said. He walked them to the door where they exchanged a low conversation.

As soon as the two men left, Harrison locked the door behind them and drew all of the blinds down.

"You're going to have to be 'appointment-only' for a few days, I'm afraid," he said. He studied my face. "All right, Scarlett?"

"Yeah, I'm fine," I said. "Just startled."

"I'd say so," Fee chimed in. "That reporter was going to run you down."

I blew out a breath.

"And, Harrison, you picked him up like he was a loaf of bread. Bagged him good, you did," Fee said with approval.

Harrison shrugged. "I play rugby. That idiot would be toast on the pitch."

Fee burst out laughing and only then did I get it. Loaf. Bagged. Toast. They were a witty bunch. I giggled but I think it was more a mini nervous fit than actual amusement.

"All right," Harrison said. "I suppose it was too much to hope that they wouldn't make the connection between you and Viv and your recent—"

"Exploits?" I supplied. My voice was dry, and he grinned at me as if relieved that I hadn't lost my sense of humor.

"They'll get tired of being camped out here," Harrison said. "But if you need anything, call me. I can fetch and carry for you if need be."

"Me, too," Fee offered.

It was awfully nice of them, but I had no intention of being held hostage in the shop. I'd had more than enough of that when I was in Florida.

"Thanks, but don't worry about me," I said. "I'll be fine."

Harrison watched me for a moment. He seemed to be studying me as if trying to get my measure. Whatever he saw reassured him, because he gave me a slow nod.

"I'll call and check on you later," he said. He strode out the front door, which Fee shut and locked behind him.

We spent the next hour and a half ignoring the phone, which we eventually had to unplug. We used our cell phones to call our customers who had special orders so that they knew pickup would be by appointment only. I gave my cell number as the number to call, hoping I was not destroying our business by closing our doors.

Fee wandered over to the windows every half hour to check on the reporters.

"Still there," she said. "Must be a slow news day in the city, yeah?"

We finished our calls and hunkered down in the back room with the shades drawn. It was depressing, but then I thought about Lady Ellis and I found it hard to complain.

There was a knock on the back door. Fee's head snapped up from where she was working on five matching fuchsia-and-black hats for the bridesmaids of an upcoming wedding.

They were pointy-brimmed and short-crowned and Fee was attaching a spray of black and fuchsia feathers to the right side of each. A cluster of jet beads nestled in the center of the feathers, and I had to admit I was very curious to see the dresses that went with the hats. I figured it would go one of two ways, gorgeous or ghastly, but at least the hats were smart.

"Could they really have come 'round the building?" I asked in a whisper. Fee shrugged, giving me a wide-eyed look.

"Bloody hell, Scarlett, let us in," a voice shouted from outside.

I gasped and looked at the door. Did the reporters know my name? I thought I was just "the party crasher."

"Don't make me start singing," another voice bellowed.

"Oh, it's Nick and Andre," I cried.

I hurried to the door and yanked it open. Nick and Andre scuttled in, and I slammed the door behind them.

Nick, bless his heart, had a bottle of wine in each hand, and Andre was holding a box from the Hummingbird Bakery just a ways up on Portobello Road. He frowned at it.

"I think your cupcakes may have gotten smashed when we scaled the wall," he said. "You've got reporters camped out front, you know."

"You brought me cupcakes?" I asked. I felt my eyes get watery.

"Isn't that what you Americans do when times are tough, eat cupcakes?" Andre asked.

I launched myself at him, giving him just enough time to move the box before it got crushed in my hug. Andre patted my back with his one free hand.

"MoonPies," I sobbed. "Usually, I eat MoonPies, but cupcakes are an excellent substitute."

"There, there, love, it's all right," he said.

I stepped back and turned to Nick. He was ready, however, having taken the opportunity to put the wine down while I was hugging Andre, and opened his arms wide.

"Come here, pet," he said. "You've had a hell of a day."

Nick knew how to give a hug. Just enough pressure, a solid squeeze and then he stood back with his hands on my shoulders so he could examine my face.

"You look knackered; let's get this wine open," he said.

I nodded and turned to find Fee watching us with a bemused stare.

"Oh, boys, this is Fiona Felton," I said. "She's Viv's assistant."

"Call me Fee," she said.

"Well, Fee, would you care for some wine and some black-bottomed cupcakes?" Andre asked.

"Sure," she said.

He turned and wagged his backside at us and we laughed, causing Nick to chime in saying, "Well, bottoms up then."

I went to the cupboard to get plates. I joined them at the table and said, "Now let's get to the bottom of this."

All three of them stared at me. Not even a chirp of amusement.

"Aw, come on, that was a good one," I protested.

"Bottom of the barrel," Fee said with a sad shake of her head. Andre and Nick broke out laughing, and I had to give it to her. It did trump my quip, but still.

"So, tell me," Nick said as he poured four glasses of wine. "Was it as bad as Andre said?"

I glanced at Andre and watched him pale from the memory of finding Lady Ellis's body. It came back in a horrific,

Technicolor flash. The sight of the gash in her side, her flesh looking like a ripped plum exposing muscle and bone, her cold pale form lying on the sodden carpet.

"Yeah, it was that bad," I said.

Nick handed me a glass and I downed it and immediately held it out for a refill. I noted that Andre did the same.

"Have the police said anything?" Nick asked.

"Not to me," I said. "They just left here a little bit ago. They searched the house."

"Whatever for?" Andre asked. "They haven't contacted me at all."

"The hat Lady Ellis was wearing," I said. "It was Viv's."

"I don't see the connection." Nick frowned.

I hesitated. Did I trust Nick and Andre not to gossip? Did it matter? If the reporters were out front, obviously, they'd made some sort of connection, even if it was just that I was on the scene when she was discovered. If they were worth their salt as reporters, it wouldn't be long until they uncovered the history between Viv and the Ellises.

"Apparently, Lady Ellis was not overly fond of Viv," I said.

"Then why hire her as a milliner?" Andre asked.

"Because she's the best," Fee said. "She's in the elite class with Philip Treacy."

"Is he still that big, even after that wedding hat of Princess Beatrice's?" Nick asked.

"That was the stuff of legends," I said. "You can't buy publicity like that. Besides, I actually liked that hat."

"It looked like an octopus stuck on her forehead," Nick said.

"The color was unfortunate," Fee conceded. "Maybe it

would have been better in a happy shade of purple or a brilliant red."

"No, it wouldn't," Nick said emphatically. "Now as I mentioned before, Lady Ellis was a client of mine." He looked at Fee and tapped his teeth with his forefinger. "I'm skilled in the dental arts, and quite frankly, I don't think I'd be understating it to say she hated everyone, especially if they were younger and prettier than her."

"But she was gorgeous," I said.

"With a lot of help," Nick said.

"Really?" I asked. "Huh, I could have sworn she was a natural beauty."

"Oh, ducks, I don't think there was a part of her that hadn't been worked over by Harley Street. She and all of her gal pals are in a never-ending quest to be the totty of their group. You should hear some of the things they do to themselves all in the name of beauty. As I understand it, she and Marianne Richards have quite the rivalry going."

I sipped my wine. Andre had plated the cupcakes and was handing them out. Fee had obligingly grabbed forks for us all, and I had to resist the urge to slam my cupcake back like a nice shot of hard alcohol. Instead, I strove to be dainty and mannerly and tucked into my cupcake with my fork.

"Any idea what the police were looking for when they were here?" Andre asked.

"They didn't say, but I imagine it would be something to tie Viv to the murder scene, something other than the hat."

Chapter 24

"Have you heard from your cousin?" Andre asked. His voice was gentle, as if he suspected the answer but was hopeful that I might have better news for him.

"No," I said.

The worry in my voice must have been evident because Fee gave me a reassuring pat on the shoulder and said, "Don't worry. She'll turn up. She always does."

As if by silent agreement, the topic was changed.

"All right, Fee," Nick said. "Let's hear your story."

"I'm only twenty-one," she said with a laugh. "I don't have a story."

"Sure you do," Andre said. "It's just a short one."

Fee blew the long pink curl that liked to hang over her right eye out of her face.

"Well, I was born and raised in Notting Hill," she said. "My grandparents on both sides of the family came here back in the sixties from the West Indies. Mom and Dad met at university, got married and had five children."

"Five!" Nick squeaked. "God bless them."

"I'm the fifth," Fee said.

"Is your family still in the area?" I asked. I had already learned that Fee had grown up here, but it had been such a crazy week, I hadn't really gotten a chance to ask about the rest of her family.

"My two sisters live in the States, but both of my brothers are here." She made an annoyed face, and I took it to mean that her older brothers were a bit too much in her business. "But they all come home for carnival in August, during the bank holiday weekend, yeah?"

"I love carnival," Nick gushed.

"This year I am staking out my spot and taking even more pictures," Andre said. His eyes were alight with eagerness.

"Which means you will be absolutely no fun," Nick said. "Scarlett and Fee, you have to be my dates for carnival. Promise?"

I hadn't been to carnival in years. It's the biggest street party in Europe, with colorful costumes, jerk chicken and plantains, and steel-band music. It is impossible not to have a great time during carnival. Now that I was living here, I couldn't wait.

"Absolutely," I agreed.

"Me, too," Fee said and clapped her hands together. "And my brothers can't give me a hard time if I'm with a dentist and my boss."

"Excellent, it's a date," Nick announced and raised his glass. We shared a toast and I tried to convince myself that at least by carnival, which was four months away, Viv would surely have returned.

It was late when everyone left. A peek out of the front door showed that the coast was clear. The reporters had decided not to rough-sleep it on my doorstep for which I was grateful.

I locked up the shop and climbed the stairs to our flat above. I crashed on the couch and tried to watch *Snog, Marry, Avoid?*, a British makeover show where they seek out bimbos and give them class, but I couldn't concentrate and the people on the show annoyed me with how ridiculous they were, and honestly they reminded me a bit too much of the rat bastard's big-boobed wife.

Images of Lady Ellis's naked body kept sneaking up on me, taunting me with her gruesome pose. I couldn't help wondering why she had been wearing only the hat. If her killer had surprised her while getting dressed, surely the first thing she'd have put on would not have been her hat, lovely as it was.

And now the police wanted to know if there was a connection between Lady Ellis and Viv. This filled me with anxiety. Ridiculous, I know, but with Viv being gone, it all just felt so wrong.

Where was Viv? Why hadn't she been in contact? And I really didn't want to hear that she was out of range or didn't have access to e-mail. Unless she was on a camel in the middle of the Sahara, there really was no excuse.

I switched off the TV and wandered into Viv's room. I had stood aside while the inspectors checked through her things. I had felt awkward about it, especially when they went through her underwear drawer. How mortifying.

Franks, the veteran, had been stoic, but Simms, the younger of the two, had turned the bright red of a traffic light, making me think his internal system was giving him the signal to stop and only sheer force of will was making him override it.

Viv's room was done in restful shades of pale blue with white trim and neat, sheer curtains over the windows. Everything was neatly put away and tidied up, not at all like Viv had been when she was younger. She used to walk into a room and explode, jacket one way and shoes another, and she never picked up.

No, this was a grown-up's room, and I longed for the days when her room was across the hall from mine and we spent all evening running back and forth until Mim finally yelled at us to settle in.

Although the good inspectors had spent quite a bit of time in here, they didn't know Viv as well as I did. She was flighty, but she was also sentimental. I went over to her bookcase and began to search through the books crammed onto the shelves. Many of them were Mim's from when this room was hers, but Viv had added her own.

I found what I was looking for on the bottom shelf: Viv's scrapbook from her years at the university. I flipped through the pages of the handmade album. Viv had been an art major with an emphasis in fashion. She had hoped to go right into hat-making with Mim, but Aunt Grace wanted her to have a full education just in case she ever decided to do anything else with her life.

Reluctantly, Viv had agreed. The pages were full of

fashion shows held at the university. Viv, now twenty-nine, looked so much younger in the photos. I couldn't help smiling at a shot of her surrounded by her models at one of her shows. I didn't see anyone resembling Lord Ellis or Lady Ellis in the photos.

Viv and I had the same blue eyes, large and round, but where I had gotten the stick-straight red hair of my father's side of the family, Viv had gotten the blond curls that both of our mothers had inherited from Mim. I used to be insanely jealous of that hair, which hung halfway down her back and seemed to lure the boys in like a creeper vine twining about them and imprisoning them in her aura, but then one day, Viv confessed that she wished she had my hair. I told her I'd gladly trade.

It was a revelation that this girl, whom I looked up to and admired, might prefer something that was inherently me. I never felt jealous again, and I was forever grateful that Viv had made me see myself through her eyes.

A yawn snuck up and punched me in the kisser, making me open my mouth so wide I heard my jaw crack. I put the scrapbook away. I saw nothing in there that answered any of my questions, and I was so tired, I didn't think I could concentrate much longer anyway.

Maybe it was seeing the body today that had me spooked, but I left a light on in the kitchen as I went up the stairs to my intensely pink room. I didn't want to wake up in complete darkness and be freaked out.

Crawling into bed, I missed the sound of the rain on the window glass from a few nights before. It would have been nice to have it drum me to sleep. I was sure I would toss and turn all night, but just like the yawn that had sucker punched me, sleep took me down for the count before I even made one toss and no turns.

I'm not a dreamer, generally, and when I do dream I never remember them in the morning. But this dream was different. It was so vivid. The pain I felt in my chest was so intense. I was wearing the aqua cloche, I was naked, and the searing ache in my lungs made me glance down and see that I had a knife sticking out from my rib cage. I looked at my hands in horror. They were covered in blood.

A panicked part of my brain kept signaling that this was a dream and that I needed to wake up—now! I felt weak, so weak, I was falling to the floor. I could feel myself slipping deeper into the blackness, but again a tiny part of me insisted that I wake up.

I put my hands up and that's when I realized there was a pillow on my face. I hadn't been stabbed and I wasn't dreaming. Someone was trying to suffocate me and my lungs were in agony from lack of oxygen! With the last of my strength, I got one foot out from under my covers and kicked as hard as I could. My knee connected with the solid weight of a person, knocking them off balance.

The pillow's grip on my face lessened and I smacked it off, taking whoever had been holding it down on me with it. I sat up and sucked in sweet, beautiful air in great gulping gasps as if there would never be enough to inflate my lungs, which had surely been on the verge of being flattened forever.

Before I could register in my oxygen-deprived brain what had just happened, there was a scuttling noise and I saw a person, dressed all in black, disappear from my room. I tried to give chase, really, I did, but my legs were like jelly and I was still sucking in air. My chest burned.

I fumbled for my cell phone on the nightstand and scrolled through my contacts, choosing the name I had typed in most recently. Despite the early morning hour, Harrison answered on the second ring.

He didn't even get a chance to speak before I blurted out, "Help! Someone just tried to kill me."

Chapter 25

Okay, I can admit it. One part of me called him to see if he was breathing heavily as if he'd just tried to smother someone and was making a run for it. Did I really think he was my assailant? No, but I wanted to be sure.

"What?" he cried.

I could hear the rustle of bedsheets as if he was moving into a sitting position. This reassured me as nothing else could have.

"Pillow over my face," I said. "They're gone now, I think."

"Call the police!" he barked. "Then call me right back. I'm on my way." He hung up.

Call the police. Call the police. My sleep-soaked, terrified brain couldn't quite register the words. I stared at my phone.

I was pretty sure it wasn't 9-1-1. In fact, I remember Mim

drilling 9-9-9 into my head, but that was for emergencies. Was this an emergency? I didn't want to get into trouble, or should I say more trouble?

My phone started to chime. I noted the number was Harrison's.

"Hello?" I answered.

"Why didn't you call me back?" he asked.

"I haven't even called the police yet," I said.

"Why not?"

"I don't want to get into trouble," I said. "With Viv missing and the Lady Ellis situation . . ."

My voice trailed off and I could hear his exasperation almost as loudly as I could hear his huffing and puffing.

"Scarlett," he said. "Someone broke into your shop and your house. They tried to kill you. Now you have to call the police. They have to investigate."

"I suppose," I said. "Can I do it when you get here?"

There was a beat of silence, and I wondered if he was going to hang up on me after demanding that I call the police again. To my surprise, he didn't.

"Are you all right?" he asked.

His voice was surprisingly gentle with concern, and for some reason it made my throat close up and I had to swallow hard before I could answer.

"I'm fine," I said. Now if English girls are anything like American girls, Harrison would know that "fine" means anything but fine. And in my case, at the present moment, it meant I was on the verge of hysterics.

"Breathe," he said. "Come on, you can do it. A nice big breath and hold it. Now let it all the way out nice and slow."

I did as I was told, realizing that English women and the word "fine" must be compatible with the American female usage. Either that or my voice was clearly borderline hysterical.

"Do it again," he said. He waited while I exhaled. "Excellent, are you better now?"

"A little," I said, feeling for the first time like I might not pass out.

"All right," he said. "Do you hear anything? Do you think your attacker might still be there?"

"Hang on," I said. "I'll check."

"No!" He shouted and I had to hold my phone away from my ear.

"Easy," I said. "I'm not deaf."

"Sorry," he said. "But don't leave your room. You don't know if it's safe."

"Oh, I'm betting even my neighbors heard that yell of yours in their sleep. I'm sure it's safe now."

"Scarlett!" He was clearly exasperated.

"Relax," I said. "I'm not going anywhere."

Which was a lie. I climbed off the bed and stood on legs that, while still shaky, managed to keep me upright. I crept toward the door.

"Scarlett, what are you doing?" he asked.

"Listening like you told me to," I said. "Now shh."

I lowered the phone so I could use both of my ears to hear. I crept up to the door. My heart started to pound in my chest. I peered around the doorjamb and noted that the light I'd left on below was still on.

It cast faint shadows up the staircase and my eyes darted

about, trying to assess what was shadow and what could be crazy-bad-person, lurking in the dark. Now my palms were sweating and my breathing was coming faster.

"Scarlett!" I could hear Harrison calling me so I pressed my phone against my belly to muffle the sound. How could I hear when he was making such a racket?

All was quiet and still in the hallway. I could just see across into Viv's old room. I wondered if I should go in there to check it out. It seemed unlikely, but how stupid would I feel if I trotted on downstairs and the person who tried to smother me came trotting down after me?

I lifted up the phone and said, "It's very quiet. I'm going to check Viv's old room."

I swiftly lowered the phone as Harrison started to protest quite loudly. The man obviously had no sense of stealth. It took some nerve-building on my part but I finally stepped out of my room. I braced myself for someone to jump out of the darkness and attack, but nothing happened.

I crept across the landing and eased my way into Viv's old room. The light from below didn't cast enough light in this room for me to see, so I quickly switched on the overhead lamp. I scanned the room. It was a generic guest bedroom now. And no, no looming bad guy lurked in the corners or under the bed or the closet.

I turned to leave, again pausing in the door to check the landing before venturing forward. Nothing.

I eased my way to the bathroom door. It was closed, so I gingerly pushed it open. It was empty, but I had to check the shower. It had a pale yellow curtain drawn across it, the perfect place for a would-be killer to hide before round two. I curled my fingers around the vinyl and quickly yanked it back, snapping off a few of its plastic rings with the force of my tug. Oops!

It was empty. No one was there but still, years of horror films had me on high alert and my heart slammed down into my belly as I registered the fact that no one was there. I felt myself go limp with relief.

I was just raising the phone back up to my ear when a heavy hand landed on my shoulder.

Chapter 26

"Ah!" I screamed as my body went rigid with fright. Then I spun around with my phone in my fist, determined to take my attacker down.

"Whoa!" I heard a yell as the person I was aiming for ducked to avoid the blow.

I went to snap kick him, but found myself snatched around the waist and dragged out the door into the landing before my foot could connect.

My back was pinned to someone else's front and I was wriggling and kicking and clawing for all I was worth.

"Harrison!" I yelled, hoping my phone was still on where I had dropped it in the scuffle. "He's got me! Hurry!"

"Scarlett, it's me!" a voice shouted in my ear. "Stop! Do not bite me!"

I had grabbed his hand and was just about to sink my

CLOCHE AND DAGGER

teeth in when I recognized the voice. I whipped my head around and we were face-to-face, with me in Harrison's arms, dangling off the ground as he held me in the air as if it were no effort at all.

"Are you insane?" I snapped. Now I wanted to hit him even more, so I did, a solid punch to the arm, causing him to drop me. "You could have said something, you know, instead of scaring the snot out of me."

"Silly me," he said. "I was trying to be quiet in case anyone was still here."

"Oh," I said. I supposed he was right, but I didn't have to admit it.

Of course, now I realized with a flush of embarrassment that I was standing in the dark in just my pajamas with a man I wasn't sure I trusted. I picked up my phone and crossed my arms over my chest.

"How did you get in?"

"The back door was wide open," he said.

I frowned.

"Someone took the lock right off of it," he explained.

"While I was sleeping?"

He just looked at me without saying anything.

"Sorry, stupid question," I said. "I'm still trying to process."

"Let's call Inspector Franks," he said. "I think the immediate danger is over, but I'm sure he'll want to know about what's happened."

"Do you think this has something to do with Viv being missing?" I asked as I followed him down the stairs without touching the railing.

157

"More likely it has something to do with Lady Ellis," he said. He paused at the bottom of the steps and looked up at me. "They tried to kill you. Why?"

My mouth went dry and I felt a little woozy.

"Blunt much?" I asked. I chose to turn my upset into snippiness. It's a self-defense mechanism. I know this and yet I can't help it.

"Sorry, that was rather tactless of me," he said. "I don't know that there's any way I could sugarcoat what happened here though."

"No, I don't suppose having someone take off an entire lock to get inside a building where they then hold a pillow over the face of the only other person in the building lends itself to a kinder or gentler description than attempted murder."

"You sound a wee bit hysterical," he said.

"Oh, I can assure you, it's more than a wee bit," I said.

I followed him through the second floor to the stairs that led below to the shop. He had his phone out and was calling in the break-in, and the attempted murder, as we went. Whomever he was talking with sounded irate, as if they didn't like having their sleep interrupted by my problem. So sorry, next time I'll try to reschedule my suffocation to a more suitable hour. Yes, still snippy.

I flipped on the light switch, bathing the shop in the reassuring brightness of electricity. I felt my shoulders drop down from around my ears. I scanned the room. No one was here.

"Thank you, Inspector," Harrison said. He leaned close to me and said, "Don't touch anything."

I glared. As if I would. I'd watched *CSI*. I knew better than to tamper with the evidence.

I went to one of the sitting areas and very carefully sat down on the edge of the couch. I sincerely doubted that the person who'd tried to kill me would have left any trace of evidence in the sitting area. It wasn't like they were here to have tea, after all.

Harrison closed his phone and joined me. I could feel him studying my face, but I was ignoring him. I was trying very hard not to feel sorry for myself and I was failing miserably.

The whole point of coming to England and working in the shop was to take my mind off the disaster I had left behind, the rat bastard, his beautiful wife, and my oh-so-public humiliation. In that regard, mission accomplished.

However, I did not like not knowing where my cousin was and that no one, save me, seemed overly concerned about her. I did not like finding clients murdered. And I most definitely did not like waking up to find someone trying to smother me.

A tiny sob bubbled up in my throat. I tried to swallow it down, but it escaped and echoed in the silence of the shop.

Harrison narrowed his eyes at me. I tried to make my face blank, but his eyes grew even narrower until they were mere green slits.

"Are you all right?" he asked.

"Fine," I lied.

A commotion at the front door brought our attention around to it. Through the glass I could see Inspectors Franks and Simms, and I was relieved to get up and let them in and escape Harrison's all-knowing look. Sympathy at this point would just make me blubber.

I used the edge of my shirt to open the door. I could hear

Harrison moving to stand behind me. Despite our differences, it was comforting to have him at my back as I had no idea how the inspectors were going to view this situation.

"Morning, Ms. Parker," Inspector Franks said. He looked grave. "I'm afraid we'll need you to come to the station with us."

Chapter 27

"What?!" I cried. Harrison muttered something even less kind beneath his breath.

"We'll need your fingerprints to differentiate them from your assailant's, assuming they left any behind," he said.

"Surely that can wait until after the sun is up," Harrison said.

Franks opened his mouth to answer but Simms interrupted. "It was the back door that they entered through?"

I nodded.

"I'll start back there," Simms said and he disappeared into the workroom.

"Have you checked to see if anything is missing?" Franks asked.

"No," I said. "I was afraid to touch anything."

Franks nodded his approval; then he turned and studied Harrison.

"When did you get here?" he asked.

There was no innuendo in his voice, but I heard the unstated speculation about the relationship between Harrison and myself. I felt my face get hot and cursed my fair skin.

Thankfully, neither of them looked at me and I was able to wrestle my composure back unobserved.

"Not long after Scarlett called me," Harrison said. "Since I live over in Pembridge Mews, I got here pretty quickly. Besides, she doesn't know anyone else, do you?"

He looked at me for confirmation.

"No one who is in my phone," I said. I made a mental note to get Andre's, Nick's and Fee's numbers tomorrow. Not that I would call them in case of an emergency, but it might prove less awkward than calling Harrison if another situation came up. Heaven forbid.

"Well, there's no sign of anything being disturbed in the back other than the lock on the door," Inspector Simms said as he joined us. "I'm going to check the upstairs."

"All right," Franks said, approving, and Simms disappeared upstairs.

I wasn't really sure how I felt about everyone going into my room, but I didn't suppose I could really prevent it, given it was the place I was attacked; besides, they'd already seen it all. I realized I needed to repaint it as soon as possible.

"Why don't you tell me what happened?" Inspector Franks asked. His voice wasn't unkind and I wondered fleetingly how bad I looked.

There were plenty of mirrors around the shop, but I was pretty sure I didn't want to know. It was bad enough I was wearing my pink pajamas with the plaid bottoms and matching Hubba Bubba bubble gum top. It just screamed maturity and mental stability.

I started with the dream that I had been stabbed. Then my slow realization that I was not dreaming, which led to kicking the person who was holding a pillow over my face away as quickly as possible. Neither Franks nor Harrison said anything, but I could see them looking at my scrawny arms, trying to see how I could have overpowered anyone.

They wisely said nothing, however, because I'd have been happy to give a demo and burn off the last of the adrenaline that still surged through me, looking for an outlet.

I explained that I couldn't remember the emergency number for the police and that I hadn't been sure it was an emergency. They both looked surprised, and I admitted I was still catching my breath. They gave me a look that said they thought I had suffered oxygen deprivation. I wanted to say, "No duh," but I refrained.

I then said that I called Harrison because he was the only local contact I had in my phone.

"And here I thought I was special," he said.

Inspector Franks snorted and I cracked a smile.

"That probably came out wrong," I said.

Harrison smiled at me in return, and I was grateful for the break in the tension.

"Well, there's no sign of anything being disturbed upstairs other than the bedclothes," Inspector Simms said as he joined us.

All three men were looking at me as if I had an explanation. Did they think I was supposed to make the bed before I called? I shrugged and they all glanced away.

"Do you keep any money in the shop?" Franks asked me after a moment's pause.

"Yes, in a safe in the cupboard in the back," I said.

"I'd like to get it dusted first," Inspector Franks said. "Then we'll check the contents, but I'm going to be honest, if they were here for your money, they likely never would have gone upstairs."

"The crime-scene techs are here," Simms said.

He strode over to the door to let them in. I watched as they came in and noted they were an unusual crew made up of one older, balding gentleman with two skinny, geeky-looking assistants.

Franks joined them and they had a brief conversation before one of the assistants went into the back room and the other assistant and the older man were led upstairs to my room. I was so not sleeping there tonight.

Harrison and I sat in one of the small seating areas and watched. While we waited I glanced around the shop. Nothing seemed out of order. The hats sat on their stands, the accessories were all neatly in their places. I noticed Ferd the bird watching the comings and goings as if amused by the human beings scurrying around him. I glowered at his beaky head.

Yes, on an intellectual level, I was aware that he was just a wooden carving, but he had an air about him that made me think he was more than a piece of knotty mahogany. I couldn't shake the feeling that he actually saw things and knew what was happening.

"Why are you glaring at the wardrobe?" Harrison asked.

"Huh?"

"You're glaring at the raven," he said. "Did it do something to offend you?"

"Not today," I said.

He raised his eyebrows in question but I didn't elaborate. I knew he had mixed feelings about me already; I didn't see any need to fan the flames of his suspicion that I was crazy.

"Do you suppose they'll have a service for Lady Ellis?" I asked.

"Undoubtedly. She was a countess and a fashion model before that," Harrison answered. He gave me a shrewd look. "Why?"

I glanced around the room. I wanted to make sure the inspectors and the crime-scene techs were out of earshot.

"I can't help thinking that it's odd that she was wearing that hat," I said.

"Do you think it's a message?" Harrison frowned. "And if so, what does it mean?"

"I don't know," I admitted. "Oh, I wish Viv were here."

"Have you heard from her?" he asked.

"No," I said. "But Aunt Grace got another e-mail, telling her she was fine. Very annoying."

Harrison blew out a breath in exasperation. I wondered if maybe he was a little tired of her shenanigans as well.

"When do you suppose they'll have the viewing for Lady Ellis?" I asked.

"Eager to see her again, are you?" he asked.

"No," I said as a shudder rippled through me. "But I feel like I have to go, as one of the people who found her."

"I heard that it might be held in the beginning of the week," Harrison said. He paused and then seemed to come to a decision. "I'll take you if you want."

"Would we be allowed in?" I asked.

"Yes," he said. His tone didn't invite questions, but I

wondered at the how. Surely a countess would merit some sort of invite-only situation.

I glanced at Harrison, thinking I should question him, but he met my glance with one of complete self-assuredness. And then I got it. He was connected. I don't know how or why, but obviously, he had connections that would get him into the viewing. Excellent.

There was no way I could explain why it was important. It was a feeling, a compulsion really, that made me think that I needed to be at the wake.

"I'll call you with the details as soon as I have them," he said.

"Thank you," I said.

The corner of his mouth turned up in a grim smile. "It's the least I can do. You've had a hell of week here, haven't you?"

Sympathy from Harrison Wentworth was so unexpected that I felt my eyes sting with hot tears. Afraid he'd rethink his kindness if I blubbered all over him, I glanced up at the ceiling, willing the dampness to roll back into my tear ducts while trying to look contemplative. I probably just looked stupid, but better that than pathetic.

"It's been a rough stretch," I agreed. "But I expect it will turn around."

With my tears safely tamped back down, I glanced back at him. He was studying me as if he found me to be a particularly perplexing problem. I gave him a small smile and he glanced hastily away as if embarrassed to have been caught staring.

"Not to squash your optimism, but I don't really expect it to get better until they've caught whoever it was who tried to kill you," he said.

It was like a blast of arctic air on my skin and I shivered.

"Do you really think they were trying to kill me?" I asked. "Maybe they just wanted me to black out so I didn't interrupt their robbery."

"Ginger, look around us." His voice was soft and kind as he called me by my old nickname. "If they were here to rob the shop, why didn't they take anything?"

I did not want to hear this. "Because I kicked them. Hard."

He sighed. "Deny, deny, deny."

"What?" I asked. "You want me to believe that someone broke in here to kill me? That's mental. Who would want to kill me?"

"Oh, I don't know," he said. His cheeks had gotten red and he looked irked. "Wild guess here, but maybe it was your ex-lover's wife."

Chapter 28

"Ah!" I gasped. "Why that's just . . . it's . . . hardly . . ."

"Problem over here?" Inspector Franks asked as he joined us.

I glowered at Harrison. So much for his sympathy. I might have known it wouldn't last.

"No, no problem," I said.

He glanced between us and Harrison gave him a blank stare.

"None that I can think of," he said.

Franks continued to study us, obviously unconvinced.

"We're ready for you to check the safe now," he said to me.

"Fine," I said. I rose stiffly from my seat and stomped past Harrison, desperately wanting to step on his toes as I went by. I refrained and felt quite smug and mature about it.

I was nearing the door to the back when I paused by one

of the built-in shelving units. I had been straightening it when Lady Ellis had come in that evening. It held a display of gloves, from black for funerals to pristine white for weddings. My favorite had been a pair of vintage Lilly Daché gray gloves with embroidered cuffs. I had been so intrigued by them, I had tried them on. But now, they weren't there.

"Ms. Parker?" Inspector Franks called me from the door. "Is everything all right?"

"No," I said. "You're not going to find any fingerprints."

His eyebrows shot up in surprise. No doubt at the surety of my voice.

"Why not?"

"Because the person was wearing gloves, my gloves," I said.

I described the missing items, the only things that had gone missing in the shop, and Inspector Franks took notes.

"Would you happen to have a picture of them?" he asked.

"I doubt it," I said. "Mim always carried accessory items, and she was partial to the vintage ones, but we've never kept a photo record of them like we do with the hats. The only possibility would be if Fee is offering the items for sale in our online store."

"Can you look into it and get back to me?" he asked.

"I'll ask her," I said.

"I'm going to have the place examined anyway," he said. "If they took the gloves after they broke in then they might have left some prints behind, at least on the door."

I nodded. Having a pillow held over my face to the point of suffocation was terrifying, hugely terrifying. But somehow having the gloves taken felt like more of a violation, or maybe it just meant that the killer was creepy enough to have broken in and then used the shop's own gloves against me. I didn't know; either way, it left me feeling more rattled than ever.

I checked the safe. It was fine. At least, as far as I knew, nothing had been touched. Honestly, I hadn't looked in the safe since I'd arrived so I could only judge by the neatness of the contents, which seemed as tidy as one would expect.

"If you hear from your cousin and she can verify the contents of the safe, that would be greatly appreciated," Inspector Franks said.

I nodded. Two hours later the police took their leave. Harrison had brewed a pot of non-caffeinated tea and we sat at the workroom table in the back while we drank.

The adrenaline that had kept me going finally departed, leaving me a soupy mess. My exhaustion must have shown because Harrison took my cup and put it aside.

"Come on," he said as he helped me up by the elbow. "Up you go."

We had propped a chair under the door handle to the back door. Not the greatest lock, but it would have to do until a locksmith could come.

I had thought Harrison would see me to the door that led upstairs and then take his leave, but instead, he walked me up to Viv's new room.

"Sleep here," he said. "I'll bunk on the couch in the sitting room and watch over you while you sleep."

That did it. The sobs I'd been holding at bay took me out at the knees, and before I could even attempt to hold them back, my shoulders were shaking, I was hiccupping and tears were running down my face as if I'd been uncorked.

Harrison didn't say a word. He just pulled me into his

solid warmth and wrapped his arms around me while I cried. A couple of times I thought I'd cried it out, but no. There was always just one more puddle to wring out of my middle. Finally, I ran dry.

"You don't have to stay," I mumbled into the soft cotton of his shirt. "But it was really nice of you to offer."

His hand was running absently up and down my back. I was tucked in against him with my head nestled under his chin, a perfect fit.

"I'm not offering," he said. "I'm telling you I'm staying. How could I live with myself if something happened to you?"

I looked up then to see his face. His green eyes crinkled in the corners as he gave me a small smile.

"Viv would kill me if anything happened to you," he said. He was joking, but it hit me like a splash of cold water.

What was I doing snuggled up against him when he and my cousin were obviously close? How close I didn't know, but obviously much closer than he and I were. I felt my face get hot.

"Viv would do you an injury, a severe one," I said, trying to joke my way through the awkwardness that suddenly felt as thick as a London fog.

He tucked a strand of hair back behind my ear. "Go get some sleep. Things will look better in the morning, I promise."

I gave him a brisk nod and fled to the big bedroom, Viv's bedroom. I paused only to fetch a spare pillow and quilt from the linen closet and hurriedly thrust them into Harrison's arms before I disappeared into Mim's old room.

I curled up on the bed, feeling like a perfect idiot. I had

just cried all over a man who couldn't stand me, who had some sort of relationship with my cousin, although I wasn't exactly sure what it entailed, and whom I didn't completely trust. It was just mortifying.

Why didn't I trust him? I wondered. I didn't really believe that he had anything to do with Viv's disappearance. In fact, I was getting the feeling that he was feeling as irked as I was with Viv.

No, it was because I felt like he wasn't telling me everything. That was it. When I thought about how I felt around him, it was this feeling that he knew things and he wasn't sharing them with me. I had no proof of it, but it was a feeling I couldn't shake.

I supposed I couldn't really blame him for not telling me everything. Here I was, this scandal-ridden American who had arrived to claim my half of an inheritance I had all but ignored until my life fell apart and I had no place else to go.

I rolled onto my back. There was a faint scent in the room of Lily of the Valley. It was the scent I always associated with Mim. Abruptly, I was spiked with a sharp spear of grief, right in my chest, and I missed her with a longing that left me bereft.

In my mind, I could see her hands, spotted with age, twisting ribbons into delicate braids of color to adorn one of her spring garden hats. She had the ability to make even the simplest hat look elegant and charming.

I wondered what she would make of this situation we found ourselves in now. Despite her own scattered artistic temperament, Mim had been very practical in her outlook on the world. She tended to see it for exactly what it was and didn't take it too seriously.

She had a silly sense of humor that frequently made itself known in her more whimsical designs. But mostly, what I missed about her was that whenever I was with Mim, there was nothing that couldn't be managed with a hot cup of tea and a hug.

Maybe that was just because I was so much younger and my problems smaller then. I knew deep down that part of the reason I had cried all over Harrison's shirtfront was because being here made me miss Mim and his had been the only warm body present to fill the void. I tried not to dwell on what a nice warm body he had, instead remembering that tomorrow I would have to go to the police station and be fingerprinted. I was dreading it.

If the reporters got wind of this, well, I couldn't even imagine what sort of sordid tales they would weave about me, because I certainly hadn't had enough of that.

A soft snore sounded from the other room. It was followed by a grunt and another snore. I wasn't sure why this made me smile, but it did. Harrison snored. I liked knowing this about him. I was still smiling when I fell asleep.

The lovely smell of coffee brewing roused me from my sleep. For a moment, I thought I was back in my apartment in Florida with my coffeepot on the timer, brewing a perfect two cups that I would then put in my travel mug before I headed out the door to the hotel I helped to manage.

The low rumble of voices busted through my happy daydream like an elephant stampede, and I snapped to a sitting position. This was a bad plan, as my head felt like someone had used it for an ax holder. The pain was deep in my skull, throbbing from my sinus cavity up through my hair follicles. It was the crying. A good crying jag, and last night's had been a doozy, always left me with a scorching headache.

Knuckles wrapped on my door.

"Scarlett, you'd better come out here," Harrison said.

"Be right there," I said. I sighed. No good-morning greeting made me suspect bad news awaited my arrival. Bleh. I was so over the bad news.

Harrison was in Mim's kitchen. Her tiny TV on the counter was on and programmed to the local news. It took me a minute to realize that the reporter speaking live was standing in front of the shop, which meant she was out front right now.

"What?"

"Shh," Harrison hushed me as he turned up the volume.

"This is the hat shop owned by Vivian Tremont, the former girlfriend of Earl Ellis of Waltham," the brunette was saying. "While it can't be confirmed, word has it that Ms. Tremont has fled the country in the wake of Lady Ellis's grisly murder and neighbors along the street here on Portobello Road have confirmed that Ms. Tremont has not been seen in days. No arrests have been made in the murder of Lady Ellis as yet, but the police were called here late last night. There is no word as to whether Ms. Tremont has returned and been brought into custody or not."

Chapter 29

The screen switched to a photo of Vivian and a dark-haired man. The man was in profile, so I didn't get the full-on smarmy face of Lord Ellis, who'd been here just days before with his wife. I could tell by the hairstyle Viv was wearing that the picture was from her days at the university when she'd gone through an unfortunate bang phase.

"Oh, for Pete's sake, that photo has to be ten years old," I cried. "Where the heck did they get it?"

"From someone who knew them then, who wanted some quick cash," Harrison said.

The reporter continued with more rumors about Vivian and Lord Ellis's alleged friendship, and at the end of it my headache had doubled in force because now I was gnashing my teeth.

"This is bad," I said. "Really bad. They're making Viv

sound like a deranged ex-girlfriend. She's going to be suspect number one."

"Not going to be," Harrison sighed. "She is."

"Oh, good grief," I said. I rubbed my temples, willing my headache to ease.

Harrison left the kitchen and returned from the bathroom connected to Viv's room with a small bottle.

"Here," he said and he handed me a bottle of Nuromol. I glanced at it. Ibuprofen tablets.

"That obvious?" I asked.

"You cringe every time you move your head," he said. "I'm assuming headache?"

I gave a small nod and then regretted it. Harrison put a mug of coffee in front of me and I loaded it with sugar and milk and used it to chase two tablets down my throat.

"Crying always does that to me," I said.

"Well, you'd better pace yourself," he said. "They've announced the viewing hours for Lady Ellis. It's going to be Monday next. Still want to go?"

"Yes, definitely," I said. "How can it be that early? Don't they have autopsy and toxicology reports to perform?"

"Apparently, Lord Ellis has put the pressure on to solve the case and has insisted his wife's body not be left overlong in the morgue. I expect the funeral will be held on Tuesday," he said.

I sipped my coffee. I wondered how Inspectors Franks and Simms were doing today. It was Saturday. I didn't imagine they would be enjoying it as such, however. Then I remembered that Saturday on Portobello Road was market day.

Normally we would prop open the front door and, weather permitting, put some racks of merchandise out on the sidewalk to lure the people swarming to the stalls of the antiques arcades. Saturday was big business in Notting Hill, which was why we were always closed on Sunday and Monday. We needed it to recover.

Today, I would not be participating. I took my mug of coffee and crossed the pale wood floor to the long, tall window that overlooked the street. There was a mob outside the store but it wasn't shoppers. Instead, it was a horde of reporters and camera crews. Great, another day of feeling like a captive in my own home.

Harrison was busily cooking up eggs and toast. I would have told him not to bother, but I was surprised to discover I was starving. Maybe what I had was a hunger headache after all.

I resumed my seat at the breakfast counter and he pushed a plate to me piled high with fluffy eggs, some fried ham and buttered toast.

"Thanks," I said. "You really shouldn't have."

"Yes, I should," he argued. "You're too thin."

"So, my mother called?" I asked. I didn't bother to temper my sarcasm.

He grinned. "Eat."

I didn't need to be told twice. He took the seat beside me and plowed into his own plate while we switched channels and noted that most of them were reporting much the same thing and from the same location below.

Only one reporter went so far as to mention me, and that would be the same one that Harrison had tossed out on his patoot. His report had pictures of me, a nice short clip of my meltdown, pictures of Viv, Lady Ellis and one of Viv with Lord Ellis.

"I should have tossed him out on his head," Harrison growled.

"You did dump him on the location where he obviously keeps his brains," I said. "Not your fault."

Harrison gave me an approving look. "Funny."

"Thank you," I said.

I could feel him watching me while I scraped my plate clean. "What?"

"You seem better today," he said. "Stronger."

"That's because we have a plan," I said. "I'm the managing type. I need to have a plan, otherwise I go bonkers."

"I get that," he said.

For a few brief moments, I felt like Harrison Wentworth and I actually understood one another. Then we had a fight.

"Scarlett, you can't cold-call your clients and accuse them of murder," he said.

We were standing in Mim's kitchen, cleaning up together and discussing what I should do next, since it was obvious I wasn't going to be able to open my doors today.

I had suggested that I call the clients known to be friends with Lady Ellis and let them know we were operating by appointment only and see if I could get any information out of them. Harrison was vehemently opposed.

"I'm not going to accuse them of anything," I said. I wiped down the counter with a sponge.

"These are wealthy, titled ladies," he argued. He put a stack of plates up into the cupboard. "You probably won't get them to answer your call. It will be their personal secretary who turns you down flat."

"No, they won't," I said. "I can work with a secretary."

"Scarlett, you and Viv are tabloid fodder," he said. "Trust me when I tell you that they won't want to come anywhere near you now."

"Don't be silly," I said. "Of course they will."

"Are you daft?" he asked. "How do you think you can possibly get them to want to have anything to do with you or the shop, given that there is a horde of reporters camped outside, Viv has been all but accused of murder and you are still tainted by the scandal you left back in the States."

"You know, I'm actually very good with people, present company excepted," I said.

He closed the cupboard and turned toward me. I met his green eyes without looking away. I was good with people. Usually. Just not him. He'd obviously never forgiven me for tossing him over, which was ridiculous given how young I was, and he probably never would.

"I know you're good with people," he said. "I've seen you in action. You can charm a honeybee out of his hive and get him to beg you to take his honey."

His lips curved up in the corners and I had the distinct impression I had just been insulted.

"Are you calling me manipulative?" I asked.

"More like lethally charming," he said.

"That doesn't feel like a compliment."

"It wasn't."

Ouch! I broke eye contact with him. The rich emerald color of his eyes was distracting and I felt the need to put some distance between us.

So much for having a meeting of the minds; every time I felt like Harrison and I might find some friendly footing, he said something that convinced me we were not friends and never would be.

"I need to call a locksmith," I said.

"Already done," he said. "In fact, he should be here shortly."

"Oh, well, thank you," I said.

See? And then he did something nice for me like sleeping on the couch, cooking breakfast and arranging for a locksmith, and I was more confused than ever.

"I'd better get dressed then," I said.

"I'll meet you downstairs." He switched off the TV and headed for the door.

"Thanks," I called after him and he nodded.

Okay, that was getting old. I really didn't want to be indebted to someone who was obviously not a fan of mine. Somehow I needed to tip the scale.

I mulled it over in the shower but nothing brilliant came to me. I would just have to bide my time and see what I could do to repay the many ways Harrison had helped me when the opportunity presented itself.

I didn't bother putting on makeup or styling my hair. It wasn't as if we were going to open today, and I didn't want Harrison to have to wait any longer for the locksmith when he probably had better things to do, like catch up on the sleep he had missed while babysitting me.

The sound of voices grew louder as I entered the back room. An older gentleman in coveralls with the company name "Titan Alarms" stitched on the left front was talking to Harrison.

"All three floors?" the man was asking.

"Yes," Harrison said.

"Hello," I said as I joined them.

"Scarlett, this is Mac. He's putting in the alarm system," Harrison said.

"Nice to meet you," I said, and shook Mac's hand. It was rough with calluses but also warm and surprisingly gentle. "What alarm system? I thought we called a locksmith."

"I'm that, too," Mac said. He had a deep voice and his accent was Scottish, with a nice thick brogue flavoring it like salt in a good stew. "I'll fix up your locks and alarm your windows and doors so no one will be breaking in here anytime soon."

"I don't think that's—" I began but Harrison interrupted me.

"Don't you think Mim would want her two granddaughters safe?" he asked.

"Of course she would, but we've never had any reason to—" I began and he interrupted me again.

"Which is why you were almost suffocated last night," he said. "With the alarm, the police would be here before the attacker reached you."

"And you called me manipulative?" I asked. "You've got a one-two punch of guilt and fear going here."

Mac glanced between me and Harrison as if trying to figure out if there was going to be an argument.

Harrison met my gaze and had the grace to look embarrassed.

"I'm not above a little good, old-fashioned manipulation, especially if I know it will keep you and Viv safe," he said.

"Bee charmer," I accused and he winked at me. Again, with the confusing signals. Was I ever going to understand him?

I turned back to Mac. "I suppose the alarm system would be for the best. Thank you."

As he walked away, I whispered to Harrison, "Can we afford this?"

"Yes," he said. "I have it all factored into the operating budget."

"Okay, then. Won't Viv be surprised?"

"Serves her right," he said. He turned and studied me and picked up a damp strand of hair. "You look younger like this, like you did when we were children."

Chapter 30

A burst of warmth hit me right in the middle and my voice was still a whisper when I asked, "Is that a good thing or a bad thing?"

His gaze met mine and a smile tipped the corner of his mouth when he said, "A good thing."

I noticed his voice was whisper soft, too.

"Harrison," Mac called, breaking the moment between us.

He dropped my hair and walked away, and I had the craziest urge to grab his hand and stop him, but I didn't; that was probably a good thing.

Harrison left shortly after that. He said I was in good hands with Mac and his crew, but I got the feeling he wanted to put some distance between us. I couldn't say that I blamed him. The combination of exhaustion and stress was undoubtedly causing us both to feel things that weren't entirely appropriate, given that we were business partners of sorts.

Fee arrived at midmorning. She looked startled to see Mac and his crew.

"What happened?" she asked.

I told her about the break-in, pleased that my voice didn't crack. In the light of day, it was refreshing to find that instead of feeling weak and vulnerable, I had a nice steam of rage blowing out of me.

Although I tried not to make it sound overly dramatic, there was no way to tell her I had almost been suffocated than to just get it out. Fee's eyes went wide and she slumped onto a chair.

"Bloody hell, Scarlett, you could have been killed," she said.

"But I wasn't. And now we'll have a lovely alarm system to keep us safe and sound."

Fee gave Mac and his crew a dubious look. She looked scared and I felt bad that she was frightened.

"If you want to take a leave of absence until everything calms down, you can," I said.

"No!" Fee shook her head. "I won't leave you in the lurch. It's just, well, I really wish Viv were here. I'm worried about her. I heard on the news today—"

"I know," I said. "I heard it, too. You know she had nothing to do with Lady Ellis's death."

"Of course, I know," Fee said, looking indignant. "But it doesn't look good for the business, does it?"

"No, it doesn't," I agreed. "So the best thing we can do is try to take care of business until she returns."

"That's aiming pretty high since we can't even open our doors, and on market day," Fee said.

"One Saturday closed won't kill us," I said. "Why don't we dig into some of the special orders and see if we can use the downtime to get ahead."

"It would be nice to get ahead," Fee agreed. "Do you have any experience blocking hats?"

"Not any good ones."

Fee tucked her lips in as if she were trying to keep from laughing.

"What?" I asked.

"Come here," she said.

She led me over to the supply cupboards where bolts of sinamay and felt in every color and the wooden forms used for blocking were stored. Fee pulled over a chair and stretched to reach the back of the top shelf. She pulled down a hatbox. It was one of Mim's original boxes before Viv had updated the design and made them more eco-friendly.

Fee handed me the box and I gave her a questioning glance.

"Open it," she said.

I put it on the worktable and wiggled the lid off. Nestled in pale blue tissue paper was a hat in an eye-searing pink adorned with feathers and flowers and gobs of sparkly crystals, you know, because the feathers and flowers just weren't enough.

"Holy hats," I said. "I made this!"

"I know." Fee clapped a hand over her mouth to keep from laughing out loud, no doubt.

I lifted the eyesore out of the box and studied the hideous shape, the sad tuft of feathers and silk flowers.

"Poor Mim," I said. "She had such high hopes for her granddaughters after her own daughters had been such a bust as milliners."

"How old were you?" Fee asked.

"I'm not sure, but it had to be about the same time I painted my bedroom that hideous pink. What was I thinking?"

Fee laughed and I joined in. The workmen looked over at us and I quickly put the hat on and gushed, "Isn't it gorgeous?"

One look at their horrified faces and I could tell this was the equivalent to "Do I look fat in this?" for them. They were clearly afraid to answer. Fee and I busted up in the face of their confusion, which caused them to turn back to their work with the speed of mice fleeing a hissing cat.

"You did a nice job on the brim," Fee said. Her eyes were kind.

"I remember this was when Mim was going through a huge sinamay phase," I said, referring to the material my hat had been formed from. "Stephen Jones brought it back from Japan in the eighties and, boy, didn't it take over in hats?"

"It's probably the most common material used now," Fee agreed. "Especially for fascinators."

"I can't believe Viv kept it all these years."

"She said she'd never bin it," Fee said. "She said it gave her hope."

"I think she needs to raise her expectations a bit higher than this."

"I think she meant it gave her hope that you'd come home."

I took the hat off and studied it. Home. All my life I'd had dual citizenship, but I'd spent most of my time in the

States. I'd always thought of myself as American, but when the going got tough, where did I run to? Mim's.

Maybe Viv was onto something. I put the hat back in the box and put it back on the high shelf. I didn't have the heart to toss it either.

The workmen headed upstairs to alarm the rest of the house. Fee was checking the work orders and pulling the needed wooden blocks from the supply shelf.

"You sure you don't want to help?" she asked. "I have three hats to form today,"

Her dark brown eyes were twinkling and I knew she was teasing me.

"I think we'll spare our customers the horror," I said.

She laughed and cleared off a section of the large work-table and set to work. I watched her for a bit. She moved with the same confidence Viv had. She cut two large pieces of gunmetal-gray sinamay and then moved to the sink to soak them in hot water for a few minutes to soften the material. Next she would pin the fabric to the wooden brim form, stretching it as tightly as she could to keep it from creasing. She would then paint it with a fabric stiffener and let it dry for twelve hours. She would do the same with the fabric on the wooden crown form.

Despite my own ineptitude, I was always amazed at the process and truly loved watching the hats come to life under the nimble fingers of a talented milliner. I was pleased that Viv had taken Fee on as an apprentice since she obviously had the same love for the art and definite skill.

While Fee set to pinning the softened fabric to the wooden form, I moved over to the desk in the corner.

It wasn't that I was ignoring Harrison's concerns, exactly; it was more that I planned to completely disregard them. With the shop being closed, it presented me the perfect opportunity to reach out to our customers, and if one of them happened to have something to say about Lady Ellis's murder, well, who was I to stop her?

I opened up the files on Viv's computer. Logic dictated that the best plan would be to call the clients she had most recently been working with. I scanned the list of invoices that were in her file by date.

I left a message for the first two, but the third one answered on the fourth ring.

"Hello?"

"Good morning," I said. "May I speak to Claudia Reese?"

"Speaking."

"This is Scarlett Parker with Mim's Whims—" I began but she cut me off.

"What do you want?" she asked. Her voice sounded suspicious.

"I wanted to inform you that in light of recent events, we're going to be open by appointment only," I said.

"You're 'the party crasher,' aren't you?" the woman asked.

"I—"

"I've seen the video. You looked demented," the woman continued. "And your cousin Vivian murdered Lady Ellis! To think I let her measure my head!"

Claudia Reese said it with such horror. She made it sound as if Vivian had tried to lop off her head while taking her measurement.

"She did not murder anyone!" I argued. My usual way

with people was abandoned as I choked back the anger in my throat like a dry biscuit.

"Of course, you'd say that," the woman said. "You're a nutter."

"I am not!" I snapped. "And if this is how you feel about my cousin and me then may I suggest you take your business elsewhere."

"Count on it!" Claudia snapped back and hung up.

Chapter 31

I stared at the phone in my hand for a beat or two. "Why . . . that's . . . just . . . oh!" I slammed my phone down, too.

"Problem?" Fee asked. She was pinning the soaked sinamay around a crown form now.

"That horrible woman just called me a nutter," I said.

"One client down," she said. She said it with a sigh that made me think she anticipated a lot more of this.

One of the workmen came back into the room and began working on the lock on the back door. He was young, and I realized that, like Fee, he was probably an apprentice, maybe learning the locksmith trade from Mac with the hope of opening his own business one day.

Well, if I didn't start getting better responses from my calls, there wasn't going to be a business for Fee to apprentice and Viv would come back to an alarm system with nothing to protect.

"Who was the woman Nick told us about yesterday?" I asked Fee. "The friend of Lady Ellis?"

"Marianne Richards," she said. She wrinkled her nose and I took it that Ms. Richards was not one of her favorites. "There's a whole pack of them. Lady Ellis and Lady Cheevers are the social leaders and then Marianne Richards, Chelsea Cline and Susie Musselman tend to follow them."

"Are they just ladies of leisure?"

"Mostly. Marianne Richards has a career but the rest, yeah, they all have too much money, not enough brains and the emotional depths of turnips."

"Okay then, somehow I need to get Lady Ellis's friends into the shop to show that they don't hold Viv responsible for Lady Ellis's death," I said.

I tapped a pencil on the desktop while I mulled it over.

"How do you plan to do that?" Fee asked.

I watched her for a moment. Her nimble brown fingers, moving swiftly over the fabric-wrapped wood. Hats!

"Fee, do we have any special stock that's been packed away?"

She tipped her head and considered me. "Meaning?"

"Special hats that were ordered but never picked up, that sort of thing," I said.

"A fair few," she said.

"Do you think you could gather five or six of them for me?"

"Whatever for?" she asked.

"I have an idea," I said. I was planning to keep it vague until I knew whether my gambit would work or not.

Turning back to the computer, I looked up Lady Cheever's number and called her. She was the remaining leader, so I figured it'd be best to get her on board first.

I dialed the number. Four rings. I braced for the voice mail to pick up but instead, a man answered. He had a pleasant voice as if talking on the phone were his profession.

"Lord and Lady Cheevers's residence, how may I assist you?"

"This is Scarlett Parker, of Mim's Whims. May I speak with Lady Cheevers please?" I asked.

"One moment," he said.

Fee looked up from where she was painting stiffener on the fabric wrapped on the crown form. She had twisted back the one long strand of hair that always fell over her eyes and she looked at me curiously. I gave her a small smile.

"This is Lady Cheevers. How may I help you?" a woman's voice asked.

"I was hoping you might have need of some hats," I said.

"Excuse me?" she asked.

"I'm Scarlett Parker from Mim's Whims. Sadly, we have several hats here that were ordered by Lady Ellis," I said. I kept my voice low with just the right amount of regret. "Given the circumstances, we would like to spare her family the painful chore of having to acquire them for no good purpose and would like to offer them to her friends instead."

"I'm sorry, are you trying to sell me my dead friend's hats?" Lady Cheevers sniffed with disdain.

"No, they would be gratis, yours for the taking," I said. "Just a token, something to remember your friend by."

I saw Fee clap a hand over her eyes and tilt her head back as if she couldn't believe the amount of stupidity she was being forced to watch.

"Oh, well, that's thoughtful of you," Lady Cheevers said. I could tell by the way she said it that she knew exactly what

I was trying to do. If I could bring her in, and the media found out, it could save our business.

"We would include, of course, Lady Ellis's other close friends."

"I am surprised that Vivian did not make the call," Lady Cheevers said, and I knew she was fishing. There was no point in not telling her the truth.

"Vivian has been out of town on business since the beginning of last week," I said.

"Oh." Lady Cheevers perked up at the sound of that.

"Yes, I'm sure once the media gets all of the facts, they will be more accurate in their reporting," I said.

"Indeed," she agreed.

"How would tomorrow be?" I pressed. "Around tea time? We'll provide refreshments of course."

"One moment. Let me check," Lady Cheevers said.

I waited, convinced she was going to leave me hanging while she came up with fifteen excuses to blow me off, but to my surprise she was back in no time.

"Yes, I'm free," she said. "I'll be there at five."

"Thank you," I said. I was a bit stunned that this was going to work. "We'll see you then."

I ended the call and turned to look at Fee.

"What are you playing at?" Fee asked.

"I'm trying to save the business," I said. "And it looks like we're having a tea party tomorrow. Are you available?"

"I can be," she said.

"Great!" I said.

The three other friends of Lady Ellis were available as well. So Sunday tea at the hat shop was a go. Now I just needed to get my supplies, hunt down some spare and amazing hats and get Fee up to speed, all of which took the rest of the morning.

"So, to recap," Fee said. "You told a big, fat lie about having extra hats that Lady Ellis had ordered so you could get her mean girlfriends to come here," she said. "How am I doing?"

"Spot-on so far," I said.

"And I can only guess that you're doing this because if word gets out that these ladies are still coming here despite the fact that one of you is a nutter and one is a killer, then you think the business will be saved."

"Brilliant, right?"

Fee crossed her arms over her chest and narrowed her gaze. "Is that the only reason?"

"I don't know what you mean," I said.

Mercifully, Mac chose that moment to appear to talk to me about how I wanted the upper levels monitored. I trotted after him, pretending that I was unaware that Fee was frowning after me.

I checked and rechecked all of the doors and windows. I did the same with the new alarm system. The small square panel indicated that all was well, but still I took an old cricket bat from my grandmother's closet and brought it to bed with me.

I slept in my old room. Well, I should say that I rested because there really wasn't much sleep happening. I thumbed through several of Mim's and Viv's mystery and romance novels but nothing was distracting me.

Every little creak in the house made me jump and clutch the bat close. I figured I must be having a mild sort of post-traumatic stress episode as every time I tried to close my eyes I felt paranoid that a pillow was going to be held down on me.

It was midnight and I still wasn't sleeping when my cell phone on my nightstand chimed. Who would be calling this late? Maybe it was Viv, she was never one to observe the no-calls-after-ten rule. I scrambled for my phone and checked the display. Not Viv, but I smiled, surprised at how pleased I was to see his name.

"Hi, Harry," I answered. "What's the matter? Did you miss my lumpy couch and want to crash on it again?"

"Not exactly." His laugh was deep and rich and tickled me right between my ribs.

"Did I wake you?" he asked. "I'm sorry if I did, but I rather thought you'd be up."

His voice was full of understanding and it made me feel better about my paranoia, as if it were perfectly reasonable to sleep with a bat in the bed.

"No, I've just been listening to the house settle and creak. It's noisier than one would think," I said.

"It has a lot to say."

"Well, I wish it could tell me who broke in last night," I said. "That would be helpful."

"The alarm system is top-notch," he said. "No one can break into your shop or your flat without the security company being instantly alerted."

"Thanks," I said. "I know that. I just wish Viv were here. It's been a week now. Why hasn't she been in touch? Why hasn't she come home?"

"You miss her."

"Yes."

"She'll be home soon," he said. His voice was so certain that I felt myself relax, believing his words even though I doubted he knew anything with any more certainty than I did.

"You're right," I said. "I know you're right."

We were both silent. There were so many things I wanted to say to him, and I realized my exhaustion at the end of a long day was making me careless with my words and feelings. I decided the best course of action was to maintain the friendly distance we'd always kept until I'd been attacked.

"Thank you for all that you've done," I said. "I really appreciate it."

"That's what I'm here for," he said. "My family has been taking care of your family forever."

There was something so comforting about his words that I felt myself sink deeper into my pillows and a yawn slipped out as my eyes grew heavy.

"Get some sleep, Ginger," he said.

"Good night," I mumbled.

I had barely hit the end button when I was out.

The shop was generally closed on Sundays, so that gave me the opportunity to clean it up. I dusted every hat, every shelf; I swept, I mopped and I even plumped the pillows.

Tea would be served on Mim's good Wedgwood country rose china. Thankfully, Fee knew how to brew a pot of tea, because it was yet another thing I had never mastered during my time here. It was a wonder Mim left me half of the hat shop, given how truly hopeless I was at respecting my own heritage.

I glanced around the store. I could see Mim here, bustling about the place, chatting up her customers about the doings of the royal family. She was a true monarchist, probably because as hat wearers they supported her business, but I think she would have been one anyway. She had great respect for Queen Elizabeth.

I wondered briefly what she would have made of the situation Viv and I were in now. Would she have been her usual pragmatic self and forged ahead or would she have been terribly disappointed in us? I hoped it was the former.

The raven was staring down at me, so I reached up with my dust cloth and gave his beak a nice polishing.

"Be nice," I admonished him.

At midafternoon, I hurried upstairs to change into more appropriate clothing. If Lady Ellis's friends were anything like her, then I had to assume they were fashionistas as well, and I was going to need to pull out some designer duds and dress to impress so as to keep on even footing with them.

The clothing of my youth had been shoved to the side and I'd hung the clothes in my suitcase up, hoping the travel wrinkles would fall out of them.

As I assessed the clothes, I knew a dress was key, but which one? Then I saw it. The dress the rat bastard had bought for me when he had taken me for a spur-of-the-moment weekend to Paris. Yes, it's really not hard to see why at twenty-five, I had been so completely blinded by him.

He was charming, attentive, funny, handsome, romantic, smart, you get the idea. I was a goner within ten minutes of meeting him. Of course, when I realized what a snake he was, all of those qualities morphed into their true meaning and I realized he was actually manipulative, obsessive, mean, expensively maintained, predatory and conniving. And now, I actually felt grateful to be free of him and wished his wife great luck with him.

One part of me desperately wanted to take scissors to the Gaultier print sheath, but I didn't. At a price tag of over six hundred dollars, I just couldn't. Instead, I'd wear it as a reminder to never get suckered again.

I styled my straight red hair loose and put on eyeliner and mascara and a pale lipstick. The dress with its geometric blues and greens made enough of a statement without me trying to match it with my makeup.

I went with a pair of platform sandals that put me an inch over six feet tall. Still not quite as tall as Harrison, but it would be nice to see him in these and be a bit more eye to eye with him, although I suspected that would only be in the literal sense as we really didn't seem to agree on much.

When I went downstairs, I noted that the reporters had cleared away from our front door. I had been worried that they would scare away Lady Cheevers and company, but either there was a fabulous news story out there that trumped Lady Ellis's death or they were taking Sunday off. Of course, in order for my plan to work, I needed someone to see the ladies in the shop. Fee and I had agreed that once they arrived, she would discreetly make an anonymous call to the paper. I sincerely hoped it did the trick.

Fee was in the back room, prepping the tea tray. We had spent the last part of Saturday, after the alarm men had gone, whipping the abandoned hats into shape, something worthy of a countess to have bought. They now sat boxed up in the front of the shop awaiting their moment of unveiling.

"Well, aren't you the fancy lady of the manor?" Fee asked as she looked me over from top to bottom.

"Did I aim right?" I asked. "Fashion-wise?"

"Nailed it," Fee confirmed. She glanced down at her own ruffle-hemmed bright blue dress. "You look like one of them, and I am feeling woefully underdressed in my bargain buy from Selfridges."

"Don't be silly," I said. "You look lovely. And you have what all of them would kill to have."

"What?" Fee asked. "A job working here?"

I laughed. "No, youth."

Fee nodded and grinned. "True enough. You can't buy that off of a fashion runway."

I helped her finish prepping the refreshments and at five o'clock, I took my place by the front door to let the ladies in as they arrived.

A buxom blonde and a classically pretty brunette were the first to appear. A driver parked in front of the shop and let them out. I opened the door as soon as they were within a few feet and gave them my most welcoming smile.

"Please come in," I said. "I'm Scarlett Parker."

The blonde smiled at me and said in a voice that was girlishly high, "I'm Chelsea Cline, and this is Susie Musselman."

"A pleasure," Susie said.

"Please come in," I said. "Fiona, my assistant, will show you where we're gathering."

As I turned back to the door, two more ladies were dropped off. One was tall and thin with black hair cut in a severe bob that paired well with the bright red lipstick she wore. The other had a certain movie-star quality about her, with thick brown hair that hung about her shoulders in luscious waves, eyebrows that had been thinned into razor-sharp arches, full lips and a tiny nose. I'd bet my dress that she was Lady Cheevers, meaning the other had to be Marianne Richards.

I opened the door and the one with the severe bob deferred to the other, letting her go first.

"Good afternoon," I said. "I'm Scarlett Parker."

"Lady Cheevers," the brunette said. "And this is Marianne Richards."

"How do you do?" Marianne asked but with no real interest in my answer, as I could see by the way she was looking over my head and into the room beyond.

"I'm so glad you both could come," I said as I closed and locked the door. "Shall we join the others?"

They followed me to the far sitting area in the shop where Fee and the other two waited. I had pulled the shades over the store windows up. I figured it couldn't hurt for people to see customers in the shop, and obviously elite customers at that.

"Oh, Elise." Chelsea hopped to her feet and hugged Lady Cheevers. "Are you feeling any better today?"

"No, but I'm trying," she said, gently hugging the blonde in return.

Fee and I stood back, watching the friends greet one another. A couple of times they watered up or choked back a sob and then complimented one another's shoes or handbag.

Fee and I exchanged a look, but said nothing, waiting for them all to settle. Once they were seated in the comfortable blue chairs, I sat, too.

"Thank you all for coming," I said.

Fee served the tea. Once she was finished, Fee excused herself from the room. I watched her go, knowing she was about to place her anonymous call to the paper from her cell phone in the back of the shop.

"First, I want to extend my condolences to all of you on the loss of your friend," I said.

Marianne's features tightened, Elise Cheevers's shoulders slumped, Susie let out a small sob and Chelsea gave a delicate sniff.

I watched each of them, looking for an opening for someone who would tell me about Lady Ellis and who might have wanted her dead. Yes, that was my ulterior motive. Yes, I wanted to have these ladies seen in the shop to show that they thought Viv was innocent and thus save the business, but I'd be a liar if I didn't hope to glean some sort of information about any possible suspects. Something I could share with Inspectors Franks and Simms to get the suspicion off Viv.

"It's so hard to believe that she's gone," Chelsea said. "Vicks was a force of nature. I can't believe she won't be around to comment on my trending hairdos anymore."

"Blue streaks are not trendy, they're tacky," Elise said. Chelsea looked hurt and then Elise reached over and patted her hand. "Well, that's what Victoria would have said, and truly it is for the best that you got rid of them."

They all nodded in agreement, and Chelsea sighed.

"She could be quite harsh," Susie said. "Remember how she positively vilified Marianne for her purple lipstick?"

"I wore it one time," Marianne sniffed. She tossed her blunt-cut bob in indignation. "She said it made me look like a circus freak, and then she went out and bought me a clown mask."

"And how about the time that she humiliated poor Susie at the RHS Chelsea Flower Show?"

I glanced at Susie and saw her face flush red with embarrassment, and she said, "I don't want to talk about it."

"She went about telling everyone that she didn't think you should be there because she feared you'd be inspired to get yet another boob job so your bustline was bigger than your gardener's prize-winning peonies," Chelsea said. There was a malicious gleam in her eye as she recounted the story. "She could be so mean. You know, it's really small wonder that she's dead."

Chapter 32

I stared into my teacup for fear that my surprise would show and I'd say something stupid, like asking them which one of them killed her. That'd end the tea party with a bang.

"The only one she never diminished was you," Susie said to Elise. "Why?"

A flash of self-satisfied smugness flitted over Elise's features but it was gone so quickly that I wasn't entirely sure I'd seen it. Then she gave a delicate shrug.

"She was too busy competing with you, that's why," Marianne said. "When you married a viscount, she married an earl. When you bought your country house, she bought a bigger one."

"Oh, I don't think—" Elise began but Marianne cut her off.

"Oh, please, it was so obvious," she said. "Whatever you had Vicks wanted, and she went out of her way to get it."

"You know, I never noticed it before, but it's true," Susie said. "If you threw a dinner party, she threw a bigger one. If you had box seats at the theater, she got a better box."

"I'm sure it was just coincidence—" Elise protested.

"I don't think so," Chelsea said. "Remember when you were written up in the society pages, a lovely article, and then she was featured the next week in an even bigger layout?"

"No, I don't believe it. Despite her flaws, Vicks was my dearest friend and not a day will pass that I won't mourn her," Elise Cheevers said, and any hint of self-satisfaction was gone. Her full lips were pressed tightly together and I sensed she was trying very hard not to dwell on the negatives about her friend.

"You're right," Susie said. "She had her kind side, too."

I waited but I noticed none of them rushed to tell tales of Victoria Ellis's largess. Fee had returned, and when I turned to look at her, she gave me a small nod.

"Well, I'll tell you one person who is not mourning our friend," Marianne said. "Her mother-in-law."

"Oh, that woman," Chelsea said. "She's vile."

"Evil," Susie agreed. "She would never forgive Vicks for refusing to have a baby because she didn't want to wreck her figure."

"Horrid woman," Elise agreed. "She hated Vicks from the moment Rupert brought her home. I believe she had her heart set on a girl he met at university."

As one, all eyes turned to me. It was like being circled by a ring of cobras, and I wondered which one would strike first. Not surprisingly, it was Marianne.

"Where is your dear cousin, Vivian, by the way?" she asked.

"Traveling," I said. "She's on a buying expedition for the shop."

"How . . . convenient," Chelsea said.

I met her gaze. Her large, blue eyes were cold and I felt a shiver crawl over my skin. Suddenly, the wisdom of inviting these ladies, friends of a murder victim who had a connection to Vivian, into the shop seemed really, really stupid on my part.

"Vivian had nothing to do with what happened to Lady Ellis," I said. I figured the offensive was the best strategy I had going. "Viv was out of the country. I know for a fact because I arrived on Monday and she was already gone."

"Of course, we aren't accusing Vivian of anything," Elise said. "Are we?"

The others all shook their heads and then Susie gushed, "Viv is just the most brilliant designer. Of course, she could never harm anyone."

"And that is why we're here, correct?" Marianne asked. "To enjoy the designs Viv created for Vicks that she will never get to wear."

"Quite right," Susie said. "Please show us."

I put my cup of tea down on the table. I felt awkward, as if this situation had turned on me and I wasn't sure how. I smoothed my dress and Fee met me by the hatboxes. She gave my hand a quick squeeze, and I appreciated the reassurance more than I could say.

Putting on my best customer-service smile, I opened the first box.

"First we have a lovely peach confection," I said. I gently lifted the straw hat with the round crown and a very wide brim, decorated with a matching peach organza ribbon and white silk flowers and held it out for the ladies to look over.

"May I?" Susie asked.

Fee hurriedly brought over a standing mirror while I handed Susie the hat. She put it on her head and turned this way and then that.

"I loathe that color," Marianne said. "But it suits you."

"It does, doesn't it?" Susie blinked her overly large brown eyes at me and I nodded. "I'll take this one. It'll be like having Vicks with me whenever I wear it."

"Excuse me." Marianne stood up and looked at me. She had a cigarette and a lighter in hand. "I need to pop outside. May I use the back?"

"Absolutely," I said. "I'll let you out. Fee, would you show them the next hat?"

Fee stepped over to the stack of boxes while I walked Marianne through the back room. Although it was almost six o'clock, the sun wouldn't set until eight, so there was no need to put on the outside light.

Marianne sank onto one of the cushioned garden chairs, and I scouted an old flowerpot for her to use as an ashtray.

"Did you know Lady Ellis well?" I asked.

"Since we were children," she said. "That's how we all know one another. We went to a girls' preparatory school together."

She flicked the lighter on and inhaled off her cigarette. The smoke blew out from her mouth in a steady stream and I could see her visibly relax.

I wasn't sure whether I should go back in and attend the others or keep Marianne company. I was sure Fee could handle it, but I didn't want to miss anything that was said.

They'd already outed Lady Ellis's mother-in-law as hating her. Who else might they gossip about?

"Was Lady Ellis well liked at school?" I asked.

Marianne stared at me through a plume of smoke. Her eyes were sharp and hard and I wondered if she was seeing through me and my intentions or if she thought I was just making idle chatter.

"Define 'well liked,'" she said. She used her thumb and ring finger to pluck a bit of tobacco from her lips while still holding her cigarette.

"It's just that when I met her, I found her to be a bit exacting," I said.

"How very diplomatic of you," Marianne said. "Her real name was Victoria Hemishem. She went to Wellstone Academy for Girls on scholarship, which meant she was very bright.

"I think that is the only reason she and I became friends. I was the brain, the one who could discuss Milton's *Paradise Lost* with her and know what I was talking about. Elise is our princess, born into title and wealth, so she gave Vicks polish."

"And the others?" I prompted.

Marianne gave me a look that said "Really?" and she took another drag off her cigarette.

"Court jesters?" I guessed.

She barked out a laugh that was low and deep, and I got the feeling she didn't laugh much. It made me feel good that I had snuck one up on her.

"Perfectly stated," she said.

We were silent for a minute. I was surprised to find that beneath the precise haircut, bright red lipstick and severe countenance, I liked Marianne Richards. Compared to the others, she seemed genuine.

As she stubbed out her cigarette into the pot, she let out a deep sigh.

"I'll be honest. I don't mourn the woman who was killed," she said. She met my gaze as if daring me to judge her. "I doubt that any of us does. But I do mourn the young woman who so courageously pulled herself out of a life of poverty and made herself one of the most influential women in London."

She ducked her head as she walked past me, and I thought I saw the trace of a tear on her cheek. By the time we had rejoined the others, she had composed herself, giving no hint of the sadness I'd glimpsed.

"We put aside this fascinator for you, Marianne," Elise Cheevers said. "It's black; all you wear is black, so it seemed appropriate."

"Thank you," Marianne said. She fingered the spray of black feathers that shot straight up from the brim in a dramatic fashion. "It's perfect."

I glanced at the four ladies and saw that they each had a hat. I wondered if I should even bother to open the last box; after all, they all had something to remember their friend by. Okay, I had a tiny twinge of guilt that I wasn't being absolutely honest about these being Lady Ellis's hats, but I brushed it aside.

Viv was being fingered as the murderer, and I had to do something to tap into Lady Ellis's inner circle and find someone else with a motive to kill her. Otherwise the media was going to keep playing the sad little love triangle to death, and Viv would be arrested for a crime she didn't commit, assuming she ever decided to come home.

"Aren't you going to show us what's in the last box?" Chelsea asked. She had helped herself to the brie and bread and was nibbling while she watched me.

"Sure," I said.

I set the box on the back of the couch and gently pried the lid off. Nestled in tissue was a very smart hunter-green wool cap. It was simple, but I liked the plaid hatband and golden acorn that had been worked into the side.

"What is that?" Elise Cheevers snapped.

"A beret," I said. I wondered if she was looking for the term for this particular hat or if the hat didn't live up to her expectation and she was expressing her displeasure.

"Well, that's not what I was looking for," she said. Two bright spots of color appeared on her cheeks and her eyes flashed.

"I'm sorry," I said. "Is there a hat you need that I can help you with?"

"No, no," she huffed, sounding even more annoyed. "I had thought you were going to share with us the hats that Vicks didn't pick up, including the one that she was going to wear to her garden party. While these are all very lovely, they aren't garden party hats."

I turned and Fee and I exchanged a wide-eyed glance. That had never occurred to me, nor her, judging by her startled glance.

I knew the police were keeping it quiet that Lady Ellis had been wearing only a hat when her body was found. I definitely did not want to be the one to tell her friends that. Instead, I decided to stick as close to the truth as possible.

"Lady and Lord Ellis picked up her hat for the garden party last Tuesday," I said.

"Rupert came into the hat shop?" Marianne asked. The ladies all exchanged amused glances. "That's not his usual stomping ground, now is it?"

Susie and Chelsea giggled, but Lady Cheevers stared at me.

"So you met him?" she asked as if she was confirming something she already suspected.

I nodded. I was not going to offer anything more than confirmation.

"I really would have liked to have seen the hat," Lady Cheevers said.

"You're obsessing, Elise," Marianne said.

"What? She made such a big show about how special it was," Lady Cheevers said. "You heard her at brunch the other day."

"That's just the way Vicks was," Susie said.

"I'm sure the hat wasn't all that," Chelsea said. As if realizing what she'd said, she looked at me and said, "No offense."

Maybe it was because Vivian was missing and I was worried that I felt the need to defend her. "Actually, it was an amazing hat, breathtaking in fact. Vivian outdid herself in its creation."

"So you did see it?" Elise asked. Her eyes were brittle and hard when she asked, "And did Vicks, Lady Ellis, seem to think it was as wonderful as you do?"

"Well, she did agree to model it for us," I said. I knew as soon as the words were out of my mouth that I had said too much, and that it was too late to turn back now.

210

Chapter 33

"What?" Elise asked.

"I was there with a photographer to take pictures of her in the hat when her body was found," I said.

My voice cracked and Chelsea reached over and squeezed my hand. I appreciated the gesture.

"Were you?" Elise asked. She stared at me for a moment and then she put her hand over her heart and gave me a sympathetic look. "I'm sorry. I didn't know. That must have been awful."

"Did she appear to have suffered?" Susie asked.

I had hoped they wouldn't press me for details. Lady Ellis had been naked with a knife in her chest and a hat on her head. Every time I closed my eyes, I saw her pale form lying in a pool of blood. What could I possibly say?

"No," I lied. "It must have been very quick."

I saw them all relax just the slightest bit. Even if they

suspected I was lying, they were willing to cling to it for the little bit of peace it gave them. I knew I would do the same.

"Oh! Look at the time," Chelsea said. "I have to meet my husband for drinks in thirty minutes."

And just like that, the four of them were texting their drivers to come and get them while Fee boxed up the hats they'd selected.

As the first driver knocked on the door, they left en masse. I noticed a cluster of reporters and photographers camped out across the street. With a quick glance at the drivers, I understood why they were so far away. I would have been across the street as well if I had to get through the brawn to get to the ladies. All of the drivers were big and beefy and looked more than capable of quelling a mob with their bare hands.

I closed and locked the door behind them and turned to find Fee wearing the beret, which no one had claimed.

"I'm glad no one picked this one," she said. "I'm partial to it myself."

I began to clear up the cups and plates. It was almost seven now and the day spent cleaning and hostessing had worn me out.

"Did I miss anything of interest while I was outside with Marianne?" I asked.

Fee picked up the remaining dishes and followed me into the workroom. I would wash Mim's china here before hauling it back upstairs.

"I don't think so," she said. "There was a bit of a scuffle over the white pillbox hat with the sheer veil. All three of them wanted it, but Lady Cheevers won that brawl. I got the feeling she has the most power in that group."

"She does now," I said. I told Fee what Marianne had told me about all of them meeting at a girls' school.

"Makes me glad I went to the neighborhood school here in Notting Hill," she said. "I can't imagine five scarier adolescents."

"A wolf pack would be more cuddly," I agreed.

I circled back to the sitting area in the shop. I wanted to pull the shades down and shut off the lights as well as make sure we'd gotten all the crumbs. I didn't scrub all day so that the place could be a mess in two hours.

When I was satisfied, I headed back to the workroom. On my way, I noticed Ferd the bird, staring down at me with his usual beaky attitude.

"I still think you'd be better-looking as a nice fat-faced angel."

I stepped close to the cupboard below him and opened the door. It was empty. The pedestal where Lady Ellis's hat had been was forlornly empty. I wondered if this was where Viv always kept her special projects. I leaned in to remove the pedestal and noted that the depth of the wardrobe seemed shorter than it should be. Then I remembered that one of the things Mim had loved about this wardrobe was its many secret compartments. Maybe that was why Ferd always looked so smug: he had so many secrets.

I ran fingers along the back wall until I found the latch in the upper right corner. Sure enough, with a press from my fingers, I heard the mechanism release and the false wall was unlocked. It opened from a hinge on one side and I swung it forward, revealing the back half of the cupboard area.

I gasped. Sitting on a hat stand was a purple flat-topped

and wide-brimmed hat that was trimmed in a luscious ring of matching feathers. It was gorgeous, simply gorgeous.

But where had it come from? I hadn't seen Fee working on anything like this. And why was it hidden? Was it being kept a secret for a reason?

"Fiona!" I called.

My voice must have radiated panic because Fee came bustling through the door from the back room as if I'd yelled, "Fire!"

"What is it?" she asked. "Is someone breaking in?"

"No, it's a hat!" I said.

She put her hand over her chest and sucked in a breath.

"A hat?" she cried. "You scared me to death over a hat?"

It was then that I noticed the wooden hat form in her hand.

"That's some advanced weaponry you've got there," I said.

"Well, it would give the bugger a blasting headache, yeah?" she retorted.

I couldn't argue it. Once she'd caught her breath, I asked, "Have you ever seen this hat before?"

She stepped closer and studied it, running her fingers along the brim.

"It's lovely," she said. "Look at the hand stitching on the brim, it's flawless."

"But why is it hidden in the wardrobe?" I asked. "How did it get in here?"

I glanced up at Ferd but he wasn't talking.

"Oh, that's just the cupboard doing what it does," Fee said. Then she gave me a startled look and clapped her hand over her mouth.

"What is that supposed to mean?" I asked.

"Nothing," she said, very unconvincingly.

"Fiona, explain," I said.

"I can't," she said. "Look, Viv must have put it in there before she left. You really have to talk to her about it. Oh, look at the time. I've got to go or my brothers will be out looking for me. Last time I turned up late for dinner they tried to have my mother give me a curfew."

"Fee, you're holding out on me," I said. I followed her into the back room.

"I don't know what you mean," she said.

And before I could detain her with any more questions, she grabbed her jacket and slipped out the back door.

"Don't forget to set the alarm!" she yelled. With a wave she unlatched the back gate and hustled down the alley.

I turned back to the cupboard and lifted the hat out. Where had it come from? I felt my insides shiver. Something was definitely not adding up.

My brain kicked my thoughts around like stray tin cans, sending them off in different directions so fast that I could barely examine them before they disappeared.

Who put the hat in there? And why? It must have been Viv. But when? Who was the hat made for? And if she did put it in there why didn't she leave a note to let someone know it was there?

Then I had a horrible thought. Maybe Viv wasn't really away. Maybe she was actually nearby, lurking and watching and killing her old boyfriend's wife!

I gave myself a mental face-slap. Now that was just crazy talk.

I put the hat back in the back of the cupboard, closing

the secret panel over it, and decided to get out of the shop. Being cooped up for the past few days was obviously making me bonkers.

I glanced out the front window and noted that the reporters still lingered. The April evening was chilly, so I grabbed my lightweight wool coat off the rack by the back door. I set the alarm on my way out, feeling very modern as I did so.

I let myself out of the narrow back garden gate just as Fee had and into the alley. No one was on the street this late on a Sunday evening, and I could hear the sounds of television broadcasts coming from above as I made my way around to Portobello Road.

My first stop was Andre's, to see if he and Nick were about. Maybe I could convince them to come to the pub with me. I had just reached the corner when a head poked out of an upper window.

"Hello, Scarlett," Nick called. "I knew I recognized that wild mane of red. How are you?"

"Looking for a dinner date or two," I called back. He was wearing a hot pink tank top and looked as if he'd been working out. "Are you and Andre available?"

"Andre's off on assignment," he said. "I was just about to start my Pilates, so yes, dinner sounds lovely. I'll be right down. Don't move."

His head disappeared back into the window and I waited for him to let me in. I followed him upstairs to their flat and saw that it, too, was thick with photographs propped against the walls.

The rest of the room looked to be a room at war. Shades of green and purple were battling it out in the furnishings, and I wondered which of them had owned the purple suede couch and which the green leather wing chair, which seemed to have nothing but disdain for each other.

He handed me a glass of red wine and kissed me on the cheek.

"Ten minutes!" he yelled. "I promise."

I sank onto the green chair and checked the box of books by the seat. They were mostly dental texts with such riveting titles as *The Color Atlas of Dental Implant Surgery*—obviously Nick's box then.

I decided this was not going to work for me as before-dinner reading material, mostly because I was sure I wouldn't understand a word. Instead, I found a stack of *Livingetc* magazines, and I wondered if these were more Andre's or Nick's or both.

I had only gotten halfway done with my wine and a third of the way through the magazine when Nick reappeared, looking decidedly dashing in black jeans and an ecru fisherman's sweater.

He held out his arm and asked, "Shall we?"

"I don't know," I said as I downed my wine. "I think I'd rather go out with you in the hot pink tank top."

"Oh, please," he said. "My public would swoon."

"Yes, you're right," I said. I put my glass in the kitchen and took his elbow. "We wouldn't want to create mass hysteria or anything."

He led me outside to the street and asked, "All right, what is your stomach's desire? Thai? Italian? You name it."

"How about a place where we can gossip?" I asked.

"You have dish?" he asked.

"I might if the ambiance were conducive," I said.

He laughed and patted my hand. "Oh, I do like you, Scarlett Parker."

We ended up in a tiny bistro, sharing an antipasto and having more wine.

Nick was a wonderful date, funny and charming, and he seemed plugged in to London society enough to know a little bit about everyone's dirty little secrets.

"So, tell me about Lady Ellis's mother-in-law," I said. "The ladies having tea at the shop today said that she hated Lady Ellis because she refused to have children, something about not wanting to lose her figure."

"Pah!" Nick waved his fork at me. "More like she didn't want to have to get knocked up by Lord Ellis as that would require . . ."

"What?" I asked when he paused.

Nick rolled his eyes and said, "Copulation."

"That sounds dirty," I said. I dabbed my lips with my napkin.

"It means—" he began but I interrupted.

"I know what it means. It still sounds dirty."

"Only if you do it right," he said with a voice even drier than our wine.

I busted up with laughter. There was just something so immensely likeable about Nick.

"Seriously," I said. "What's the mother of Earl Ellis of Waltham like?"

"As in, do you think she's capable of murder?" he asked.

"Well, that was a straight shot into the heart of the beast," I said.

"She loves her boy," he said. "She thinks he married beneath him and then the tart won't even pop out an heir."

He set his fork down and leaned forward. "I've only seen her across the room at a few events, but she's downright scary."

"So then she could—" I began but he interrupted me.

"She'd never get her hands that dirty," he said. "She would hire someone to do it for her."

"But who?" I asked.

"That's the million-pound question, isn't it?" he asked. "Maybe you should just trot over to her mansion with a hat and see if you can get her talking."

"Are you mocking me?" I asked.

"Not at all, I have great confidence in your ability to mine information from the gentry," he said. He took a bite of pasta, chewed and swallowed and said, "So, how was the tea party anyway?"

"Interesting," I said. "I had a nice chat with Marianne Richards."

"Oh, I like her," he said. "She's a doctor, you know."

"No, I didn't," I said.

"Formidably intelligent," he said.

"Yes, well, that means she would know exactly where to shove the knife, doesn't it?"

Nick raised his eyebrows. "Marianne Richards, cold-hearted killer, interesting. But she's a head doctor, not a medical doctor."

"Oh," I said. Was it wrong that I felt disappointed? "Mari-anne did tell me that Lady Ellis went to their school on scholarship, but that she worked very hard to blend in, using

Lady Cheevers as her main social crutch, but the others as well."

"Lady Cheevers." Nick nodded. "She didn't quite live up to her potential."

"Meaning?"

"Married a viscount, had the requisite two children, but seems to lack the social panache of Lady Ellis."

"Marianne said she was the one who gave Lady Ellis her polish," I said.

"Undoubtedly," he said. "Without Lady Cheevers opening doors for her, poor little Victoria Hemishem never would have bagged Lord Ellis, who I believe was enamored with your cousin at the time."

"So I've been told," I said.

"But then, Rupert did date half of London before finally settling on Vicks," he said. "Rumor has it, she was the only one who could tolerate his all-consuming hobby."

"Rupert Ellis has a hobby? Do tell." I leaned closer. "What sort of hobby?"

"Oh, no, you have to guess," he said.

I took a bite of my gnocchi with gorgonzola and thought about it. I swallowed and said, "Stamp collecting?"

"No." He continued eating while I sipped my wine and pondered what sort of hobby would make an earl ineligible for marriage.

"Tatting?"

"Ha! No, but points for creativity," he said.

"Fly-fishing?"

Nick shuddered. "No."

"Oh come on," I said. "You have to give me a hint."

"Sorry, you're going to have to dig deep to figure it out," he said.

"That was a hint, wasn't it?" I asked.

He raised his brows but said nothing.

"You're killing me here," I protested.

He barked out a laugh. "You have no idea, my dear."

"Scarlett Parker, are you flirting with my boyfriend?" Andre asked as he took an empty seat at the table.

They exchanged a quick kiss and I smiled. "As if I could."

"Then this must be Nick's way of stealing my best girl," Andre said.

"Your best girl?" a voice asked from behind me. "I thought she was my best girl."

I tipped my head back and saw Harrison leaning over my chair. His green eyes were sparkling and I felt my breath catch.

"Sorry, fellas, I'm nobody's girl and happy to keep it that way," I said, pleased that my voice sounded amused.

The waiter arrived and cleared our dinner plates. Both Andre and Harrison passed on ordering an entrée but joined us for coffee and dessert.

"So how did you two meet up?" I asked.

"Nick texted me that you two were here, and when I passed the shop, I saw this sad lunk outside and invited him to join us," Andre said.

"'Sad lunk?'" Harrison asked. "I suppose I've been called worse."

"Well, I'm glad you're here," I said. "Nick is holding out on me, maybe you can help me pry the information out of him."

"What information?" Harrison asked.

"The passion of Lord Ellis," I said.

Andre and Harrison glanced at Nick, who gave them a mild look.

"Scarlett wanted to know why Lord Ellis married Lady Ellis, and I told her that Vicks was the only one of his many girlfriends who could tolerate his hobby."

"I've already covered stamp collecting, tatting and fly-fishing," I said.

"It's much more grave than that," Nick said.

We waited while the waitress delivered our tiramisu and coffees.

"Coin collecting?" Andre asked.

"No."

"Dollhouses?" I asked.

"No." Nick smirked. "Come on, it's a dead bore for most of us but he's buried in it."

Andre and I exchanged a confused glance, but Harrison laughed.

"Is it the sort of hobby that might rub off on you?" he asked.

Nick grinned and said, "Indeed."

Harrison looked at Andre and me and said, "Lord Ellis is a taphophile."

Chapter 34

"Oh, my," I said. I put my hand over my mouth. I had no idea what this meant but it definitely sounded way more perverted than "copulate."

"He's into gravestones," Nick clarified.

"As in the ones in cemeteries?" Andre asked. At Nick's nod, he added, "Weird."

"So, you can imagine that it would take someone with a real eye on the bottom line to agree to spend her life with a man who likes to spend his free time in graveyards doing headstone rubbings."

"He didn't strike me as the sort who would enjoy that type of thing," I said. Thinking back on it, Lord Ellis seemed more like the sort to enjoy gambling, a good cigar and a pretty woman, and not necessarily in that order.

They were all looking at me.

"He came in with Lady Ellis when she picked up her hat," I said. "He seemed very smooth."

"Really?" Nick asked. "The few times I've met him, 'smooth' is not the first word that comes to mind."

"Was he into graves when he was friends with Viv?" I asked Harrison.

He was sipping his coffee, but paused to shrug. "I don't know. She never really talked about him or Lady Ellis much."

"Viv isn't one to pay attention to what's going on around her," I said to Nick and Andre.

"I know the type," Nick said with a sideways glance at Andre, who was studying the room about us as if considering it for a photograph.

"What?" Andre asked. Obviously, he'd just become aware that he was the subject of Nick's comment.

I smiled as they squabbled good-naturedly. I turned to share the joke with Harrison and found him watching me with an intensity that made my heart skip a beat and then pound twice as hard as if to make up for it.

"What?" I asked, repeating Andre's question.

"I . . . nothing," he said. "It's nothing."

He forced a smile and turned back to the table, engaging Nick in a discussion of Kensal Green Cemetery, one of the seven magnificent nineteenth-century cemeteries in London, and the one closest to Notting Hill. It was also known as All Souls and was where the rock star Freddie Mercury was buried.

I tucked my spoon into my dessert. It was delicious. I found I wanted to look at Harrison again to see if I could figure out what he'd been thinking, but I was feeling unaccountably shy, not a normal state for me, and so I kept my attention on my dessert.

I didn't believe that Harrison had anything to do with Viv's disappearance anymore. Well, I was pretty sure at any rate. I couldn't imagine that he would be actively trying to find her and helping me put in an alarm system if he was involved in some nefarious way. Well, unless he was a complete psychopath. Now I did glance at him.

His dark brown hair was brushed back in its usual careless way. I got the feeling Harrison wasn't one to spend a lot of time primping. His eyes sparkled as he and Nick traded more puns about graveyards. Dig it?

His brows rode low over his eyes as if he were in a perpetual state of concentration. His nose was long but took a slight detour as if it had been broken. His lips were full and parted over a generous smile. There was an innate honesty to his face and a sense of integrity that was unyielding. I got the feeling that Harrison said what he meant and he meant what he said. Quite simply, I trusted him.

"Isn't that right, Scarlett?" Andre's voice brought my attention back to the table.

"I'm sorry?" I said.

"She wasn't listening," Nick said. "She was too busy checking out the only available male at our table."

"Nick! That's just . . . well, inaccurate," I protested. I felt my face get hot with embarrassment.

I could tell Harrison was looking at me, but I refused to look at him, as if I'd combust from sheer mortification. Instead, I turned to Andre and asked, "What were you saying?"

He smiled at me, but I glowered and he sobered up immediately.

"Sorry." He cleared his throat. "I was saying that the house the Ellises live in would certainly make one consider putting up with someone else's eccentricities if the payout was that they got to live there."

"It was a gorgeous home," I agreed.

Andre went on to describe the interior to the others while I finished my dessert, scraping the dish clean. Nick snatched the check before the rest of us could grab it. And in moments the four of us were making our way back to Portobello Road.

We saw the police car lights flashing up ahead but still, it took me a moment to register that they were parked in front of Mim's Whims.

My first thought was that they were there to tell me they'd found Vivian. My second thought was that if it were police who had come to tell me about her, then the news was bad.

I broke into a run, not easy to do in super-high heels, but still I ran. I heard shouts behind me but I didn't wait for the others. Terror had me moving at a clip. Vivian had to be okay. I wouldn't accept any other explanation.

Harrison caught me by the elbow but didn't slow me down, instead he spotted me as we ran. My heart was pounding triple time and I'd broken into a sweat. The cold air was making my nose run and I didn't have a tissue, so I had to snuffle repeatedly to keep my nose from dripping all over my coat.

A constable was standing at the front, and he held out his arms as if to keep me from plowing into the shop. I stopped, and it was then that I could see through a gap in the shades that the lights were on and the police were inside. It took only a glance to see that the place had been ransacked, as in turned over, or, more accurately, destroyed.

The white straw hats Viv had strung to hang at different levels in the front windows to look as if they were floating had been left alone and they hung like the ghostly remains of the hats that had been tossed about the shop with little or no regard for their value or craftsmanship. It looked as if the person had been in a temper: chairs had been turned over, drawers and shelves emptied, their contents strewn across the floor.

"Vivian," I said to the constable. "Is Vivian here? Does this have to do with her?"

The constable gave me a confused look and I wanted to yell at him to get with it.

"Vivian Tremont is the owner," Harrison explained from beside me. "Is she here?"

"No, sir," the constable answered. "We found no one on the premises when we responded to the call."

"Scarlett, what happened?" Andre and Nick caught up to us. Nick was winded and huffing and puffing but Andre looked fine.

"At a guess, I think we were robbed," I said.

I glanced at the front door and saw Inspector Franks inside. He gestured that the front door was still locked, so I quickly fished out my new key and unlocked the door. It took longer than usual as my fingers were shaking.

I pulled the door open and Inspector Franks joined us out front.

"Ms. Parker," he said.

"Inspector," I returned. I was pleased that my voice wasn't as trembly as my insides.

"What happened, Inspector?" Harrison asked.

"By the looks of it, a burglary," Franks said. He looked

tired and I wondered if he was getting sick of me yet. I doubted even a good Stetson would make him look kindly on me.

"When the call came in to the station from the security company, one of the constables realized it was your shop and called me," he said.

I looked past him and saw Inspector Simms, working his way through the shop, assessing the damage.

"Can I ask where you were, Ms. Parker?" Franks asked me.

"Having dinner with friends," I said.

"That would be us," Nick said. He had a steely look in his eye as if daring Franks to doubt him.

"And me," Harrison said. "In fact, I met Andre, here in front of the shop, just a little over an hour ago, and there was no indication of any disturbance."

"How did they get in?" I asked.

"Smashed a window in the back," Franks said. "They must not have realized you've had an alarm put in. Still, they were long gone by the time we arrived."

"Well, at least I know the system works," I said. My voice was faint. The thought that I could have been suffocated again or worse ran through my mind and I trembled as if my body was shorting out in fear.

I felt Harrison's hand tighten on my arm. I leaned into him to let him know I was okay.

"We have them sweeping for fingerprints, but given that we didn't find any last time, I doubt we'll have much better luck this time, assuming we're dealing with the same person."

"We are," I said. "It's too coincidental not to be."

"I agree," Harrison said. His voice was tight as if he was really angry and it was taking every bit of his self-control to keep it in check.

"I'll need you to check to see if anything is missing," Inspector Franks said.

"Of course." I turned to Andre and Nick. "Thank you for dinner and everything."

I hugged them both and Andre put his hands on my shoulders and said, "We have a guest bedroom. Why don't you plan to sleep at our place?"

"Oh, thank you," I said. I put my hand on his cheek. "But I don't want to leave the shop or the flat unattended."

Both Nick and Andre looked ready to argue, but Harrison cut in and said, "I'll stay with her."

They gave him a look and he added, "On the couch, of course."

"Call us if you need us," Nick said.

"I will, I promise."

Harrison and I watched as they wound their way around the police cars and continued toward their flat. Their heads were pressed together and I wondered if they were discussing what a truly unfortunate friend I had turned out to be. They'd only known me for a week and every time they turned around I was involved in some new drama. It was getting embarrassing.

It didn't take long to assess the situation. Whoever had done the damage had never made it upstairs. Obviously, the alarm system worked well enough to have scared them off pretty quickly. Still, the mess was depressing. It was a good thing we were closed tomorrow. I had a feeling I was going to need all day to clean up.

Nothing seemed to be missing, but given the mess, I'm not sure I would have noticed anyway. I didn't tidy up, thinking I'd see if Fee could pop in tomorrow and let me know if she noticed anything in particular being gone.

Harrison boarded up the window with some old shelves Mim had stored in her garden shed. I held the boards while he nailed them, and even though they didn't cover the window completely, I figured it would be tough for anyone to squeeze through the two-inch gaps.

Harrison swept up the glass once the police said it was okay to do so. While he dumped it in the trash, I set about making a pot of tea.

Inspectors Franks and Simms left with their entourage. They promised to be in touch if they found anything, but I wasn't feeling very optimistic.

"Come on," Harrison said as he pulled out a seat at the worktable for me. "Have a seat. Have some tea. It'll calm your nerves before bed."

"Not to be argumentative," I said, "but I don't think anything is really going to calm me down."

"Don't worry," he said. "I'll be here to watch over you."

The words were so comforting that I felt my throat get tight with an excess of emotion.

"You don't have to do that," I said. "I'll be fine."

"I know," he said. "I'm not doing it for you. I'm doing it for my own peace of mind. You can't deny me that, now can you?"

Oh, how manipulative, making me feel guilty if I didn't let him stay.

"Well played, Harry," I said.

He lifted his cup at me in a toast and then took a long sip. "Hey, is this your first pot of tea?"

"Yes, I think it is," I said. I hadn't really noticed that I was making tea. I had just needed something to do.

"Not bad," he said.

I tasted mine and was relieved to discover that I hadn't messed it up.

"Seriously," he said. "I want to stay. I'd worry."

I glanced quickly at the window.

"Oh, not about anyone breaking in," he said. "I think the fact that they never made it upstairs shows that the alarm system works. But I'd be worried that you were frightened and that's unacceptable."

"Thanks," I said. "It's very kind of you."

He waved off my thanks, but still, I realized I was racking up quite a lot of debt with him. There had to be some way I could show my gratitude for his help.

"What are you thinking about?" he asked.

"That I need to find a way to thank you for all that you've done," I said.

To my surprise, Harrison Wentworth actually blushed.

"Not like that!" I snapped.

He gave me a sheepish grin that was ridiculously charming and shrugged and said, "A man can dream."

Now it was my turn to blush.

"Just drink your tea," I ordered.

"Yes, ma'am," he said. But I noticed when he lifted the cup to his lips, he was grinning.

Chapter 35

This time I slept in my old room and insisted that Harrison take the bedroom on the main floor. I simply couldn't have him sleep on the sofa, which was too short for him and unforgiving in its firmness. And given this new and somewhat alarming tension between us, I felt the distance of separate floors might be required. No, not for him; definitely, for me.

I was only a few weeks out of the worst breakup, as in most public and most humiliating, of my life. I was not, I repeat not, going to get involved with the first good-looking, okay, hot, man who came along. Just because he had wicked green eyes and a lovely, deep, gravelly voice and a bod that—whoa, stop right there.

I was not going to start thinking of Harrison that way. Other than some fuzzy childhood memories and the recent week we'd spent together, I hardly knew the man. The fact that I was even thinking about him just proved that what my mother had said was true. How had I never really noticed before that I always had a boyfriend? It wasn't on purpose. Or was it?

This was more self-analysis than I wanted to delve into at the moment. No, my time would be much better spent trying to figure out who had killed Lady Ellis, who had tried to kill me and why was my shop under siege?

I couldn't hear Harrison snoring from up here. Crazy as it sounds, that bummed me out. There was something comforting about having audible proof that I was not alone in the flat. I tossed and turned a bit and finally punched my pillow until I'd flattened it enough.

I stared into the dark, wondering if I didn't hear him sleeping because he wasn't asleep. Maybe he was having the same hard time that I was. It was quite the adrenaline rush to come home and find your business has been violated, and twice in one week made it particularly disturbing.

An image of Harrison lying awake downstairs flashed through my mind. Nope. I was not going downstairs to check on him. That would only invite the sort of trouble of which I was determined to steer clear. No men. Not for a while, at least a year. Oh, that seemed unduly harsh. Six months. I cringed. That seemed a long time to go without a date, but not impossible. Okay, six months it was.

I turned over the idea in my head. Six months without a man calling or sending flowers or taking me to dinner. Hmm. Then I thought of the humiliation of walking into that reception at the hotel and seeing the enormous cake with the diamond necklace sitting on it and seeing the man I thought I loved smooching his wife.

The wife he was supposed to be separated from, the one

he described as controlling, who didn't understand him and support his dreams like I did. I could feel the bile rise up into the back of my throat and my chest got tight as if a giant hand had reached inside and squeezed my insides into mush.

A year. I was definitely taking a year off from men. I never, ever wanted to feel so stupid and worthless again. And the next man I got involved with was going to be worth loving, this I promised myself and felt infinitely better for it.

I turned my attention back to the situation at hand. Someone had broken into the shop. The question that gave me the willies, of course, was, had they come looking for me? Given that someone had tried to suffocate me, this did not seem an unreasonable thing to wonder. But since they never made it upstairs from the shop below, I wondered. Maybe they hadn't been after me this time. Maybe they had been looking for something in the shop. But what?

The wake tomorrow should be informative. I wanted to see the ladies from the tea today at the wake. Did I think any of them had anything to do with Lady Ellis's death? I suppose it was possible. Marianne had all but admitted that Victoria Ellis was no longer the friend they had once enjoyed.

But if they disliked her so much, surely they could bow out of the friendship? And yet, they had all shown up today to pick over her leavings. Was it sentimentality that made them do so, or were they more like vultures, picking at the carcass of their dead friend? Hard to say.

It was not the best thought to lead me into dreamland, and my unconscious made powerful work of it, giving me dreams about the rat bastard being chased by a vulture, which turned out to be me.

I awoke to the smell of bacon with my heart thrumming through my chest like a train in the tube. I was sweating and shivering at the same time. I splashed cold water on my face and headed downstairs. I needed coffee with the strength to disintegrate a spoon.

I didn't care that I had a wicked case of bed head or that I was in my bubble-gum pajamas. Having sworn off men was liberating like that.

I found Harrison in the kitchen, sipping a cup of coffee and looking as bleary-eyed as I felt.

"Morning, Harry," I said.

"Harrison," he grumbled.

"Sleep well?" I asked.

He looked me up and down and a small smile played on his lips. "About as well as you, I'd say."

"In that case, I'm sorry," I said.

He gave me a sympathetic look and poured me a cup of coffee, which he pushed toward me. "Bad dreams?"

"You could say that," I said. "How about you?"

"No, not bad dreams," he said.

He didn't say anything more, and I almost questioned him, but he had an intense look on his face that made me hesitate, so instead I doctored my coffee and tried to ignore the fact that my face felt warm.

"What's your agenda for today?" he asked.

"Clean the shop," I said with a sigh. Remembering how much work I'd put in yesterday to spiff it up made me irritated, so I tried to put it out of my mind. "And then we have the viewing tonight?"

"I'll collect you at half five," he said. "All right?"

"I'll be ready."

"Eat," he ordered. "Judging by the mess downstairs, you're going to need your strength."

He handed me a plate with a bagel loaded with bacon, a fried egg and cheese and I glanced at him through my eyelashes.

"You're quite handy to have around," I said.

He stared at me for a beat and then his gaze strayed to my lips. His green eyes scorched, and I realized it was me. I did that. I was flirting with him. What was wrong with me?

"And I mean that in the most casual-friendship sort of way," I said. I sat up straight and tried to look stern, as in not flirtatious. Good grief, I was going to have to relearn my very way of talking to men.

When I glanced back at him, he was smiling at me as if he knew what I was doing and it amused him.

He tucked into his bagel and I did the same, relieved that the nuclear reaction between us, if not totally gone, had definitely slipped back down to DEFCON five, maybe four.

True to my word, I spent the day cleaning up. Fee came by but couldn't identify anything that might be missing. I could see she was as freaked out as I was that there'd been two incidents in a matter of days. I didn't know what to tell her to reassure her, except that she would never be in the shop alone.

She waved me off, but I think she was trying to be brave. She stayed to help clean but I shooed her out after an hour, knowing that she had studying to do.

I called my mother and my aunt. I did not tell them about the break-in. I figured it would only worry them needlessly. There was no news from Viv and now it was officially a week that she'd been gone, and I hated to think the worst, but where could she be that she hadn't heard about what had happened to Lady Ellis?

Nowhere. The planet just wasn't that big anymore. I realized this was why Inspector Franks was so suspicious. He had to be thinking that Viv's history with Rupert Ellis and the fact that she went missing when his wife was murdered was too convenient.

I decided to wear my all-purpose black chemise dress, very Audrey Hepburn, to the wake. I twisted my red hair up into a sleek knot on the back of my head and chose a pair of black pearl earrings with a matching strand for around my throat.

These were a gift from the boyfriend before the rat bastard. Seth. He had been a medical student, completely committed to his studies with very little time for a girlfriend. I was twenty-four when we broke up, mistakenly thinking I had met my soul mate in the rat bastard.

As I fastened the pearls, I hoped Seth had met someone more deserving and had finished medical school. Then I had to wonder why hindsight was always twenty-twenty.

A glance at the clock told me that Harrison would be here any moment. I zipped the back of my dress, getting it halfway up my back. I tried to get the zipper all the way up, but to no avail. I just couldn't contort myself to pull it up. I tried to remember how I usually got my zipper up, and I realized I usually had a boyfriend to finish it for me. Suddenly, I felt like such a loser.

"Scarlett!" Harrison's voice called up the staircase. "Are you ready?"

"Just about!" I yelled.

I tried reaching over my back, but my fingers just brushed the zipper but couldn't grab the tab. I tried pushing it from the bottom. No luck. It was just out of reach. A thick strand of hair fell out of the knot on my head and swung across my cheek as I tried another round of gymnastics to get my zipper up.

"I'd be happy to help you with that, you know."

I snapped my head around to find Harrison, leaning against the doorjamb and watching me as if I were a show and, judging by his smile, a comedy.

I blew out a breath. "Fine. Thank you."

The words came out grudging and I turned my back to him. In the mirror I watched him walk toward me. His fingers barely brushed the skin of my back as he moved the zipper up and fastened the clasp at the top of the dress.

"Better?" he asked. His usually low voice was even more gruff and when our eyes met in the mirror, I could feel the tension between us rocket back up to DEFCON one. Uh-oh.

"Much, thanks," I said. I quickly stepped away from him and slipped on my black pumps. One year, I told myself, one whole year with no men.

Newly resolved, I turned back to face him with a polite smile on my face.

"Ready when you are," I said.

He tipped his head as he considered me, as if trying to get my measure. Then he gave me a rueful smile and gestured for me to lead. I did, fully aware that his eyes were on me all the way down the stairs, which naturally led me to repeat the phrase "Please, don't let me trip" in my head until I was safely on the floor below.

* * *

Harrison drove us to the funeral home. He had a dark blue Audi that he'd parked in front of the shop. I still wasn't used to sitting on the left side as a passenger. It felt awkward, and I remembered that it always took me a while to adjust. Usually just when I had gotten used to it, I went home. This time I wouldn't be.

We were quiet as we navigated the traffic. I had read Lady Ellis's obituary in *The Times* this morning and I knew that the wake and funeral were to be private. I wondered how Harrison had gotten us included in the visitation.

I wanted to ask him, but he seemed to be concentrating on something else. He was quiet and he stared out the front window with absolute concentration that did not invite questions.

The wake was being held at a very posh funeral home in Kensington. It was valet parking, so as Harrison pulled up, my door was opened by a young man in a dark gray uniform. He handed me out and Harrison met me on the other side, handing his keys to the young man.

I stood on the curb, looking at the squat, redbrick building in front of me. A forest-green awning was set out over the walkway to the door. It occurred to me that the last funeral I had been to was Mim's, in a parlor much like this one, but closer to Notting Hill.

Suddenly, I missed her so much it squeezed the breath right out of me and I gasped.

"Are you all right, Scarlett?" Harrison asked. He took my elbow and turned me to face him so he could examine my face.

JENN McKINLAY

The knot in my throat was tight, so I took a deep breath and let it out slow.

"I'm okay," I said. "I just haven't been to a funeral since Mim passed five years ago. The grief kind of snuck up and kicked me in the pants."

He looked at me for a moment and then smiled. "You do have a way with words."

I sniffed and opened my eyes wide, trying to stem back the outer signs of my inner sadness.

"It's okay," I said. "I'm good now."

Harrison gave me a small smile and took my hand and wrapped it around his elbow.

"Lean on me if you need to," he whispered in my ear.

I pushed the thick strand of hair that fell over my eyes aside and nodded.

Together we made our way up the carpeted walk to the door, where another man dressed in gray opened the door for us.

I don't know what I had expected when I heard that the wake was private and for family and friends only. No, that's not true, I expected it to be a small gathering. Instead, it looked as if the funeral home had opened up all of their rooms to make one large room. Seats were placed in rows up by the casket and more were then scattered throughout.

It was elbow-to-elbow, knee-to-knee thick with people. The scent of expensive perfume and cologne fogged the room, making it stifling. I was glad I had Harrison to lean on because I felt suddenly light-headed and a bit dizzy.

"All right?" he asked.

He leaned close when he asked and I was relieved to

breathe in the fresh, clean scent of him as if it repelled all of the others away.

"Yeah, it's just more crowded than I thought," I said.

"She was a countess," he said. "A certain crush is to be expected."

"Can we hang back and watch people for a bit?" I asked.

"Sure," he said. "Follow my lead."

He steered me through the throng. Not to just any spot on the wall but to the one that gave us the best view of the grieving family and friends.

"Excuse us," Harrison said as he propelled me between two young men in suits. "She's feeling quite ill."

Both men jumped back as if afraid I'd be sick on their shoes. I gave Harrison a dark look but went with it, because there was no denying that it was working.

"Try to look wretched," he said.

I put my hand to my forehead as if warding off a head-ache and said, "You have a devious side to you, don't you?"

"Do you think so?" he asked. "I thought I was just quick-witted."

"That, too," I agreed. "So who do we see with the family?"

Harrison leaned against the wall beside me as if waiting for me to compose myself. I used the hand at my forehead as a shield and glanced through my fingers to check out the people up by the casket, which I noticed was open. That threw me.

I suppose it shouldn't have; given that her fatal wound had been in her torso, there really wasn't a reason not to have an open casket, but somehow given that the last time I had seen her she was nude with a knife hanging out of her middle, I wasn't really sure I could handle looking at her again.

"Are you okay?" Harrison leaned in close again and his eyes looked concerned. "You do look a bit wrecked."

I blew out a breath and whispered, "Sorry, murder-scene flashback."

He nodded but I noticed he glanced around to make sure no one heard me.

"Focus, Ginger," he said. "Can you see the people sitting to the right of the casket?"

"Yes, there's a thin, pale-looking man in an ill-fitting suit, an older woman dripping diamonds and an older man with an unfortunate toupee."

"That would be Lord Ellis and his mother and step-father," he said.

"What?" I dropped my hand and stood up on my toes to get a better look. I stared at the thin, pale man. I could defi-nitely see him as the sort who would be at home in a grave-yard. I could not, however, see him as the man who had been married to Lady Ellis. He was lacking the distinctive thick lips for one thing.

Harrison slid in front of me, blocking my view, or more accurately blocking me from view as I was undoubtedly making the teensiest bit of a spectacle of myself.

"What is it?" he hissed.

"That's not Lord Ellis," I said.

Chapter 36

He peered back over his shoulder and then back to me. "Yes, it is."

"But he's not the man who came to the shop with Lady Ellis," I said. "When she came to get her hat she was with a different man."

"It could have been a driver," Harrison suggested.

I snorted. "He was no driver."

Several heads turned in our direction and I put my hand back to my forehead as if I were going to burst into tears at any moment.

"Are you sure?" he asked.

"Yes, he was definitely not working-class," I said. "He had a way about him, a smarmy I-know-something-you-don't-know way. It was very off-putting."

"Lover?" Harrison asked.

He was jostled from behind and had to brace himself

against the wall with hands on either side of me to keep from flattening me. We were now standing just inches apart and I felt my pulse pound in my ears until it drowned out all sound.

He glanced down at me and for a second neither of us drew a breath. He shook his head and took a quick step back.

"Come on," he said and he pushed off the wall and took my elbow. "Let's go where we can talk."

We worked our way through the crowd, obviously swimming against the tide, until we entered another room that had been set aside for light refreshments. Several long tables were prepared with food and drink and were surrounded by guests who had already paid their respects and were now sharing their memories of Lady Ellis. The room was full of soft murmuring, the occasional sob, and gave off an overall feeling that this was the room to see and be seen in.

"Is it just me or is there another agenda going on in here?" I asked Harrison. He shook his head.

"It's not you. It's as if they're all trying to figure out where the paparazzi are so they can have the most advantageous placement."

We each grabbed a crystal glass of watery punch. I wondered if Lady Ellis's mother-in-law had been in charge of refreshments. It seemed likely given that if it had been anyone who knew Lady Ellis, it would have been an exotic beverage, reflective of her personality, not watered-down and lacking in sparkle.

"So, you're quite certain that wasn't the man who came into the shop with Lady Ellis?" Harrison asked.

"Positive," I said. I scanned the room. "I don't see him

here. I didn't see him in the other room either, but I wasn't really looking for him."

Harrison scanned the room with me. There were all ages here, all dressed their best, all waiting for their photo op.

"What about the mother-in-law?" I asked. "If she can walk around under that poundage of diamonds, she is definitely strong enough to run a long knife through a skinny woman's chest."

"That seems far-fetched," Harrison said. "It's well known that she hated her, but enough to kill her?"

"I don't know, no grandbabies might do that to an old girl," I said.

We were both silent while we watched the crowd.

"I suppose it could be one of her childhood friends," I said. "Although, when I had them over for tea none of them seemed particularly lethal."

"Excuse me?" Harrison asked and turned to face me. "Tea? When did you have her friends over for tea?"

"Yesterday," I said.

"And you're just telling me about it now?" he asked.

"Well, in my defense, the break-in threw me off track yesterday," I said.

I noticed the muscle in his jaw was clenching and unclenching. At a guess, I'd say he was miffed. That's a nice way of saying "furious," isn't it?

"You could have mentioned it at dinner," he said.

"I forgot," I said. It was true. Once Andre and Harrison had shown up at the restaurant all thought of the tea and Lady Ellis and who might have killed her had fled my mind.

I decided not to dwell on the whys and wherefores of that realization.

"It was nothing, really. Fee was with me," I said. "We had some hats that could have been Lady Ellis's that we thought her friends might want to keep as mementos, so we invited them—"

"What do you mean 'could have been Lady Ellis's'?" he asked.

"Um." I sipped my punch. "When I say 'could have been' . . ."

"You mean you lied to them to get them to come over—why?"

"I thought it would be good for the business if people saw or heard that Lady Ellis's friends were still coming into the shop, and there did happen to be several reporters lurking about," I said. It sounded so coldhearted. I did feel ashamed, truly.

"Shrewd," Harrison said. "And incredibly stupid."

"Stupid?"

"Didn't it occur to you that one of them might be the killer?" he asked. "That you were putting yourself and Fee in terrible danger by inviting them to the shop when it was closed?"

I raised my glass and held it in between us as a buffer to keep him from looming over me, which it looked like he was about to do.

"No, it did not," I said, which was a big fat fib. I remembered all too clearly hearing her friends talk about her and thinking any one of them could have murdered her. "I mean honestly, these are her childhood friends, why would they—"

"Scarlett Parker?" a voice called from behind Harrison.

My eyes went wide and so did Harrison's. I peered over his shoulder and saw Marianne standing there with Chelsea and Susie.

"And look at that, there they are," I muttered to Harrison.

All three were dressed in dark-hued dresses that accentuated their figures and were appropriately somber for the funeral of their friend. Susie's mascara had run, giving her a bit of a Goth look, and Chelsea's nose was bright red. Marianne looked even paler than usual, which was the only evidence of her grief.

"Scarlett, why, it's so nice of you to attend the wake for Vicks," Susie said. She gave me a nice air kiss and the heavy floral scent of her perfume hit me like two fingers in the eyes.

"Yes, so thoughtful," Chelsea muttered with an air kiss for my other cheek.

Marianne just looked at me with an eyebrow raised. She was not the air-kiss type, for which I was grateful. I blinked furiously to keep the tears back from the perfume assault, but I figured if one did escape at least I would fit in with the mourners.

"She was a loyal customer," I said. "And I wanted to be sure to pay our respects."

Marianne gave me a doubtful look, but then turned to take in Harrison, from head to toe, in a very thorough perusal. I found I wanted to stand in front of him and protect him, but I resisted.

"May I introduce our business manager, Harrison Wentworth," I said.

Susie gasped, Chelsea's eyes went wide and Marianne cocked her head to the side, "Not *the* Harrison Wentworth, the wizard of the *Financial Times*?"

Harrison gave her a charming smile. "Afraid so."

"And he's your business manager?" Marianne persisted.

I gave her a bewildered shrug, because I'm quick on my feet like that. Then I glanced at Harrison. Obviously, he was a bigger deal than I realized, and he never mentioned to me his revered status as a financial wizard. Huh. Was that why I'd always gotten the feeling he was keeping something from me? Interesting.

"Our families go way back," Harrison said. "My family has always managed the finances of Scarlett's family."

"Well, any friend of Scarlett's is a friend of mine," Marianne said. She looped her arm through his and before I was quite sure what had happened, she'd walked off with him.

"She always does that," Chelsea whined.

"Only because Vicks is dead," Susie said. "She'd have made off with him before we even knew who he was."

"Made off with who?" a voice inquired from behind me.

I turned to see that Elise had joined us. She was looking picture-perfect in a knee-length navy dress with cap sleeves and a cute ruffle at the waist. Like Marianne she seemed pale and her eyes were puffy as if she'd just recently recovered from a crying jag.

"Marianne just took off with Scarlett's date," Chelsea said.

"He's not my—" I protested but no one was listening.

They all turned to watch Marianne with her head pressed close to Harrison's. I felt a flutter of annoyance. Marianne was the one I had liked the most, so I really didn't appreciate her making off with my escort.

"You see, girls, this is what happens when one chooses to be smart and decides to have a career instead of marrying a nice eligible man when she's in her prime. She is reduced to hitting on men at funerals." Elise said it loud enough for Marianne to hear her.

Marianne gave her a dark look and then took Harrison's arm and led him back to me as if he were a pet poodle she had taken out for a stroll but found wanting.

"Excuse me," a low voice broke into our little group. "Don't I know you?"

I turned to find a short chubby man with sweat stains under his armpits, staring at me. He had unkempt, black wiry hair on his head and face, more on his face than his head to be truthful, and he looked as radiant as if he'd just found a winning lottery ticket.

Before I could open my mouth to utter a word, he wrestled a small camera out of his pocket and was holding it up to my face. Then I recognized him. He was the reporter that Harrison had tossed out of the shop the other day.

"The party crasher here at Lady Ellis's funeral," he chortled. "This is going to make me, Bernie Lutz, a fortune. Hey, love, any chance I can get you to throw some cake?"

Harrison jumped in front of me and held open the sides of his jacket shielding me from any shots from the icky man's camera.

"Time to go," he said, and he ushered me away from the group.

"Hey, you told me she'd be okay with this," the man whined.

"I guess I was wrong," a voice answered.

It was Elise's voice. Why would Elise tell him I was okay with having my photo taken and at a funeral, no less? I barely knew the woman but it hurt me that she judged me to be such a media hog. Is that how people saw me? Was fleeing my home country not enough proof that I was not into being the viral flavor of the month?

We were hurrying out of the funeral home with the photographer hot on our backsides when I saw him. He wore a dark suit and he stood at the back of the room, leaning against the wall as if he didn't have the strength to stand on his own two feet. I stopped when I saw him, and Harrison stumbled into my back.

I met the gaze of the man I had believed to be Lord Ellis and all I could think was that he no longer looked smarmy and condescending but rather, he looked shrunken, as if the weight of his grief diminished him.

"Ginger, we have to go." Harrison prodded me forward a few steps into the crowd. When I looked back the man was gone.

Not so the photographer. We lapped the reception hall once in our effort to lose him. I kept an eye out for the man who'd been with Lady Ellis when she picked up her hat, but I didn't see him again. The photographer, however, kept popping up until Harrison surprised him by doubling back through a door we'd just gone through. The door caught the photographer on the chin and knocked him out cold.

Harrison took the opportunity to hustle me outside to the valet. He pushed me into the shadow of a large yew shrub.

I don't know what he said to the valet but the boy took off at a run and was back with the car in moments. Harrison pulled me out from the bush and assisted me into the car. We zipped out of the parking lot as if the hounds of hell were chasing us.

We were silent for most of the ride, not relaxing until we were near Portobello Road and the shop.

"I'm pretty sure you lost him," I said.

I turned from looking out the back window to glance at Harrison. His gaze kept flitting up to the rearview mirror, checking to verify that the photographer was nothing but a memory.

"I'm sorry that happened to you," he said.

"At least he didn't get a picture," I said with a shudder. "That would have been a nightmare."

"Is that what it was like afterwards?" he asked.

"Somewhat," I said. "There was one photographer who climbed onto my balcony, but other than that it was just the phone calls from television and radio stations who wanted to interview me and lawyers who wanted to represent me. I unplugged my phone and didn't leave my apartment for three days."

"Probably a good strategy. You don't deserve to be treated like that," he said. He glanced at me when he said it, and I could see the sincerity in his eyes. For some reason, it made my throat get tight.

"Thanks," I said.

My voice was raspy with emotion and I realized I was choked up because it mattered to me what Harrison thought of me, and I was glad he didn't think I deserved what had happened to me, even though I had treated him pretty badly when we were kids. I probably didn't deserve to have him as my friend now but, oh, I was so glad he was.

"So, Marianne, vampire?" he asked.

The laugh that burst out of me short-circuited the tears that had threatened, which I suspected was Harrison's purpose.

"Worse," I said. "She's a psychiatrist."

"Oh, eek," he said with mock alarm.

He parked the car a few spots down from the shop. He got out and before I found the latch on the unfamiliar car, he opened it for me and gave me a hand out.

"She trotted off with you before I could even try to save you," I said as we walked toward the shop.

"I felt like the prize bull at an auction," he said.

"Really?" I asked. "I pictured it as more of a poodle-snatching."

"Hey!" he protested, but he was laughing, which made me laugh in return.

It felt good, cathartic even, since I had spent most of the evening on the verge of tears for one reason or another.

His arm slid around my waist as if it were the most natural thing in the world and we were still chuckling as we approached the shop.

"Harrison!" a voice shouted.

I glanced up and saw a woman, dressed in a retro, pale pink dress with a fitted bodice and a skirt that flared out at her waist and stopped at her knees. On top of her head, she wore a matching pillbox pink hat with a big, white lily on it.

The woman broke into a run and Harrison dropped his arm from about my waist and opened his arms wide as if this was a familiar greeting for him. The woman launched herself into his arms and he spun her about two times before he gave her a fierce hug, a quick kiss on the lips and gently put her down. Then he yelled at her.

"Where the hell have you been, Viv?" he asked.

Chapter 37

It was only then that I recognized my cousin.

"Vivian!" I gasped.

She spun to face me.

"Scarlett!" she cried in return and snatched me close.

I was not as prepared as Harrison and was crushed by my cousin's enthusiastic greeting.

"It's you!" she cried as she jumped back and grabbed me by the shoulders. "I can't believe it. You're finally here."

"Finally?" I asked, feeling a flash of irritation. "I've been here for a week."

"Really? Has it been a whole week?" She looked to Harrison for confirmation.

"Yes," he said. "A very long week."

What the heck did that mean? I felt my irritation double as Viv had no idea what she had put us all through and

Harrison sounded as if he'd been tortured during her absence by my stay.

"I figured something must have happened," she said. "I've been sitting out here for an hour, afraid to go in."

"Why?" I asked.

She pointed to the small sign the alarm company had put in the window.

"You're here a few days and we have an alarm system?" she asked. "Don't tell me the horrible paparazzi followed you from the States?"

"No, it's worse than that, I'm afraid," I said.

Harrison opened the door to the shop and we each grabbed one of the suitcases Viv had left by the door. She led the way with her big rolling bag.

"I'll get these," Harrison said. He turned to reset the alarm and lock the door behind us. "You two go ahead upstairs."

"You're going to check the perimeter, aren't you?" I asked with a smile.

"Isn't that what pet poodles do?" he teased, returning my smile.

Viv looked between us as if she was missing something, and I immediately felt as if I had overstepped my bounds.

"Come on, let's get you something to eat," I said.

"I'm so glad you're here." Viv squeezed me tightly to her side.

Abruptly, all of the worry and irritation I'd felt toward her fled and I was really glad I was here, too, with her in our shop.

"Me, too," I said. But then I scowled. "You still have a lot of explaining to do. I've been worried sick about you."

We entered the flat and Viv pulled her hat off and shook out the long blond corkscrew curls that I had envied since childhood.

"I know, I know, and I'm so sorry," she said. "But I was on a hero's, well, a heroine's quest and I couldn't turn back."

"Quest for what?" I asked.

"It's better if I show you," she said.

Harrison came banging up the stairs, carrying the three bags as if they were nothing. Show-off! I had broken into a sweat just lugging the one bag into the shop.

Viv hurried over to the mid-sized of the three vivid floral bags. She placed it onto its side on the floor and unzipped the top. Her face glowed. I'd seen this look before when she was caught up in a creative episode.

I peered over her shoulder, disappointed to find nothing but clothes, but then I noticed that there was another compartment and then another.

"Clever bag," I said.

"I like to keep my treasures to myself," she said.

Harrison gave her a look, and I wondered if there had been some issues with Viv's expeditions before.

She pulled out a cloth case that was tied shut and then closed the lid on her bag. She carefully pulled the ties open and unrolled the cloth. Then she folded back another plain cloth. Nestled between the two fabrics was an array of feathers that were breathtaking in color and iridescence.

"Oh, my," I breathed.

"Are those real?" Harrison asked. "They're stunning. What bird did they come off of?"

"Believe it or not," Viv said. "I had to track my way through the jungle to a rare feather ranch."

We both looked at her.

"I swear on it," she said. "It exists, but it is tucked deep in the cloud forest in Africa, which is why I had such spotty mobile service."

"What do you mean, a rare feather ranch?" I asked.

"A friend of mine from Dubai told me about it," she said. "There's a ranch owned by a retired Hollywood actor. He quit movies and devoted his life to trying to save several endangered species of bird. He raises money by auctioning the exotic feathers that the birds lose. No plucking allowed. Believe me, I saw what happened to one of my fellow bidders when he was caught trying to encourage a feather off of a Seychelles Paradise-Flycatcher."

She shuddered and I stared at her as if she'd gone mental.

"Do you mean to tell me that you disappeared for a week, to go chase feathers?" I asked. "You knew I was coming— you couldn't have waited?"

"The auction was happening at the end of the week," she said. "I had to get there immediately."

"See?" Harrison asked. "No impulse control."

I glared at him. I really didn't want to hear it right now.

"What?" Viv asked. "Surely you knew I'd be back as soon as I could."

"You left me no information," I said. I could feel my temper beginning to heat. "You couldn't have told me where you were going and why?"

"No," Viv said. "You know what this business is like. I couldn't risk another milliner scooping me. I mean look at these feathers. They're a treasure. This one alone cost fifty pounds."

She pointed to a gorgeous blue feather that flashed with green and gold when the light hit it just right.

"It's lovely," I said. "But still—"

"Oh, come on," Viv cajoled. "It couldn't have been that bad with me gone. You had Fee, who is wonderful, and Harrison, who is wonderful in a completely different way."

They exchanged a smile, and I couldn't believe he wasn't more irritated with her. He seemed indulgent with her disappearing act but the more I thought about it the madder I got. One week, no word and I'd discovered a dead body, almost been suffocated in my bed and the shop had been ransacked, not to mention being worried about Viv, and here she was just fine after a wonderful quest off in Africa.

I stepped away from the sofa for fear I might snatch up one of the pillows and clobber her with it.

"Well, I'm so delighted that your week went so well," I said. My voice dripped sarcasm and Viv gave me a wide-eyed look of surprise. "Because here it's just been coming up roses, or more accurately, a dead body wearing your hat."

"Scarlett, are you feeling all right, love?" Viv asked. "Because that made absolutely no sense whatsoever."

"You tell her," I growled at Harrison.

"Tell me what?" she asked.

"Viv, Lady Ellis was found murdered," he said.

"Victoria Ellis? Rupert's wife?" she asked with a note of disbelief.

"Yes," Harrison confirmed.

"What? Why? I don't understand," she said. She turned and frowned at me as if I could help her make sense of it all.

"It gets worse," I said. Seeing her bewilderment, my anger was doused. I sat on the floor beside her. "When I went over to her house—"

"Why would you go to her house?" Viv asked.

"Photo shoot," I said.

"Photo shoot of that cow?" she asked.

"Well, when I couldn't find the hat she ordered," I said, "I had to come up with some way to appease her vanity and luckily, Andre was willing—"

"Who the hell is Andre?" Viv squawked.

"It's a long story," I said. "Longer if you keep interrupting me."

"Luckily, I have plenty of time," she said.

"Then let's eat while we talk," Harrison suggested. "Because I, for one, am famished."

He took to the kitchen while Viv and I moved to sit at the kitchen table.

"Handy to have someone around who cooks, isn't it?" Viv asked me.

"Yeah, Harrison is worth his weight in gold," I agreed.

"You didn't think that at first," he said. "She thought I had something to do with you being missing."

"I did n—" I cut myself off. There really was no point in denying it. "Okay, I did, but you have to admit, it seemed odd to have you picking me up when I expected Viv."

"But I asked Harrison specifically because you knew him," Viv protested.

Harrison uncorked a bottle of wine and poured us each a glass. Then he looked at me and said, "It would have helped if she remembered me."

"You didn't?" Viv asked.

"No, but in my defense it's been years and I was kind of caught up in my own personal crisis," I said.

"Bet you haven't had much time for that," Viv said.

She had a knowing look about her and for a moment I

almost wondered if that had been her plan all along, to stick me with the insanity of the shop so I didn't have time to brood. Well, hadn't that plan just backfired on us all?

"Scarlett has done amazingly well in the shop," Harrison said. "She even sold a hat to Mrs. Looksee."

"You didn't!" Viv cried.

I grinned. I couldn't help it. "Wedding hat in lilac."

"Well done," Viv said and she raised her glass to me.

The three of us toasted and after a sip, Viv said, "All right, I'm ready now. Tell me about Victoria."

While Harrison whipped together a fettuccini dish with a delicate cream sauce and chicken and broccoli, I filled Viv in on all that had happened. Harrison stuck in the facts that I missed and by the time he was serving us each a hot plate, Viv was fully informed.

"Suffocated?" she kept asking. "Someone broke in and tried to suffocate you?"

She had asked this about five times and grew alarmingly pale each time she asked.

"It's okay," I said. I reached out and laid my hand on her arm. "I'm fine."

"I just . . . if anything had happened to you . . ." She took a long sip of wine and blew out a breath.

"It didn't," I said.

We were halfway through dinner when there was a banging on the door downstairs.

"Who would be here at this hour?" Viv asked.

"It's not our friendly burglar," I said. "He never knocks."

"I'll check it out," Harrison offered. "You two finish eating."

As soon as he left, Viv leaned close and asked, "What do you think about our Mr. Wentworth?"

"Harry?" I asked. "I mean, Harrison. He seems very efficient."

"Efficient?" Viv asked. "He's adorable. Please tell me you noticed."

Oh, geez, what was I supposed to say? Were Viv and Harry an item? He had said they weren't, but maybe she thought they were. Did she want my approval? Yeah, he was handsome and likeable, charming even. I felt a flash of heat when I remembered his help with my zipper.

"Yeah, he's really nice," I said. Lame, so lame.

Viv looked like she was about to call me on it, when Harrison appeared in the doorway. He did not look happy.

"Viv, the police are here," he said. "They want to talk to you."

Chapter 38

"Oh, all right," Viv said. She took one more bite of her meal before she rose from her seat.

"Viv, you know what this is about?" I asked.

"Well, I imagine since it is well-known that Victoria loathed me, they need to question me about the murder," she said. "I can't believe she was only wearing the hat I'd made for her. Small wonder they want to talk to me."

She didn't look overly concerned but paused and took a folder out of her bag and handed it to Harrison. Then she followed him down the stairs to the shop. I took a second to fortify myself with a big gulp of wine before I followed.

Detective Inspectors Franks and Simms were shaking hands with Viv when I joined them. We all took a seat and Inspector Franks took the lead in the conversation.

"I'm sorry to bother you upon your return, Ms. Tremont," he said.

"How did you know she was back?" I asked.

"We flagged her passport, so we'd be alerted if she came through customs," Franks said.

"It's no bother," Viv said. "My cousin and Mr. Wentworth explained the urgency in the matter."

Inspector Franks looked at Viv and was immediately rendered a kinder, gentler version of himself. There was something about her long blond curls, framing her heart-shaped face and her big blue eyes, that did in every man with a pulse. Poor bastards didn't stand a chance.

I glanced at Simms to confirm, and yep, he looked as besotted as Inspector Franks.

"Well, we won't keep you," Franks said. "Just a few questions and if you could stop by the station house tomorrow, we'll need to take some fingerprints."

"Just to rule you out," Simms assured her.

I glanced over Viv's head to where Harrison was sitting. He looked like he was trying not to laugh and somehow that made me smile. He met my gaze and gave me a wink and I returned it, which made him duck his head as if he was trying to keep from busting up.

"Now could you tell us your whereabouts on Friday last?" Inspector Franks asked.

"I was at a rare feather ranch in Africa," she said.

"A what?" Simms and Franks asked together.

"Here, I have receipts," she said. She took the folder from Harrison's hands and said, "These should catalog my whereabouts quite thoroughly."

Franks took the folder and flipped through it. "You really were in Africa."

Viv nodded.

"I'll be happy to make copies for you," Harrison said. "But as her financial manager, I'd like to keep the originals."

Franks studied him for a moment. Harrison did not get the dewy-eyed look that Viv got from the detective.

"All right," he said.

"Now if you could just go over your whereabouts one more time, Ms. Tremont," Franks said. "And in detail."

"I'll go get some tea," I said. I had a feeling neither detective was eager to tear himself away from Viv.

It was an hour later when the detectives took their leave and Harrison followed shortly after. I showed Viv how to work the alarm and we set it and hurried up the stairs.

We both put on our pajamas but then met up in the sitting room.

"Fancy some telly?" Viv asked.

I would have refused, given that I mostly wanted to talk with her about the past few days, but her eyes were already drooping and I realized she was probably horribly jet-lagged. It would be rude to keep her up just because I needed to talk.

We sacked out on Mim's sofa, Viv on one end and me on the other with our feet meeting in the middle; within fifteen minutes Viv was sound asleep. I got up and fetched the blanket off her bed. I stretched out her legs and tucked her in, knowing that if she still slept as deeply as she always had, she wouldn't wake until morning.

Unlike Viv, I didn't feel sleepy. In fact, I was restless. Every creak and shudder that the building made caused my shoulders to tighten. It was as if I were waiting for something but I had no idea what.

I trotted back down to the shop. Fiona and I had done a wonderful job of restoring order. In fact, we had taken the opportunity to set up some new and wonderfully eye-catching displays. At least, I thought so.

The shop was silent. I glanced over at the wardrobe. Ever alert, Ferd was staring out across the place as if keeping watch. I remembered the fateful evening that Lady Ellis had come to pick up her hat.

It reminded me that I couldn't find it in the computer. I needed to ask Viv about that. Were there customers she didn't put in or who had a special file?

I crossed to the wardrobe and noticed there was a gouge in the dark wood as if someone had tried to pry the doors open. I didn't remember it being there and I ran my fingers over it. Then I remembered that on the night the place had been ransacked the only thing that had been untouched was the wardrobe. But we never locked the wardrobe, so why would someone have to pry it open?

Stepping back, I glanced up at Ferd. "What happened that night? Why do I get the feeling you're not telling me something? Something important."

He didn't answer, but I got the weirdest feeling that I needed to open the wardrobe. I pulled the iron handle and the door opened easily. I pressed the latch at the back and moved the panel aside. Sitting on the pedestal in the hidden compartment, just as it had been yesterday, was the purple hat.

"Scarlett? Is that you?" Viv called from upstairs.

"Yes, it's me," I called back. I was afraid I'd woken her up and felt bad about it.

"What are you doing?" she called.

Really? We were shouting at each other from separate floors? It reminded me of when we would have one of our yelling conversations when we were teens, and Mim would look at us with one eye closed tight as if the closed eye was too busy warding off an incoming headache to be functional in the sight department. Again, the memory made me miss her so much. What I wouldn't give for just one more hug from Mim.

"I'm looking in the wardrobe," I yelled, but my voice tapered off on the last word as Viv entered the room.

Her hair was tumbled around her head and she was yawning. So I guess she wasn't the deep sleeper that she'd once been. Maybe it was just part of being a grown-up. No more untroubled sleep.

"I'm sorry, did I wake you?" I asked.

"No, the lump in the couch took care of that," she said. "But you weren't there when I woke up and then I heard voices down here. Who were you talking to?"

"Ferd," I said.

She looked at me in confusion. I pointed up at the raven, and she smiled.

"If he were a real bird, I expect he'd plop some droppings on you for that moniker," she said.

"I just noticed that the cupboard door is gouged," I said. "I don't think that was here before the break-in. But I haven't locked the cupboard, so I don't understand why they thought they had to gouge it open."

Vivian glanced into the cupboard and then she paled.

"What is that doing in there?" she asked.

"The hat? I just found it yesterday," I said. "I'd forgotten about the hidden compartments in this cupboard. Why did you hide it in there?"

"It was supposed to be a secret," Viv said. "But you told me Lady Ellis was wearing the hat I made for her when her body was found. So, why don't the police have it?"

"Why would they?" I asked. She wasn't making any sense.

"Because that's the hat I made for Lady Ellis," she said.

Chapter 39

"No, it can't be," I said. "I sold her the hat you made for her and it looked nothing like this."

We stared at each other for a moment and Vivian looked fully awake and very ill at ease.

"What did the hat you sold her look like?" she asked. "Can you describe it?"

"It was blue," I said. "Well, no, not blue exactly, more like an aqua or a teal. It was a cloche, really lovely."

Viv frowned at me. "Why would she pick up a cloche? She specifically wanted a wide-brimmed hat that would frame her beautiful face, her words not mine. A cloche wouldn't do that."

"I don't know," I said. "Nothing makes sense. I thought she was accompanied by her husband that day, but I just found out at the wake that it wasn't Lord Ellis at all but rather some smarmy man. Except he didn't look smarmy at the wake today, he looked sad."

"Smarmy?" Viv asked.

"Yes," I said. "He had thick lips that he licked repeatedly. I got the distinct feeling he enjoyed the misery of others, especially if he was the one making them miserable."

"Lord Cheevers, Elise Cheevers's husband," Viv said. She hurried over to the counter where she'd left her cell phone. She quickly opened an Internet browser on it. In seconds she had brought up pictures of the man I'd met with Lady Ellis that fateful night she'd come to collect her hat.

"That's him," I said. My insides clutched as I got a bad feeling about the whole situation.

"This is so strange," Viv said. "Why was he with Lady Ellis? And why did they buy the wrong hat?"

"You know, Viv, not to be critical," I said. "But if you'd put Lady Ellis's order in the database, I might have been able to find the right hat for her, especially if you noted that you were keeping it in the back of the wardrobe."

"I did. She is in the database," Viv said.

"No, I looked under 'Lady,' 'Ellis' and 'Victoria,'" I said. "There was no listing."

"That's because she's listed under another name," Viv said.

"What other name?"

"It's of no matter," Viv said. "It's a nickname. Now back to the hat . . ."

"Oh, no, you don't," I said. I put the hat on an empty shelf and stared Viv down. "What nickname?"

"It's in the 'K's,'" she said.

I had thought it would be in the "B's," as in the word for a female dog, so now I was utterly confused.

"I call her 'Knicks,'" Viv confessed. "Not to her face, of course."

"Of course," I said with a laugh. "Care to explain?"

"Her knickers are always in a twist; 'Knicks' rhymes with 'Vicks' so it just seemed to fit."

"Anyone else in there under a nickname?" I asked.

"No, I think she's it," Viv said. She looked down at the floor and then up at me with a grin. "I'm sorry she's dead, truly, I am, but she was an awful person. She married Rupert for his title and status and treated him abominably."

"Then why take her on as a client?" I asked. "You are famous enough for your creations not to have to take on people you don't like."

Viv sighed. "Rupert asked me to do it and I just feel so badly for—"

"For what?" I prodded her. "For not loving him back? Viv, it's not your fault you didn't feel that way and he went and married someone awful. He should have stuck to his love of headstones."

"You heard about that?" she asked.

"The press made quite a story out of it," I said. "Earl obsessed with graveyards comes home to murdered wife."

"Oh, poor Rupert." Viv cringed. "He really is the nicest person."

A knock at the door made us both start. The shades had been drawn on the large windows and on the window of the door, so we couldn't see out.

"Who could be here at this hour?" I asked.

"Maybe it's Harrison," Viv said.

"No, he would use his key," I reasoned. "Maybe it's the police."

I approached the door, fearing it was the sweaty photographer from the wake. Yuck. I pushed the shade aside and peered out front. No one stood out there waiting to come in. It was then that I noticed a shadow against the door glass. Someone was slumped against the bottom of the door.

"Viv, someone is out here. I think they're hurt!" I cried.

I had the alarm deactivated and the dead bolt halfway unlocked when Viv hurried to my side.

"Don't open the door!" she cried. She was looking past me, but it was too late. I had already pushed the door open a crack. It was yanked from my hands before I had a chance to pull it shut or refasten the lock.

"Well, look who's returned!" Elise Cheevers said as she strode into the shop. "Vivian Tremont, and here I thought you'd fled the country after murdering your longtime love's wife."

I glanced past Lady Cheevers at the closing door. No one was out there, so it had been Elise slumped against the door. She had tricked me.

"Elise," Viv said, her voice remarkably steady given the odd situation. "You are aware that we're closed?"

"Oh, this won't take but a minute," Elise said. She looked at me with scathing contempt. "*You* sold my hat to Vicks."

"I did?" I asked.

"Yes, Vicks called me the next day and told me all about the pathetic little shop girl who sold her this fabulous teal cloche," Elise said. Her eyes blazed. "That was *my* hat."

I looked at Viv for confirmation but her lips were pressed together in a look that said she was trying not to lose it. I could tell by the horrified expression in her blue eyes that she felt the same sense of danger I was feeling. There was definitely something wrong with Elise Cheevers, and even with all of my people skills I had no idea how to manage her. I glanced back at Elise and saw the fury in her eyes, and I realized this wasn't about a hat. This was about having everything you ever wanted scooped out from under you by the person who was supposed to be your best friend. Suddenly, it all made perfect, insanely perfect, sense to me.

"It was you, wasn't it?" I asked. "You killed Lady Ellis."

Elise Cheevers laughed. It was the sort of cackling laugh that made your skin ripple with dread.

"Figured that out, did you, ducks?" Elise slurred her words and I wondered if she was drunk. That would actually be a good thing because I figured we could overpower her if she was impaired. Otherwise, she might just be crazy strong and then we'd stand no chance of taking her out.

"Elise, I appreciate that you and Knicks, uh, I mean Vicks had your issues, but it has nothing to do with us," Viv said.

She moved to stand beside me as if we were a wall that Elise would have to get past.

"Oh, it has everything to do with you," Elise said.

"Really, Elise, I've had a long day and the shop is closed," Viv said. She moved toward Elise with her arms out like she was herding geese across a busy street.

Elise pulled a sharp knife out of her bag and held it straight out at Viv. I reached forward and yanked Viv back before she was impaled upon the point.

"I'm sorry, but this has to be cleared up tonight," Elise said. She began walking forward, knife in hand, giving Viv and me no choice but to keep backing up. We kept moving back until we found ourselves in the workroom, pressed up against the center table. "You see, you two are my only loose ends."

"I'm not following," I said. It was a blatant stall tactic. For I can assure you, with a knife that big pointed at us I was following this conversation more closely than I had ever followed anything in my life.

"You are the only two who know that the hat on Lady Ellis's head at her time of death is not the hat she ordered, which is a minor detail that could cause an unfortunate amount of suspicion to come my way," Elise said. "Well, you two and my husband, but he's of no consequence anymore."

The look of evil satisfaction in her eyes led me to believe that whatever had happened to Lord Cheevers had been about as pleasant as what had happened to Lady Ellis.

"But he was at the viewing . . ." I trailed off. Damn it, when would I learn to keep my mouth shut?

Elise gave me a frosty look. "Yes, the poor man was so grief-stricken over his lover's death, but you knew that, didn't you?"

"I don't understand," I said. This time it was true. I had a feeling her crazy train had hopped the tracks.

"How did it feel to almost have your life snuffed out?" Elise asked.

In a flash of memory, the burning sensation in my lungs returned, but this time the terror that had gripped me turned into rage.

"You think I had something to do with Lady Ellis and Lord Cheevers buying your hat?" I asked. "It was a mistake, an honest mistake."

"No, you see, it wasn't," Elise said. She turned the knife as if enjoying the play of light upon its blade. "They did it on purpose. They did it to hurt me. Vicks always wanted whatever I had. I should have known that eventually, she would take him, too, and you helped them. After all, you are quite the home wrecker yourself, aren't you?"

"But I didn't know . . ." My voice trailed off as I realized that in her crazy mind I had been a part of her husband and her best friend's plot to hurt her. And given that she knew about my own personal scandal, I didn't think there was anything I could say to prove otherwise.

"Elise, this is madness," Viv said. "Scarlett didn't know the hat was yours. She didn't even know who your husband was. They tricked her as well."

Elise stared at me as if trying to see into my soul. I could hear the ticking of the clock on the wall and feel every beat of my heart in my chest.

"It doesn't matter," Elise said. "I knew when you got back, Viv, that you would figure out that Scarlett sold the wrong hat to Vicks. I did try to find the hat once to spare us all but no luck. If that bloody wardrobe hadn't been locked, none of this would have been necessary. I'm afraid my temper got the better of me when I couldn't open the cupboard."

"You ransacked the shop?" I asked. "After the tea, when Lady Ellis's garden hat wasn't among the ones I offered?"

Elise gave me a bored look. "Viv once told me she kept all of the special hats in the wardrobe, and I knew that's where Vicks's hat would be. Do you remember?"

Viv nodded, but I wasn't sure if it was because she remembered their conversation or because she was trying to pacify Elise.

"When you said it was Lord and Lady Ellis who had been in the shop, I realized you didn't know who the man with Vicks really was. I thought I might not have to kill you after all," Elise said. "But then you saw my husband at the wake, and I knew you would figure out that he and Vicks were a pair and that the person most likely to kill Vicks would be me. I didn't know you were back, Viv, so this just makes things all the easier."

"Elise, you don't have to do this," I said. "You can declare it a crime of passion to have killed your husband's lover."

"And my husband?" she asked.

Viv and I exchanged a wide-eyed glance and then turned back to her.

"Yes, I'm afraid he's suffered an unfortunate accident. After the wake, he was so distraught, I offered to make him some tea. That will be the last time he puts his thick lips on any of my china," she said with satisfaction.

There was no way I could hide my look of horror. Elise narrowed her eyes at me.

"Oh, please, he got off much easier than Vicks. I made her wear the hat. I wouldn't let her put anything else on, and then after she confessed to sleeping with my husband, I stabbed her."

Elise smiled to herself as if pleased. "It was a poor decision to leave the hat on her head, but I felt there was a certain poetic justice to it; besides, I had to hurry before the house-keeper found me."

"But surely, if you've killed your husband, someone will notice his absence and you'll be caught," Viv said.

"No, I made sure everyone thinks he's on a business trip to the Continent. That should buy me a little time. Now there is a grass shack in some small village in Thailand calling to me and I must go."

"You're mad," Viv said. "Four murders? How do you possibly think you'll get away with four murders?"

"Oh, but I'm not going to murder you," she said. "No, you're going to have a horrible accident."

"What are you talking about?"

"A tragic fire," Elise said with a mock-sad face. "The beautiful cousins were just reunited when a horrible fire engulfs their home and the two women and their hat shop are scorched beyond all recognition."

"Scorched?" Viv and I asked faintly.

"Cooked, toasted, fried," she confirmed. "Let's go upstairs and set the stage, shall we?"

Viv looked at me and I knew what she was thinking. If we went upstairs, we were done for. She tipped her head imperceptibly toward the table. Fiona had left several wooden hat forms she'd been using on the table. I frowned at Viv. I had no idea what she was thinking.

"Go on, upstairs with you," Elise ordered. "I have places to go and people to see."

"I wonder what Mim would say about this," Viv said.

"Who cares?" Elise asked.

"It's just that she was so particular about her things in the shop," Viv said. "Remember, Scarlett?"

She looked again at the table and then at me. I was standing closer to the table so I knew she was trying to tell me something. And then, I remembered.

One summer on my vacation to London, Viv and I had taken a few of the wooden hat forms for brims that Mim kept in her storage closet to the park. We used them as toy boats in the fountains and as clunky Frisbees. We tied one to a tree branch and used it as a swing.

Mim had been furious. These had been two of her favorite hat forms and we had battered them beyond repair. We'd spent all of the next day scrubbing every floor in the three-story house. Lesson learned.

That being said, I had developed a knack for flinging the round wooden form pretty far. Is this what Viv wanted me to do now? Did she think I could grab it and hit Elise with it before she stabbed one or both of us? I didn't think it was possible, and even more than not wanting to be stabbed myself, I really didn't want Viv to be harmed. I'd just gotten her back.

"Scarlett!" a voice called from out front. It sounded like Nick.

"Oy, Scarlett, you've left your door unlocked," Andre called after him.

Elise whipped her head in the direction of the door. As soon as she did, I snatched up one of the circular hat forms and heaved it at her arm. There was a solid *thunk* and with a yelp, Elise dropped the knife. Viv dove forward and sacked Elise in a tackle worthy of an American football player. I kicked the knife away.

Nick and Andre dashed through the open doorway, yelling, "What the bloody hell is going on?"

Elise was struggling but Viv had her pinned. I snatched some ribbon from the table and used it to tie Elise's hands and feet. When I stood, I saw my friends staring open-mouthed at us.

"Oh, Nick, Andre, you're here," I said. "Excellent timing. My cousin Vivian has returned."

They stared at Viv and then at me and then Elise, who was struggling and cursing on the floor, trying to wrench her hands free of the ribbons.

"Pleasure to meet you," Andre said as he extended his hand to Viv. "Although, you seem a bit tied up at the moment."

Nick chuckled and said, "No, she's just stringing you along."

Vivian laughed and said, "I'm a frayed knot."

The three of them were hooting, when I said, "I knew you were all bound to get along."

They all stopped laughing and looked at me. "Aw, come on. That was a good one. 'Bound'? You have to give it to me."

Nick shook his head and threw an arm about me. "Don't unravel on us now, Scarlett."

The others laughed and I pouted.

"Come on," he said. "Let's go call the police."

"Fine," I said.

We called Inspectors Franks and Simms and Harrison and all three arrived within moments. Simms bagged Elise's knife and hauled her off to the station with a couple of uniforms while Franks stayed to interview us.

Andre and Nick made their departure when it was apparent that this would take a while. They promised to return the next day to get the full story.

When Harrison finally walked Inspector Franks to the door, the detective was positively beaming, and as the door shut after him, I heard him break into a rich baritone as he belted out an Alan Jackson song.

Vivian gave me a perplexed look.

"He fancies himself a country-western singer," I said. "We really should go and see him at the pub sometime."

Harrison collapsed onto one of the empty chairs, looking relieved. "Is it finally over?"

"Yes, I do believe the mystery of who killed Lady Ellis is solved," I said. "But there is one thing I'm unclear on."

"What's that?" Viv asked.

"I still don't understand about the wardrobe," I said. "Elise said it was locked the night she broke in to search it for Vicks's hat."

"And?" Viv prodded.

"And, I've never locked it and I don't think Fee did either," I said. "So how could it have been locked?"

Viv and Harrison exchanged a look and then Viv got up and started whistling. She didn't say a word. She just disappeared through the door that led upstairs and finally even her whistle faded into nothing.

I turned to look at Harrison. "What was that about?"

"No idea," he said. He rose from his seat and headed for the door.

"Harry, what is going on?" I demanded as I followed him. "You and Viv are keeping secrets. Even Fiona said something about the wardrobe just doing what it does. What did she mean?"

Harrison turned to face me, and I felt caught in his emerald-green gaze as he asked, "Are you staying?"

"What do you mean?" I asked, but he didn't explain. Instead he turned and continued to the door.

"Come on, Harry," I cajoled. "We've been through so much together. Tell me."

He was almost at the door when he turned abruptly and I slammed into him. He caught me by the arms and steadied me on my feet.

"It's Harrison," he said, but he was grinning as he laced his fingers with mine. "Who do you suppose would lock the wardrobe to keep a hat safe?"

"I don't know. Who?" I asked.

"Think about it," he said. He stepped forward and kissed me gently on the forehead. Then he let go of my fingers and strode out the door.

I stomped my foot. This was positively maddening. I locked the door and set the alarm. As I crossed the room to go upstairs, I glanced at the wardrobe.

"All right, Ferd," I said. "You win this round, but I'll have your secrets yet."

It may have been a trick of the light, but I was quite certain this time that he did wink at me, and then the faint scent of Lily of the Valley filled the air. It was Mim's scent. The same scent I had smelled in my room after Elise had almost suffocated me. But instead of feeling the grief of Mim's loss this time, I felt engulfed in warmth like I was being hugged. I stood perfectly still until the scent dissipated.

"Mim?" I asked. There was no answer. Duly spooked, I raced up the stairs, slamming the door behind me.

Viv had obviously gone to bed, so I tiptoed up to my own room as quietly as I could with my heart racing and my knees trembling. I was being ridiculous. I knew it, and yet, I couldn't seem to help it.

Then I thought of Mim and her no-nonsense ways, and I stiffened my spine. I was no coward. Was I going to stay and find out what my cousin wasn't telling me? That Mim was still here in some mystical way? That it was Mim's ghost that had locked the cupboard and comforted me when I needed it?

Embraced by the hideous pink as I walked into my room, I smiled as I switched off the light.

"Heck, yeah," I said out loud. "I'm staying."

Turn the page for a preview of
Jenn McKinlay's next Hat Shop Mystery . . .

DEATH OF A MAD HATTER

Coming soon from Berkley Prime Crime!

"Take it off, Scarlett. You look like a corpse."

My cousin Vivian Tremont stared at me in horror as if I had in fact just risen from the grave.

"Don't hold back," I said. "Tell me how you really feel."

"Sorry, love, but pale redheads like you should avoid any color that has gray tones in it," Viv said. Then because calling me a corpse wasn't clear enough, she blanched.

I crossed the floor of our hat shop to the nearest free-standing mirror. Our grandmother Mim had passed away five years ago and left her shop, Mim's Whims in London to the two of us. Viv was the creative genius behind the hats, having grown up in Notting Hill just down the street from the shop, while I was the people person, you know, the one who kept the clients from running away from Viv when she got that scary inspired look in her eye.

Being raised in the States, I had chosen to go into the

hotel industry. Things had been going well until I discovered my rat bastard boyfriend was still married. At Viv's urging, I escaped that fiasco and came here to take up my share of the business. So far London had done quite a lot to take my mind off my troubles. Viv in particular kept me on my toes, making sure I didn't lose my people skills.

In fact, the last time she'd gotten swept up in an artistic episode, she'd tried to convince the very timid Mrs. Barker that wearing a hat with two enormous cherries the size of beach balls connected by the stems and with a leaf the size of a dinner plate would be brilliant. It was—just not on Mrs. Barker's head.

It had taken me an afternoon of plying Mrs. Barker with tea and biscuits and pulling Viv into the back room and threatening to put her in a headlock to get them to an accord. Finally, Mrs. Barker had agreed to a black trilby with cherries the size of golf balls nestled on the side and Viv had been satisfied to work her magic on a smaller scale.

I ignored my dear cousin's opinion and stood in front of the mirror and tipped the lavender sun hat jauntily to one side. It was mid-May and summer was coming. I'd been looking for a hat to shade my fair skin from the sun and being a girly girl, I do love all things pink and purple.

"Oh, I can just see the headstone now," a chipper voice said from behind me. "Here lies Scarlett Parker, mistakenly buried alive when she wore an unfortunate color of sun hat."

I glared at the reflection of Fiona Felton, Viv's lovely young apprentice, in the mirror.

Viv laughed and said, "I can dig it."

"In spades," Fee quipped back.

"Fine," I said. I snatched the hat off my head. "Obviously, the hat is a grave mistake."

They stopped laughing.

"Oh, come on, that was funny," I said. They shook their heads in denial.

"You need to bury that one and back away," Viv said. They both chortled.

"I think you're being a bit harsh," I said. I replaced the pretty hat on its stand and shook out my hair.

"No, harsh was that hat on your head," Fee said. She smiled at me, her teeth very white against her cocoa-colored skin. Her corkscrew bob was streaked with blue, she was always changing the color, and one curl fell over her right eye. She blew it out of her face with a puff of her lower lip.

"But I need a sun hat," I complained.

"Plain straw would look nice," Viv said. "Maybe with a nice emerald ribbon around the crown."

"I'm tired of plain and I'm sick of green." I knew I sounded a tad whiney but I didn't care. I was jealous of Fee and Viv. Fee's dark coloring looked good with everything and so did Viv's long blond curls and big blue eyes, which she had inherited directly from Mim. So unfair!

The front door opened and I glanced up with my greet-the-customer smile firmly in place. It fell as soon as I recognized the man who walked into the shop.

"Oh, it's you, Harry," I said with a sigh.

Harrison Wentworth, our business manager, gave me an annoyed glance.

"Harrison," he corrected me. "Pleasure to see you, too, Ginger."

I felt my face get warm at the childhood nickname. Yes, Harry and I had a history, one in which I did not come out very well.

"I didn't mean anything by it," I said. "I was just hoping you were a customer so everyone could stop telling me how gruesome I look in lavender."

"I didn't say you were gruesome," Viv corrected me as she rearranged the hats on one of the display shelves. "I said you looked like a corpse. Good morning, Harrison."

She stood on her tiptoes and kissed his cheek.

"Now that's a proper greeting," Harrison said, giving me a look.

"Hello, Harrison," Fee said. She also kissed his cheek and smiled at him. He returned the grin. I glanced between them. They seemed awfully happy to see each other.

Harrison was Viv's age, two years older than my modest twenty-seven, but Fee was only twenty-one, entirely too young to be considering a man in his advanced years, in my opinion. And no, it had nothing to do with the fact that Harry and I had a history, if you consider me standing him up for an ice cream date when I was ten and he was twelve and breaking his adolescent heart a history. I did mention that I didn't come out very well in it, didn't I?

As Fee stepped back, Harrison looked at me expectantly. Before I could stop myself, I found myself looking at him from beneath my lashes and giving him my very practiced, secretive half smile. Sure enough, the man looked as riveted as if I had just propositioned him.

Ugh! Honestly, I am a dreadful flirt. It's like breathing to me and I don't discriminate. I flirt with everyone, kids, pets, old ladies, men, you name it. Probably, that's why the hospitality industry was such a natural fit for me. I am very good at managing people.

I blame my mother. After thirty years of marriage, she still has my dad wrapped around her pinky and it's not just because of her charming British accent either. My mother is an incorrigible flirt.

After my last relationship disaster, however, I made a promise to myself that I would go one whole year without a boyfriend. So far it had been two months. Prior to that the longest I'd gone was two weeks. Shameful, I know.

I shook my head and forced myself to give Harrison my most bland expression. He looked confused. I really couldn't blame him.

Mercifully, the front door opened again and this time two ladies entered. I charged forward, relieved to escape the awkward moment.

"Good afternoon, how may I help you?" I asked.

"You're not Ginny." The older of the two women frowned at me.

"No, I'm Scarlet and this is my cousin Vi—"

"Ginny!" The older lady shot forward with surprising speed and hugged Vivian close.

Vivian looked startled, but she hugged the woman back, obviously not wanting to offend her.

I quickly examined the two ladies. The older one had gray hair and wore a conservative print dress that had Marks & Spencer all over it, while the younger woman, a pretty brunette who looked to be somewhere in her twenties, was much more fashion forward, wearing a tailored Alexander McQueen chemise.

"You haven't aged a day," the older woman exclaimed.

She cupped Vivian's face and examined her closely. "How have you managed that?"

Vivian gave an awkward laugh as if she was quite sure the woman was teasing her but the woman frowned. "No, really, how have you managed it?"

"Um, my name is Vivian," she said. "I think you might be confusing me with my grandmother Eugenia, everyone called her Ginny."

The older woman stared at her for a moment and then she laughed and said, "Oh, Ginny, always such a joker. Didn't I tell you, Tina?"

"You did at that, Dotty," the other woman said as she stood watching.

"Oh, heavens, where are my manners?" Dotty said. "Ginny, this is my daughter-in-law Tina Grisby. Tina, this is my friend, the owner of Mim's Whims, Gi—"

"Everyone calls me Viv," Vivian interrupted as she extended her hand to Tina. "This is my cousin Scarlett, our apprentice, Fiona, and our man of business, Harrison."

"You changed your name?" Dotty asked Viv. "How extraordinary."

Viv stared at her for a second and then clearly decided that it did no good to insist she wasn't Mim.

"Yes, I feel more like a Viv than a Ginny," she said.

"Huh." Dotty patted an errant gray curl by her temple. "Maybe I'll change my name. I always fancied myself a Catriona."

Tina gave her mother-in-law an alarmed look. "Dotty, we really should explain our purpose so that we don't keep these kind folks from their business."

"Yes, you're right," Dotty said. "But I do love the idea of a new name."

"Are you in need of a hat for a specific occasion?" I asked, thinking to get the conversation on track. "Fee, would you bring us some tea?"

"Right away," she agreed.

"I'll just go and attend the books," Harrison said. "If you'll excuse me, ladies."

I watched as he and Fee shared a laugh as they left the room and wondered what they could be discussing that was so amusing. I suspected it was me in my lavender hat.

"Don't you agree, Scarlett?" Viv asked. She was seated in our cozy sitting area with the Grisbys and all three of them were watching me.

"Um," I stalled and when I glanced at my cousin, she had her lips pressed together as if she was trying not to smile. I sat down quickly.

"The Grisby family is hosting a tea in honor of Dotty's late husband and they are thinking they'd like it to have an Alice in Wonderland theme," Viv said.

"Oh, I like that idea," I said. "How can we help?"

"Well, it's to be a fund-raiser so that we can name a wing of the hospital after my late husband," Dotty said. "Each family member will host a table and we'd like them to wear a hat that can be tied to a character from the book."

I glanced at Viv. Being the creative quotient in the business, this was really her call.

"When would you need these by?" she asked.

"We're hoping to have the tea in late June," Tina said. She gave us an apologetic look. "I know it is short notice."

"Ginny doesn't mind, do you, dear?" Dotty asked. She patted Viv's hand as if they were old friends.

I tried to remember Mim mentioning Dotty Grisby, but I couldn't bring the name up in any of my memories. Of course, given that I was only here on school holidays, I wouldn't have as broad a frame of reference as Viv would. Judging by Viv's surprised expression when Dotty had hugged her, however, I was betting Viv didn't remember her either.

Fee came out with a tray loaded with tea and biscuits, some cheese and fruits. The Grisby ladies enjoyed a cup each and nibbled some of the food. It was agreed that Viv would work up some sketches and they would come in to see them next week.

Dotty took Viv's arm as we walked them to the door. The older lady looked so happy to see her dear friend that I was glad Viv had decided to go along with Dotty's faulty memory. I fell into step beside Tina.

"Your cousin is being very kind," Tina said. "Please tell her that I appreciate it."

"I will," I said. "It must be hard to watch Dotty struggle with her memory."

"Honestly, she's been like this since her husband left her thirty years ago. Her reality is different than everyone else's and as my husband explained it to me, it is just better if we go along with her."

"Thirty years ago?" I asked. "I'm sorry, but did I understand that she wants the wing of a hospital named after him?"

"Yes, well." Tina lowered her voice. "They never divorced. He lived in Tuscany with his mistress until he died a month ago. She always told everyone that he was away on business, and I think she managed to convince herself that was the truth. One does wonder though . . ."

"What?" I asked.

"That if that is why she is slightly addled," Tina said. "She never got over him leaving her."

A driver was outside waiting for them and Viv and I waved as they drove away.

Harrison came out from the back room. "The books are done for this week and I'm pleased to announce you're still in business. How did it go with the Mmes. Grisby?"

"They want a tea party à la Alice in Wonderland," Viv said. "It'll be tight but I think I can get it done."

Harrison made a face.

"What? I think it will be great fun," I said.

"You would," he retorted. I was pretty sure this was an insult but I didn't press it.

"What about you, Viv?" Harrison asked. "How do you feel about it?"

She was quiet for a moment, staring out the window as if contemplating something. When she turned around she gave us a wicked smile.

"If it's a mad hatter that they want then it's a mad hatter that they'll get," she declared.

I exchanged an alarmed glance with Harrison. Between Mrs. Grisby's dottiness and Viv's Cheshire Cat grin, I was beginning to feel as nonplussed as Alice when she fell down the rabbit hole. Oh, dear.

"[McKinlay] continues to deliver well-crafted
mysteries full of fun and plot twists."
—*Booklist*

FROM *NEW YORK TIMES* BESTSELLING AUTHOR

Jenn McKinlay

Going, Going, Ganache

A Cupcake Bakery Mystery

After a cupcake-flinging fiasco at a photo shoot for a local
magazine, Melanie Cooper and Angie DeLaura agree to make
amends by hosting a weeklong corporate boot camp at Fairy
Tale Cupcakes. The idea is the brainchild of Ian Hannigan, new
owner of *Southwest Style*, a lifestyle magazine that chronicles the
lives of Scottsdale's rich and famous. He's assigned his staff to a
team-building week of making cupcakes for charity.

It's clear that the staff would rather be doing just about
anything other than frosting baked goods. But when the
magazine's features director is found murdered outside the
bakery, Mel and Angie have a new team-building exercise—find
the killer before their business goes AWOL.

INCLUDES SCRUMPTIOUS RECIPES

jennmckinlay.com
facebook.com/jennmckinlay
facebook.com/TheCrimeSceneBooks
penguin.com